The Saint & the Sinner
Blood Week

By J.D. Martin

www.jdmartinbooks.com

Chapter 1

Some men will do anything to get what they want. The pain of others has no bearing on their decisions. The only thing that matters is achieving their goals, and the methods to get there are of little consequence. Under the night sky with the dim illumination of the waning-gibbous moon, one such man rose from the grass with the smug grin of accomplishment.

Reaching sure footing, his unfastened pants drooped around his knees, exposing his backside to the light. Surrounding trees cast shadows across the paleness of his cheeks that were visible for only a moment before he pulled up his jeans. The metal of his buckle clinked together as he pulled the leather strap of his belt through it. Stuffing a pair of lime green panties in his pocket, the man peered down at his latest conquest and was filled with pure satisfaction.

A skinny blonde lay before him with a disheveled skirt that exposed her to the world. Her manicured pubis pleased him as she rolled over to her side. Trying to cover her shame and fear brought the man further satisfaction. The features of his unshaven face were hidden in darkness as he was backlit by the night sky. Regardless of how she felt at the moment, her admirer couldn't remove the smile from his face.

They met earlier that night in a bar a few blocks away. He'd seen her from across the bar as she entered and he immediately wanted her. She was in her early twenties with a fit physique that accentuated her bosom. Her hips were hugged by a checkered miniskirt that exposed the centers of her milky thighs which connected to smooth and shapely legs tucked into black heels.

Not one to waste time, he moved to where she sat with friends and offered to purchase their first round of drinks. He introduced himself as Justin and began the game. As the evening went on, he continued courting her until he'd finally been able to separate her from the herd like a lion going in for the kill.

A couple hours and many cocktails later, she started to feel the effects of everything she'd consumed. Standing with Justin near the bar, she began to stumble from the effects of what had been hidden in her beverages. With her unaware of what was happening, Justin asked if she wanted to go for a walk in the park to which she agreed.

Normally she would never leave with a stranger, but everything around her was spinning slightly from her inebriation. Escorting her out the front door, Justin marveled at his prey. He noticed the way her body moved as she traveled down the sidewalk. Her skirt was just short enough to give the illusion you might catch a glimpse of her ass each time she took a step.

Once they were deep in the park, he wrapped his arms around her and steered her to a small area of grass and trees that was devoid of spectators. With the drug's fallout in full effect, it didn't take much to have his way with her. The fight was minimal, allowing him to reach climax quickly with the evidence secure in his hand.

Taking the used condom with him, Justin decided to part ways with the foggy-headed mistress. Once he'd gotten what he wanted, there was no further use for her. Barely conscious of her surroundings, the woman rolled her head to the sky in a stupor, tears lining her grass-stained cheeks. Turning away from the girl crying in the dirt, he said "Thanks for the ride, babe" and walked away.

Basking in what had been a chance encounter, he strolled down the deserted sidewalk with a spring in his step. He couldn't wait to brag about the bitch he'd picked up. Justin would tell his friends of the slut that was aching for a good sticking. He would say that he was all too happy to scratch her itch, and that she was such a freak that she'd fucked him in the park where anyone could have seen. Drunk on his own power, he tossed the condom in a receptacle along the sidewalk and began looking for his next conquest.

Across the street from where he gave into primal passions, he spotted a figure leaning against a wall. Justin couldn't make out the face of the man shrouded in the shadows, but it caused him worry. They weren't far from where he left that girl, and he wondered if the man might have seen any of the night's public display.

It was then that a thought caught him by surprise. Could that be him? The odds were ridiculous, but it was about that time of year. Justin knew that the odds of running into him had to be astronomical. For all Justin knew, the guy didn't even exist. The vigilante from the news could easily just be a media ploy for ratings. He'd never met anyone who could verify the guy even existed. Although, supposedly the vigilante never left any witnesses to make that assertion anyway. Just in case, Justin made a quick turn and hastily walked in the opposite direction.

Glancing behind him a few times, he no longer saw the shadowed figure. In a wave of relief, he chose to dismiss the thought. After all, it was so dark out, what could the guy have even seen? Like a caged beast craving another meal, he turned at the next corner to head towards the club district. With all the ladies there, he was sure to find further sustenance. The dance clubs were always full of eager young women ripe for the plucking, and he planned to bag him a fresh one.

The subtle sounds of deserted streets were soon overtaken by a dull thumping in the distance. Loud rhythmic bass slowly increased in volume as he rounded the last corner and found himself on club row. Taking a moment to choose which club to patronize, he was interrupted by a fresh piece of cotton candy jaywalking across the street. Another early-twenties girl, she wore a black form-fitting spaghetti strap and tight jeans tucked into knee high leather boots. Her golden hair was in curls that bounced with each step.

As she stepped onto the sidewalk, she spotted him and gave a smile and a wink. That was it for him, as the decision was made. Before the night was over, he would have her.

It looked like luck was about to strike twice this night as he couldn't wait to sample the sweet sugar tucked in those tight jeans.

Her boot heels clicked across the pavement as she strolled towards the entrance of Friction, one of the many dance clubs along the row. Watching her enter, he followed her inside to go make a new acquaintance.

The music was deafening as it beat against the side of Justin's skull. It came in just shy of shattering his eardrums. Exiting the hallway that led into Friction's main dance floor, he entered a whole new world. The expansive room, formally a manufacturing warehouse, shook with the beat of the music. The only light in the room came from a mixture of neon signs along the walls, spotlights on the DJ, and green lasers slicing along the dance floor. It was enough to bathe the area in a dim hue allowing everyone to move about the floor without falling over one another.

He looked around for his black-clad beauty but was having trouble locating her. Justin had entered only a moment after her, so he knew she was around, but there must have been a hundred people on the dance floor alone. This made it difficult to separate the needle in that haystack. Noticing that the bar sat slightly higher than the rest of the room, he figured it to be a good vantage point to find her.

The wood on the bar had been painted black in an attempted to cover the wear-and-tear it had seen over the years. Since Friction had only been open a couple years, the materials were most likely recycled from the bar of a former club. It gave a rustic contrast to the flashiness of the rest of the space.

At the higher level, Justin watched the people on the floor grinding to the music. They rubbed their partners in ways that would make their parents cringe, but the display only brought him excitement. The live Skinimax show made him smile.

Ordering a beer, he continued scanning the crowd in hopes of finding what had brought him. As he searched, his gaze locked with the eyes of a man staring right back at him. His pulse jumped a beat as it looked like the man had been watching him, but a shift in the dancers below and the face was gone. Justin tried to find him again but didn't see him anywhere. Eventually, he realized that he must have been mistaken. The lights could play funny tricks in a place like this.

The song ended just as his beer arrived and was followed by a blood-curdling scream that echoed throughout the room just as he was taking his first drink. Slipping from his hands, the bottle bounced around splashing beer everywhere. Before he could ask, the scream dissipated and the DJ yelled "LETS GO!!!"

The bass slammed hard from the speakers to an electronic rhythm that rose in frequency before dropping again. The people in the pit responded by cheering as they jumped up and down. Looking at his bartender in shame for his party foul, Justin requested another beer.

"You aren't used to this music, are you?" the man asked as he handed him another bottle and began wiping away what was spilled.

"What makes you say that?" The drink master glanced over the edge of the bar at the bottle by Justin's feet then looked back at him with a smirk. "Okay, you got me," said Justin as he retrieved the dropped bottle and handed it to him to discard. "I wasn't expecting to hear a woman screaming like that. How is that even considered music anyway?"

"Yeah…you definitely aren't part of the club scene. It's called dubstep and most of the joints have guest DJ's playing it nowadays."

"It's not horrible but it should come with a warning label. It's crazy what people will listen to." The bartender laughed as he returned to his duties helping another customer.

Drinking his beer, Justin listened to the sounds and watched the floor. As if out of nowhere, the crowd split to reveal a sight that sucked the air out of the room. She drew all attention her direction as she exited the dance floor.

The girl he'd been searching for stepped up next to him and asked for a Coke. It was like the lamb stepping up for the slaughter. After looking everywhere for her, she had simply walked right to him. He couldn't ask for a better setup.

"Mmmm….if only," he spoke aloud as his eyes wandered the landscape of her body. This got her attention and she looked at him with a smirk.

"If only what?"

"If only you were a bad girl."

"And why is that?" she laughed.

"Because then you might be willing to moan for me."

"Is that what you use to pick up girls?"

"Well it certainly gets my point across," he smiled.

She stared at him for a few seconds as her eyes searched his and pondered what to say next. Seemingly coming to a conclusion, she leaned forward slowly and put her lips to his ear. She let out a slow moan heavy with her breath that felt warm on his earlobe. "Who said I wasn't a bad girl already?" she whispered before pulling back away again.

Licking her lips, she chugged her soda and walked back to the floor and struck up with a dancer in need of a partner. The boy was eager to oblige the blonde beauty and stepped from the edge of the floor to join with her.

With the music pounding, she began grinding up against him to the beat. Justin watched her unblinking as he craved to take her as his prize. She straddled the boy's leg and slid her crotch up and down his thigh, arching her back in a way that accentuated her curves. Her hands were in constant motion sliding through her hair, across the side of her neck, and down the crease between her breasts. Turning her back to the boy, she pressed her ass into the front of his jeans and pulsed to the beat.

While giving the young boy the best dance of his life, she passed the occasional glance towards Justin. She knew she was being watched and seemed to enjoy the voyeurism. Although she could have easily disappeared back into the crowd, she kept her show right on the edge, making sure to keep her audience completely immersed in her vision. Justin was captivated.

As the song finished, she left the boy who frowned at her dismissal. She moved her attention to a voluptuous brunette that had just descended into the pit. Whispering into her ear, they both glanced up at the bar. Turning this one-woman show into a duet, they both locked eyes with Justin as they gyrated together.

As the next beat dropped, it caused the crowd to bounce around with their arms in the air. The ladies rubbing their perspiring skin against each other; lips mere inches away from touching. It all became too much for him. No longer wishing to be a bystander, he pushed away from the bar and joined them.

As Justin descended to the dance floor, the blonde spun around putting her back to the brunette. She caressed the girl's face from over her shoulder while rubbing her back against her. Justin approached the two of them with one thing on his mind. When close enough, he placed his hand on her waist and pulled the blonde over to him. Swaying with her to the pulsating rhythm, he leaned forward to kiss her, but she dodged effortlessly and whispered into his ear instead.

"Am I really so captivating?" she asked.

"Honey, you're the only woman here worth my attention."

With a smile she responded, "Flattery will get you everywhere with me, stranger." Placing a hand on his neck, she slid her tongue from his cheek to his ear, ending with a kiss on his lobe. "How about we finish this show elsewhere?"

"Oh, I think that's the best idea I've heard yet." Taking her hand, he led her off the floor towards the exit.

Back outside, Justin put his arm around her neck as they walked side-by-side and tried to grab her breasts. She pushed his hand away before he could get what he wanted. "What happened to the next episode of this show, sweetness? Don't you want to moan for me again?"

"Not here," she said coyly. "I have a car down the street."

Getting the picture, he proudly displayed a grin as he followed her towards her vehicle. He was amazed how easy this one had been. She must be truly hurting for it to be so easy.

The further they walked, the more he started to feel strange. He began to feel a little groggy and stumbled a few steps before using a wall to balance himself. Noticing his stumbling, the girl put an arm around him to help guide him towards the car. "It's only another block away," she said. "Everything will be better once we get there, baby."

He wanted to believe her, but he had to increasingly rely on her support to walk with each step. The closer they got to the car, the more he couldn't keep himself upright. Justin wasn't sure what was happening. He'd only had a few beers the entire night and only one in the last hour.

As they arrived at the back of a black sedan, the blonde beauty had had enough. "You know what? I'm done carrying your drunk ass!"

Letting go of him, the man fell hard and slammed into the sidewalk. "This was as far as I needed to get you anyway. I'm out of here." Trying to clear the blur from his vision, he tried to make sense of what she was saying as she started walking away. As the sound of her heels got fainter, he was left alone on the pavement; or so he thought.

"Something tells me she didn't leave satisfied. Do you make a habit of leaving women with less than they expected? Eventually the rumor will get out and you will be the laughing stock of the female community." Struggling to see who was speaking to him, Justin rolled around trying to focus. The newcomer leaned down over him and spoke so only he could hear.

"Poor Justin, don't you know you should always keep an eye on your drinks? I suppose not, seeing as you were spending all your energy on watching that young woman. You didn't see me slipping you something special, did you?"

"Flunitrazepam has quite the kick when mixed with alcohol doesn't it? Of course, you already know that, don't you? Oh, where are my manners, I'm talking like an egghead when I should be using laymen's terms. I'm sure someone such as yourself is more familiar with the term rohypnol."

"Who are you?" Justin mumbled quietly.

"That's not what's important right now. What is important, though, is how you got here. We'll review that after we take a quick drive together. You're up for that right? In your state, it would seem that you could use a designated driver, and I'm happy to volunteer."

Opening the trunk, the stranger spread out the plastic inside to cover as much of the interior as possible before turning back to Justin. "I must apologize ahead of time as you won't be riding shotgun."

The man hoisted Justin up, dragging him over the bumper and rolling him into the compartment. After folding his legs in with him, the man shook his head at the limp body in the trunk. "The accommodations might not be to your liking, but you'll have to deal with it for now. However, as you're probably seconds away from unconsciousness, we can just assume you won't remember the ride anyway. Sound good?"

Justin peered up at the person speaking and realized that it was him. This was the man he'd heard about on the news. The vigilante was real. Justin tried to plead for his release, but the words wouldn't form on his lips. He felt unconsciousness take him as the man closed the trunk lid, placing him in total darkness.

Chapter 2

The clock on the dash read 11:37pm on a Sunday evening as the black sedan coasted along a deserted East 12th Street. Surrounding buildings reflected off the freshly waxed side panels. The late model Ford crept along while the air conditioner attempted to overcome the intense heat and humidity infecting the night air.

Every year around this time the high temperature became nearly unbearable, but luckily the city was at the tail end of the latest heat wave. It meant that the cooling system was working overtime. Even with the sun down, the heat was enough to cook an egg on the street.

A popular coffee shop known as the Java Break was a few streets over. The driver knew that the shop's owner arrived each morning at 4:00am to prep his store to open at 5:30am. Research was the key to his actions on that night, and knowing the area's daily routine was pertinent information to have.

Impressive so was the black bean coffee and croissant he'd purchased on his first visit that he pondered the possibility of another stop there soon. He decided to stop in tomorrow to celebrate the start of another week.

This whole block was a string of locally-owned locations catering to a wide range of needs. A hair salon, legal counsel center, and a Laundromat were just a few of the stores along the block. These businesses were still making it for now, but they had seen better day. Judging from the abundance of graffiti in the area and buildings boarded up, the neighborhood wasn't the greatest. However, some of the best of a city's culture often came from neighborhoods like this.

A few stray dogs ate from a toppled trashcan by the deli. One looked up from his evening meal as the car passed by, and for an instant his eyes seemed to glow as they reflected the light from the street lamps.

The vehicle slowed, turning into an alley that ran between the Java-Break and the Laundromat. It ended at the rear of the building where it opened to a row of yellow lines for employee parking. Brake lights bathed the walls of the empty lot in red as the car came to a stop in one of the many unoccupied spots. Some fresh graffiti decorated the wall in front of the vehicle.

In large letters, the wall read "12th Street Ryders"; a small gang of primarily Mexican descent with territory spanning five blocks of town. Rumors had surfaced that the Ryders started some old-school notions of forcing shop owners to pay protection money, but so far, the rumors hadn't been confirmed.

The sedan's door opened and a man in a dark hoodie, blue jeans, and black boots exited. With the hood pulled over his head, his face remained hidden by the accompanying shadow. Reaching under the seat, he found a small cardboard box that he'd hidden beneath it. Inside were disposable gloves that squeaked together as he pulled out a fresh pair.

After sliding the gloves over his hands, he closed the door and walked to the rear of the car. He inserted his key into the lock of the trunk and eased it to the right until it clicked. The latch released the lid and it popped up a few inches. Removing the key and placing it in his pocket, he lifted the lid open to find his guest still unconscious inside. "Right where I left you."

In the rear of the trunk was a black pack that he pulled out and slipped onto his back. Taking a quick look around to ensure he was alone, he lifted Justin out and tossed him over his shoulder before closing the lid. Across the lot, he spotted the black cast-iron ladder that led to the roof.

At the bottom of the ladder, he dropped the dead weight to the pavement. Justin moaned as his limp body came to rest on the sidewalk with a thud. His captor reached into the bag and pulled out one end of a very long rope that he tied around Justin cinching it tight beneath his arms.

He left Justin lying there while he climbed to the roof where he rigged up a pulley and brought sleeping beauty up to join him. At the top, the unknown figure began preparing the rest of his venture.

Removing the pack from his shoulders, he dropped it to the hard surface of the roof and knelt over it. Unzipped, he retrieved a roll of duct tape that he then carried over to his friend. Binding his hands and feet together, he finished with a strip over Justin's mouth. This meant it was time for the fun part.

Returning the roll of tape, the man pulled out a small white package that he bent in his fingers causing it to crack. He waved the smelling salts beneath Justin's nose until he awoke with a shake.

"It's about time you wake up. You slept all the way here." Justin slowly came to recall what had happened that night. He realized he was laying bound before his kidnapper and he struggled to escape the bindings, but it was fruitless.

"You are wasting your time with that. But don't worry, I brought you here for a reason. What do you say we have some fun tonight?" He freed the rope that had still been secured under Justin's arms and carried it to the opposite side of the roof.

He began fastening it to the opposite side in a series of knots. "You know, I've heard things about the girls you choose to socialize with." Tightening the final knot onto a metal rail, he turned and continued, "I couldn't help but wonder why you left out so many details about your supposed conquests when you bragged about them."

Returning to Justin's side, he leaned down to him. "Would it shock you to hear that I know exactly how you get these girls?"

He grabbed Justin by the throat, his voice coming through grit teeth while the captive choked behind the duct tape over his mouth. "Tonight, you learn what you put them through."

Releasing him, the man stood and dragged Justin by his ankle across the roof to the front of the building. Propping him up, he tore open the man's shirt before digging through his pack again. Coming back with something small clutched in his hand, he spoke to his captive audience.

"So how about I tell you a little about myself and then we'll come back to you?" After a brief pause, he continued, "I made a decision many years ago to start an entrepreneurship of sorts. The only problem was it took a very long time to train for the position. It's not like most careers where you can be up and running in a few weeks. Not to mention the fact that this business carried with it an abnormal amount of risk."

He chuckled to himself before beginning again. "You know it's funny that I speak of the risk since I do my best to avoid it. I plan everything to perfection to make sure I can do my work without interruption."

"You see, Justin, I can't stand the filth that has overridden this city. Even worse is that not a single soul was doing anything about it." Light reflected off the item in his hand as he continued, "Well no one until me. If we want a better world we need to reach out and seize it. Don't you agree?"

He paused and stared into the night sky before closing his eyes, tilting his head back, and inhaling deeply. The night was crisp with just a hint of dew on the air. Finally, a cool breeze was beginning to take the edge off the heat.

Adrenaline pulsed through the man's body like the injection of a drug. His breath quickened and there was a tingling to his skin. He smiled slowly and looked down at Justin. The light from a nearby streetlamp glistened across his face and Justin began to squirm against the tape with more effort.

"Well, I needn't keep you in suspense. That would be rude of me. I'm here to put things right for those that can't. The police seem to have an inability to do anything about the laws you break, and that ends here."

"You see, the same laws protecting your victims also protect your freedom." Kneeling close to Justin, the man pulled out what had been shimmering in the light and showed it to his prey.

The mere sight of it made Justin flush with fear. He attempted to turn away from it, but his binds and the wall behind him kept Justin close.

"You see this?" The man rotated the thin metal that sparkled in the moonlight. "This is a number ten scalpel with a palmar grip. It's like my paint brush where as you are my canvas. You should be proud," he said, running the metal lightly across Justin's exposed stomach. "Once I display you across the front of this coffee shop, you'll live in infamy."

Justin whimpered as tears fell along his cheeks. "I'm honored that my art moves you so, but I don't want to keep my fans waiting. What do you say we get started with the first stroke?"

Justin's fear finally received its realization as the blade sliced into his chest. He tried to scream, but the duct tape across his mouth allowed only muffled grunts. The skin burned where the sharp steel separated it into pieces. The skin parted like an invisible zipper had been holding it together. The movement was effortless, and the skin separated with the ease of butter.

"Don't worry. I promise that it will all be over soon. Once I sign my work, I will let you down from this rooftop. You understand, I have to make sure credit is received for all this trouble I'm going through," he stated calmly.

After a few more seconds, the artist leaned back to inspect his handiwork. "Looks great! You should see yourself right now; quite the masterpiece Justin. Now to keep my promise, it's all over."

Grabbing the rope he'd tied to the front of the coffee shop, he wrapped it back around Justin. Once it was secure, he lifted Justin up to the edge of the roof and leaned in close to Justin's ear. Choosing his words carefully, he lost the calm demeanor that he'd been carrying and spoke with quiet rage.

"You have made many mistakes throughout your time in this world Justin. With all your chances to turn everything around, you continue to inflict pain on others. That ends tonight."

With a flick of the wrist, his blade sliced deep into Justin's neck. With a large grin, he rolled the man over the ledge and shouted, "Look out below!" Justin fell to the length of the rope, and his body jerked hard at the end. Swinging like a human pendulum, blood splashed onto the pavement.

"Qui tacet consentire videtur. Blood Week has begun."

Chapter 3

I watched as the car pulled up to the intersection. The setting sun reflected off the blue paint causing flecks of silver to sparkle like stars in the night sky. The man driving leaned over to the woman with him and kissed her on the cheek. As he pulled away, an arm came in through the window and pressed a cold barrel to his temple. I wanted to scream for help, but before the words could come out, I felt the pistol on my skin.

Death's goodnight kiss was puckered and ready to bid me farewell. I felt the cold leather of the steering wheel between my fingers. Before I could save myself, the trigger pulled and released the firing pin into that ignited the metal tube in a flash of light. Instantly, I was back on the sidewalk watching the struggle as a loud bang was followed by the interior of the windshield splashing red.

Time inched by as it appeared to stop in that moment. Everything froze for that instant before death. The slug shrieked in the night as it bored into flesh and bone. The geyser that was his life sprayed out like a fire hose as the force of the bullet snapped his head to the side and caused the man's dying body to fall into the passenger's lap.

Again, I tried to stop what was happening. The man was lost, but I could still save her. I ran towards the vehicle, my chest heaving with the effort, but I didn't get any closer. From across the street, I could feel the life draining out as the blood spilled onto the floorboards. The woman was screaming as the gun turned on her. I ran harder as my vision began to blur from the strain. Reaching out as if my fingers could somehow stop all that was happening, the gun rang out for the second time as I shot up from the sheets screaming.

The buzz of the alarm filled the dark bedroom with the sharpness that I always woke up to. The bedsheets were damp with sweat and tangled in knots around my legs. I reached out and smacked the snooze button before falling back onto the warm pillows. Normally it would be nice to fall back to sleep for a few minutes before rolling out of bed, but I didn't want to risk returning to the nightmare.

As I lay there, a bright light pierced through the darkness like a knife. The warm beam came shimmering through a crack in the drapes and scraped at my exposed pupils. I squinted and raised my hand as if to bat the light away. The unwelcome sun ushered in a new dawn that I wasn't ready to greet. On normal occasions I would call myself a morning person, but I hadn't been sleeping well with the anniversary coming up.

It had been almost two weeks since I'd had a good night's sleep. Like so many other things, there was a cure for situations like this; I needed a cup of coffee.

After rolling out of bed, I made my way to the kitchen where the coffee maker lived. The pre-programmed timer was just about finished making me a fresh cup to cure my morning woes. I'd always found the single-cup coffee makers more convenient since nobody ever drank an entire pot alone before it went bad. In an age of instant gratification, I felt impatient as I waited for the dark brew to finish. Rubbing my face, I breathed in that earthy aroma that permeated through the apartment.

Opening the fridge, I grabbed the bottle of creamer and pulled the sugar from the cupboard. I heard a ding that told me my cup was done. After adding a shot of creamer and two sugar cubes, I walked out on the balcony to start my daily routine.

Viewing the cityscape was a longstanding morning ritual with my coffee. My loft apartment was on the fifth floor of the Walnut building, which offered a terrific view of downtown. Normally I'd prefer to be a little higher, but the balconies were all on the fifth floor and I liked the location. So, this is where I stayed.

I could've gone anywhere with my inheritance like New York or Los Angeles, but Kansas City had a special place in my heart. It was where I'd spent my entire life, and I couldn't see myself ever choosing to leave. Sure, it didn't have the sleekness of Manhattan or the consistent weather of L.A., but it's a place all its own.

With the jazz clubs of 18th & Vine, the delicious staple known as Kansas City BBQ, or the gorgeous view that changed dramatically through the seasons; this place was my home. Being such a wonderful place to live was only the start. To leave would also mean leaving them behind.

Like me, my parents spent the majority of their lives in this city. They met in college and, at first, they couldn't stand each other. One of their first conversations ended with my father getting slapped. Mom said he fancied himself a ladies' man but he didn't actually know how to speak to a woman. It often led to him getting into situations like their first encounter. However, seeing as they had mutual friends, they were forced to spend time together.

Eventually, their time together began to melt the iceberg between them. A fondness grew that eventually led to dating, marriage, and a son. I couldn't imagine two people more in love than my parents, which neither of them saw coming after that initial introduction. They both had very lucrative professions, but still found the time for family. My mother was a physician at a large hospital and my father had his own law firm. It provided a comfortable life that wasn't meant to last.

My trust fund was released to me on my 21st birthday, allowing me to continue living that comfortable life. That money purchased my condo and gave me the view that accompanied my morning coffee. There were more lavish places I could've lived in, but something about the Walnut building spoke to me. It kept me in the heart of downtown while also whispering of a bygone era. It was a place that fit me.

Out on the horizon, the sun continued inching out its own bed, painting the sky orange and yellow. I could feel the warmth from the light as it reached my perch. As it crept higher, all the morning colors would fade, which is why I took the time each morning to appreciate it. Even if it was only for a brief moment, it was peaceful.

Finishing the last of my coffee, I stepped back inside and placed the cup in the sink before heading for the shower. I had an appointment before work, so I needed to get the day started.

Thirty minutes later, I wore a towel around my waist staring into a large walk-in closet. I tried to decide on a wardrobe from the options before me. A wide arrangement of suits, shoes, and accessories were lined up for my selection. After some contemplating, my choice fell upon a three-piece charcoal fabric with thin pinstripes.

Adding in a burgundy button up and a silk neck tie of red, black and silver gave me a good start. I finished with a steel watch with brown band, and a matching belt and shoes.

After removing the selected garments from the closet, I tossed the towel aside to get dressed. Donning the fashion of the day, I left the jacket lying on the bed and walked to the wall opposite the walk-in. I couldn't complete the ensemble without two very important elements that accompany every outfit I wear.

On the wall was a four-foot impressionist's interpretation of a couple walking along a lake in mid-autumn. The use of red, yellow, blue, and purple on the surrounding trees was a constant conversation piece. I could've gone with the good old dogs playing poker, but this painting preached of a better time.

Swinging the painting open on the hinges hidden behind it revealed a one-foot square safe. Pressing my thumb to the dark glass plate at the center scanned my print and caused clunk as the bolt released. Inside was a set of leather hoops that I slipped over each arm.

After fastening the buckles to my belt, I slipped my thumbs up the front to smooth it. Next, I pulled out a steel magazine with fifteen .40 S&W hollow points and a Glock 22 hand gun. I slid the ammunition into the weapon, chambered a round and ensured the safety was on before placing it in the holster secured to my left side by the shoulder straps. This kept the weapon readily available while also hiding it under my suit jacket when I wore it.

The last item I pulled from the safe was a golden shield emblazoned with KCPD attached to a black leather clip. Securing my badge to the right side of my belt, I closed the safe and restored the painting to its original position.

Stepping into the bathroom, I inspected myself to make sure everything was in its place. My skin contrasted to my dark brown hair that gave a mixture of bed head and sophistication. It spiked a bit in the center but was meticulously styled so. My clean-shaven face emphasized my square jaw. When I had tried out a beard, a woman had described me as a lumberjack. It was funny at the time, but I preferred to be clean cut.

Satisfied, I grabbed my wallet and cell phone from the nightstand and placed them in my pockets before picking up my jacket and exiting the bedroom. Checking my watch, I left the apartment with plenty of time to make it to my appointment.

Chapter 4

A twenty-minute drive took me to Elmwood Cemetery where I stood in front of a pair of headstones. The burial grounds were one of the older cemeteries of the city. Located on Truman Road, it had been in use since the mid 1800's. After serving the city for so long, it had eventually made its mark by being listed on the National Register of Historic Places.

On the grounds were a collection of stone structures that decorated entrances to mausoleums as well as the Armour Chapel that was being restored on the 43 acres of land. I'd donated to their cause last year in an effort to keep the grounds clean for my parents to have the best resting place possible. The two stone slabs jutting from the earth carved with the names Douglas and Erica gave me a vested interest in the facility.

Sixteen years ago, these two left a fifteen-year-old boy alone in the world, and today was the anniversary of their passing. Each year, I came to visit with them. I knew it was silly to cling to this ritual, but it seemed even sillier to talk to them anywhere but here. Perhaps I shouldn't talk to them at all. Obviously, they couldn't respond, but people do things like this more for themselves than anything else. I was no different.

"Hey Mom...Dad...hard to believe it's been another year." Leaning down I placed a single tulip in front of each stone. "The time has just flown by, hasn't it? I've kept fairly busy at the precinct; even received an accommodation from the mayor back in March. Exceptional service...line of duty...blah blah," I said, laughing to myself.

"You remember when I told you about my partner Hadley? He retired a few weeks ago and I have a feeling that the captain will be surprising me with a new partner soon. She has been exceptionally nice lately, so it's got to mean bad news is on the way." I chuckled and placed a hand on each stone. "I miss the both of you."

I rubbed my fingers along the smooth stonework before kneeling in front of them. I felt the etching in the rock that held their names. Closing my eyes, "I hope you're in a better place."

Kissing the tips of my fingers, I touched my parents' names and held them there for a moment. After making my peace, I stood back up and spent a moment in silence with them before walking away.

On the way back to my car, I passed a woman crying over a fresh grave. From the head stone, I assumed this was a wife mourning her lost husband. I didn't want to be disrespectful, so I averted my gaze and finished the trek to the vehicle. Not being in a sports car mood this morning, I chose the Tahoe from the garage to drive to the cemetery. Back in the SUV, I noticed on the dashboard clock that my shift started in fifteen minutes. Pulling away from the curb, I realized I still needed to grab breakfast.

Turning a corner, I spotted the street vendor that was there each morning selling bagels and crepes. Stopping alongside him, I asked for a blueberry bagel and handed him a few dollars. My way came a fresh bagel freckled with blueberry spots wrapped in a brown napkin. With breakfast in hand, I thanked him and continued towards the precinct.

A few blocks down, I turned into the underground garage and parked just as my cell phone rang. The name Stacey Hawthorne flashed on the screen. Detaching the smartphone from the dash's hands-free device, I tapped the green button.

"Good morning Captain," I answered.

"Hey Alex, visiting the folks?"

"Yeah, I actually already left. Just got to the precinct."

"Perfect timing then," she laughed. "Could you meet me on the observation deck?"

"Why?" I asked, my voice dripping with suspicion.

"Just get your ass over here," she said before hanging up.

"Sure thing, I'll be right over," I said to the phone as I put it in my pocket. Exiting the truck, I pressed the lock on my key fob and ascended the parking-garage stairs to street level.

Stepping out onto the sidewalk, I watched cars fly by while I waited for the crosswalk signal. I glanced to the right and the monument that stood in front of police headquarters caught my eye. It was a life-sized statue of a policeman carrying a small child. It stood atop a stone pedestal with the names of 119 men who had given their lives in the service of the city through the years.

Some of the names dated as far back as the late 1800's when the department was founded. When the monument had been erected, enough room had been left on the base to honor each officer that died in the line of duty. Each time this happened, their name was added to the list so we could always remember their sacrifice.

The traffic came to a halt as the light changed and I crossed the street to the building on the other side. City Hall was 29 stories from the ground up and at the top was an observation deck that took in the city from all sides. It was built around 1937, so it had seen quite a bit of the good and bad during its tenure. It was a neoclassical Beaux-Arts style brown stone with lines of windows reaching all the way to the roof. The building was wider for the first six stories, serving as a base to the remaining twenty-three floors of the skyscraper.

Along the top of the base were relief sculptures depicting the history of Kansas City during its settlement. Although City Hall wasn't the tallest building in the city, it still dominated the skyline due to sitting atop a large hill. It really was an awe-inspiring sight , and right now the captain was at the top of it.

My history with Captain Hawthorne went back to before she had the title. Stacey had known me my entire life. She grew up with my parents and had been a friend of the family for years. She'd even watched me as a kid when they had gone on some of their weekly dates. This was before I was old enough to stay home alone, but even when I had come of age, she still checked in on me from time-to-time.

Once they were gone, this surrogate mother/child relationship began between us that continued to this day. Knowing me for so long, she also knew of my love for the view that the observation deck gave of downtown Kansas City. Every time she had bad news for me, she gave it to me on the observation deck to soften the blow. For some reason, that view always calmed me.

At the top of the stairs, I pulled open the main doors and stepped onto the green marble of the main lobby. The room was filled with the click and clacks of shoes on the hard surface as everyone hurried to wherever they needed to be. As I was going up, I walked directly to the closest elevator.

Usually someone from security would escort visitors to the top and give them a brief history lesson as they took in the surroundings. I came here so often that most of them had come to know me. They were aware that I was a homicide detective stationed across the street, so I simply gave a nod to the security personnel as I passed by.

The brass doors of the elevator were etched with an assortment of transportation. There were square panels with planes, boats, cars, and even trains like those that come into Union Station each day. Pressing the call button, the doors immediately opened and I stepped in. I pushed the floor for the observation deck and waited as I began to ascend. Although it was the highest floor the elevator went to, it still wasn't at the observation deck. You actually had to walk up a single flight of stairs to reach the door that led to it.

"Hey Cap, how's the view today?" I asked, stepping through the door.

"Alex, I couldn't ask for a better one. We've got clear skies all the way out to the horizon" she replied handing me a warm cup of coffee. Her auburn hair rustled in the breeze. She had it up in a ponytail, which was her usual style choice. It was all business, but still kept something feminine with how it revealed her neckline. The number of days behind her were starting to show with the lines around the edges of her eyes.

While I know they bothered her, the freckles on her face were usually her main complaint. Although I told her that they were one of her best qualities, she usually called me a liar and changed the subject to something else like how her weight wasn't as under control as it used to be. She wasn't fat by any definition of the word, but her edges had begun to soften over the years.

Although I was aware of her concerns in these areas due to our closeness, she didn't talk of them often. She carried herself like a true leader. The respect of her peers and direct reports was more important than what they thought of her looks. I was proud of her accomplishments and her abilities, regardless of anything else that she may view as blemishes.

After taking a sip, I got the ball rolling, "So what's the bad news?"

"Just because I invite you up here, does it have to always be bad news?" she asked with a wry smile.

"Most definitely" I laughed.

"Don't be an ass, Alex. No, I was just thinking about your folks and decided to take a look out over the city. They really loved it here. And seeing as I was going to be up here already, I figured I'd have you join me."

"This is where the bad news comes in, right?"

"Oh hush," she said smacking my arm. After a brief pause, she continued, "Come to think of it, I did want to tell you that your new partner's transfer came through." I knew it had to be something.

"His name is Marcus Delgado and his flight from Fresno should be landing at KCI any minute. He'll be here in a couple hours, which gives you just enough time to review his jacket. I left it on your desk."

"In that case, I should get back there and start reading. I'd like to know at least a little about him before he arrives."

"I'll walk with you," she said heading towards the door. Opening it for her, Stacey stepped through and I followed her down the stairs to the elevator.

On the way back to the station, the conversation mainly consisted of the past and my parents. Sometimes it seemed like she missed them almost as much as I did.

The elevator at the station opened on the second floor to homicide's bullpen. Entering a room filled with seasoned veterans of the force, I made my way to my own little slice of real estate. On my desk was a thick folder filled with all the information we had on my soon-to-be partner awaiting my review. Sitting down, I opened the file and began reading.

Marcus was a Latino, born and raised in Fresno, California. Being a third-generation police officer, it was safe to assume he knew his way around the force. I discovered that he was named after his grandfather who happened to start the family's occupational tradition. Delgado signed up for training the day after his 19th birthday and has now been on the blue team for fourteen years; four as a detective. His 33rd birthday and anniversary with the Fresno PD would have been in three months.

The file showed him to be a decorated officer, but it didn't mention a reason for his move to Kansas City. It also didn't list whether the change in scenery was requested or mandated. I made a mental note to ask him the circumstances behind the move when I met him. It looked like he wasn't coming alone either. Delgado was accompanied by his wife Rita, and seven-year-old daughter Victoria. I couldn't help but wonder what made him decide to pluck his family out of the life they knew and move them halfway across the country.

While I brushed up on all that was Marcus Delgado, a man sat on bench on the other side of the room with cuffs on his wrists and a beat cop standing next to him. The arrestee, a balding Caucasian that looked to be in his mid-twenties, still managed to have a goatee to make sure there was at least some hair on his head. He also had an eyebrow ring above his left eye that looked infected. Wearing ripped blue jeans, white sneakers, and a faded green t-shirt, he sat on the bench while waiting to be interrogated.

Glancing up at this man from my study materials, I took notice of his demeanor and realized something was wrong with the way he was looking at the officers around him. I saw his eyes narrow just as he bolted upright, catching the officer guarding him across the nose with his forehead. Turning to run, a hand grasped his chest and shoved him over an outstretched leg that forced him off his feet. The startled runner got a first-hand lesson about gravity as it pulled him down to the hardwood floors with a loud thud.

Wincing, he tried to catch the breath that had been knocked out of him. Coughing, he slowly opened his eyes and looked up to find his vision blocked by the barrel of my gun staring down at him. Standing over him I stated, "Not your smartest move pal. Did you really think you were going to get out of here? You're in a room full of cops, moron." Taking a step back, fellow officers hoisted him to his feet and carted him off to holding.

"Thanks." replied the officer as he stood up nursing a bloody nose.

"No problem. Are you ok?" I asked the patrolman as I holstered my weapon. He gave me a nod, but it was clear that his pride had been hurt more than anything else. "Well, make sure to get yourself checked out by one of the EMT's." With another nod and an awkward smile, he turned and walked down the hallway.

Getting back to my chair, I took a sip of coffee and continued boning up for the upcoming exam. I barely finished a sentence before a duffel bag plopped into the chair next to my desk. Looking up, I saw the face from the file I had been reading standing before me.

Marcus was of medium build, wearing navy blue slacks, and a white button-up shirt. The cut of his biceps could be seen pushing up through his sleeves. This evidence convinced me that he could handle himself in a rough situation. Although, the belly was pushing on the buttons of the shirt slightly. The man had power in his physique, but there was a small keg hiding what was probably once a six pack. Either way, it's good to know ahead of time if your partner can watch your back, and by the cut of this man there wasn't a doubt.

His clean-shaven face was smiling back at me as he offered out his hand. "I guess that guy didn't know that Van Damme worked here, huh?" Laughing, he struck a tough guy pose straight out of an 80's action flick before extending his hand to me again.

I chuckled as I rose up to shake his hand. "Well, I did watch a lot of *Bloodsport* when I was younger." Taking his hand, I continued, "Pleasure to meet you Marcus, I'm Alexander Saint."

"It's nice to meet you too. I see you've been reading up on me," he said while gesturing towards the open file. Reaching into his bag, he pulled out a similar envelope, holding it up to me. "That makes two of us. It's always good to know a little about someone you're supposed to trust with your life."

"Yeah, I've barely had a chance to scratch the surface. I thought you wouldn't be here for a few hours. Didn't your plane just land a little while ago?"

"Actually, my wife and daughter arrived on the plane this morning. I came in yesterday afternoon so I could finish a project I'd been working on. My wife's parents live in Olathe, so I stayed on their couch since our house won't be ready until this afternoon. I've come up a few times over the past few weeks getting things ready."

"So, do you know the area well then?"

"A bit. We'd fly up here a few times a year to visit her parents so I know enough about the city to get by."

"Seems like a lot of money to spend on airline tickets," I said.

"Oh, no joke. Frequent flyer miles accumulate like crazy with how much we flew back and forth. We've been doing it for six..." Delgado was interrupted by Captain Hawthorne stepping out of her office and calling for attention.

Every set of ears in the pen turned to hear her as she reported, "It's that time of year again folks, and the first day is already on top of us. Our first body has been discovered at a café a few miles from here." Turning, her eyes fell on me. "Saint, the body was found on East 12th Street near Main. You and Delgado get down there, show him the ropes and see if our man has decided to slip up this year."

I stood up, grabbed my jacket and began putting it on as I walked towards the exit. "On our way, Captain." Marcus followed in stride as we reached the elevator and I pressed the down button.

"I guess we'll have to save the get-to-know-you festivities for later," said Marcus. "What was Captain Hawthorne talking about? She made it sound like you guys have a serial killer.'"

"Looks like we found the first thing you'll be learning about this city that you didn't already. Know. Marcus, you chose a hell of a time to join our precinct." Entering the elevator, I pressed the button for the garage and said, "You may regret not waiting for the fall once this week is over."

Chapter 5

On the ride to the corner of 12th and Main, I gave Delgado the CliffsNotes on what had been a thorn in the KCPD over the past few years. Kansas City was the home of a murderer who had been leaving bodies all over the city. Every year around this time, another body would appear that started a weeklong period of death. Then, the killer would disappear for another year.

The news had begun referring to this time of year as Blood Week. Today marked the beginning of the fifth anniversary of the first week. A new body would be found each day for the entire week; each of them mutilated and displayed in public spaces to ensure they're found quickly. While the police department was trying to catch them, there was growing support for the killer around the city.

The person had become somewhat of a legend because the dead bodies were always criminals. Because of this, arguments have begun to whether the police should bother putting a stop to it. You would think that stopping a killer would be a simple decision. But the actions of this one created discord among citizens with a divisiveness that created a lot of fanfare for the news outlets to cover.

Ridding the streets of filth was commendable under the right circumstances, but the vigilante was circumventing the law. On the one hand, this person was clearing the streets of murderers, drug dealers, gang bangers and the like, but was murder okay when the targets were the criminal elements? This is where the public debate continued to rage.

"Sounds complicated," said Marcus. "I can see both the good and the bad that would surround something like this. I'm honestly not sure how I would feel about it."

"A lot of people are conflicted. But then there are those on the outskirts that feel very strongly about one side or the other."

"What is the PD's stance on it?" asked Marcus.

"Officially, we are trying to bring him into custody. He's broken the law and that is something he'll have to answer for."

"And unofficially?"

I sighed, "That's even more complicated."

Marcus pursed his lips. Taking a breath, he turned towards me. "And where do you stand?"

"I just follow the captain's orders, and right now we're to work the case." Delgado looked out the windows, realizing that was all he would get on the matter. He realized that he would have to make up his own mind on the subject. In the meantime, Marcus appeared to understand that my advice was sound. Follow orders and work the case.

A quick chirp of the siren alerted officers on crowd control to slide the barricades aside as we pulled up to the crime scene. Dead bodies always managed to draw a few onlookers, but this one had pulled in more than its fair share; not uncommon for one of the Blood Week victims. While most killers hid their bodies, this one chose to display them. Whether as a message to the city or just to taunt law enforcement, the vigilante never left anything behind that could identify them.

Parking the car, Delgado and I exited the Tahoe to join in on the fun. A huddle of uniforms stood in front of the coffee shop and above them was a white male, covered in dried blood, being lowered to the ground. Most of the blood came from the victim's neck, which had left a large pool on the sidewalk that had expanded to the surrounding cracks. It was still tacky in places, but the majority would take a lot of cleaning to remove. The evidence of what happened here would not be quickly forgotten.

Marcus and I arrived near the pool just as the body reached the pavement. After performing a preliminary report on the body—checking lividity and liver temperature—the coroner waved over her assistant. They both lifted the body up and placed it into a body bag while we waited to speak with them.

The coroner wore dark blue scrubs with sleeves that stopped just below the shoulder. Small beads of sweat formed on her cheeks from the heat. Her fair skin was taut over her athletic frame as she assisted in sliding the body into the zippered bag. Once the body was secure, she removed her gloves and ran her fingers through her hair to secure any of the brown strands that had attempted to escape her pony tail.

"Morning Saint," she said as she finished with her hair. "Aren't you looking good today?"

"Well, you know, a girl has to keep her figure in check," I said posing. Delgado snorted as I stepped over to stand next to our resident coroner. "What do you have for me, Amy?"

"Not much. Your John Doe died between eleven last night and one this morning. He has small cuts to the upper right of his chest, but it was the one to the jugular that is our COD. I'll know more once I get him back to the morgue."

Flashing a smile, I pulled out a small notepad and wrote down the information. After a pause, I stepped closer and quietly asked the question everyone wanted to know. "Do you know if it's him?"

"I think so, but I can't say for certain until I get the body on my table and clean him up. That looks like his pattern," she said, nodding towards the cuts on the chest, "but I won't know for sure until the dried blood is washed off. I'll have more for you in a couple hours."

"Alright, I'll check in with you there once we're done here."

With a smile that could melt the coldest hearts, she added "I look forward to it."

As the body was taken away, I heard my name from behind me. "Detective Saint?"

"Yes", I said turning to see where my name came from. I found a tall, slender officer with chestnut skin looking a bit shaken. I ventured a guess that this was his first dead body, or at least his first murder victim. I didn't recognize him and I tried to make myself familiar with as many of the uniforms in my precinct as possible, so I figured he must be new. "What can I do for you officer?"

"Umm, I was the first responder, sir. I was told you'd probably want to speak to me."

"Of course, officer….?" I trailed off as I clicked my pen to write down his information.

"Kitna sir…Oswald Kitna"

"Oswald? That's not a name you hear everyday"

"I know; caught a lot of slack in school about it. My friends all call me Dokie."

"Dokie?" asked Marcus.

"As in Okie Dokie."

"Oh, I get it," he said. "Because of your initials O.K., right?"

Dokie nodded. "Well, Dokie," I began, "this is my partner Marcus Delgado, and it would seem you already know my name. Can you run the two of us through everything from when you got the call until now?"

Officer Kitna stated he had been on a standard patrol of the area when a call came over the radio that a body was found at the Java-Break on East 12th Street. Since he was only a few blocks away, he responded that he'd check it out. He knew that homicide would be coming down too, but it was always a good idea to get someone on scene as soon as possible.

Dokie didn't see anything when he first arrived, so he thought it might've been a bogus call for the newbie. Some of the veterans on the force were known for hazing anyone fresh from the academy. That was until he found the pool of blood on the sidewalk when he walked up to the coffee shop. He became fairly sure it wasn't a prank at that point. However, there wasn't a body to go with the blood. It was possible that someone had moved the body, but he didn't see a trail going in either direction.

Again, thoughts of an elaborate prank filled his head. You could buy fake blood in stores that looked incredibly realistic, and Kitna wasn't experienced enough to tell the difference. He was just grabbing his radio to report in when he felt something wet hit his arm. Seeing as it had rained a bit the night before, he assumed it was water dripping from the awning over the entrance. But then he realized that this store didn't have an awning, and noticed the drop on his arm was dark red.

Curiosity was followed by disbelief as he slowly started to look up. Oswald said it felt like a scene right out of a bad horror flick. The blood dripping down alerted him to the body hanging above. It was classic slasher film, and he was the latest star. He found the body hanging from the roof with tiny red droplets trickling down to the sidewalk like a leaky faucet.

Kitna immediately grabbed the radio on his shoulder and called in to confirm the body. He requested homicide and the coroner brought in. He then went into the building and spoke with Mr. Williams, the owner of the coffee shop. I stopped Okie Dokie before he went any further as I preferred to get the accounts of Mr. Williams directly from him. He finished by stating that he was inside getting the statement from the owner until he'd seen me speaking with the coroner.

Thanking Officer Kitna for the information, I nodded to my partner who was also writing everything down. It was nice to see my partner didn't waste time working into his new position. Too often people try to acclimate to the people and area before jumping into the mud of the job. It was clear that Delgado wasn't one of them. Finishing his note, we moved inside to speak with the owner.

Inside we found a few uniformed officers conversing while sipping cups of coffee. I noticed a short, balding man with copper skin wearing a white apron and carrying a tray of assorted pastries around to them. When he spotted us, he set the tray on a table near the officers. Smiling at them, he gestured with his palm for the officers to have their pick. Turning back, he quickly walked towards us as he noticeably avoided looking at the scene out front. He greeted us with a smile that that made the lines in his face join with the grey in his goatee to show his age.

"Good Morning, gentlemen. What can I get you?" With all that was going on in and out of his store, it was amazing to see the man taking the time to be so kind.

"Morning. I am Detective Saint and this is my partner Detective Delgado. Are you Mr. Williams?"

"That's me, but seriously, what can I get you?" Before I could say that I didn't need anything he added, "I insist."

"Well..." I started.

Delgado leaned in to me and whispered, "I'd recommend the black-bean coffee." I stood slightly puzzled as to how he'd know what to recommend. Catching on, Marcus filled in the blanks. "I've been here a few times with my mother-in-law who works a few blocks from here at the elementary school. She introduced me to it."

With his sound advice, I decided to indulge. "I'll take a cup of black-bean coffee with a croissant, please."

Mr. Williams nodded politely as he poured me a cup and retrieved my pastry from the tray. Afterwards, he turned to my partner, "and for you Detective?"

"The same, thanks." While he took care of the order, Delgado turned back to me. "I had some of the coffee recently and it was amazing. I was actually hoping to get more, but hadn't had the chance yet." After taking care of us, I asked Mr. Williams what he recalled from that morning.

"I arrived at 5 this morning with my wife just like every weekday. We officially open at 6:30, but we have to prepare the store for our breakfast customers before opening."

When they arrived, he pulled his car down the alley and parked behind the building. After walking back to the front door, he noticed a puddle just outside the entrance. It was still dark, so he couldn't make out what it was. But he could tell it was thick when he'd accidentally stepped in it. Once inside, his wife went to the kitchen to bake the morning pastries while Mr. Williams turned on the lights and retrieved an old mop.

After filling a bucket with warm water, he went back to the storefront where he found red foot prints on the white tile. It had been dark when they walked in since the lights were behind the counter. This was the first he'd seen of the color.

Mr. Williams mopped up what he thought to be spilled slushy or something like that. Once the floor and the bottom of his shoe was clean, he flipped on the coffee grinders and placed clean trays in the display case for when the first batch of pastries were ready. He began to go on a tangent about how the key to his famous black-bean coffee was the fact that he ground them fresh each morning. Getting him back on track, he stated that he moved the coffee grounds to a filter and put them in the brewer before going back out to the sidewalk.

It was when he got back outside with the mop that he saw a ripple in the puddle. At first, he ignored it and started to wet his mop, but then he saw it again. Looking up, he could see something was there but the sun hadn't quite peaked over his building enough to make it out. Mr. Williams returned to the store and turned on the neon sign to add some much-needed light.

With 'Java-Break' flashing through the front window, he was finally able to see what was making the puddle. He rushed back into the store to tell his wife, and shortly afterwards they dialed 911. While on the phone with them, the sun had crept high enough to cast a ray of light to illuminate the body hanging from his roof.

He told me that the first officer arrived about a quarter after six; fifteen minutes after he'd found the body. Since he was unlikely to get any real business that morning—shutting the place down due to a crime scene had that effect—and he didn't want everything he'd prepared to go to waste, so he decided to serve breakfast to all the men and women in blue.

Feeling bad that Mr. Williams had lost a day's business, I thanked him for his statement and his hospitality with a tip of $100. Delgado dropped a twenty as well and asked where the roof access was located.

"Yes, it's right down the alley," Mr. Williams said.

I thanked him again before continuing the investigation. Following Delgado, we passed the uniforms on crowd control and turned down the alley. Walking alongside the Laundromat, Marcus kept his eyes fixed to the ground along the edge of its wall while I did the same on the Java-Break side. It was another mark of a seasoned professional. We didn't need to discuss this tactic beforehand; it just happened.

As we surveyed the alley, I found newspaper pages, coffee cups, napkins, an old McDonald's bag, and a fresh pile of dog shit. Marcus' discoveries were similar, although he was lucky enough to find a used condom. It looked like it had been discarded recently since it was one of the few items in the alley that wasn't covered in dirt and grime.

He flagged a forensics analyst bag and tagged it, but I didn't expect it to be of much use. It was hard to believe that our victim was having sex here just before dying. Getting your throat slashed would have been a hell of a way to climax, but human relations didn't usually go down the same roads as the praying mantis. It would certainly make men reconsider their decision on the possibilities of a one-night-stand.

Delgado and I reached the parking area at the back of the alley at the same time where a forensics tech was examining the ladder that led to the roof. Looking flustered, he kicked the box at his feet that contained his tools for acquiring and testing samples.

"Damn it!" He sat back on his heels and stared at the ladder. "Hey Detectives?" Judging from his elevated voice, the tech didn't realize we were standing right behind him.

I cleared my throat, startling him. "Oh, detectives...I can continue dusting but I doubt we are going to find any prints. It looks like he may have been wearing gloves. I found a piece of what looks like blue nitrile. It was caught on a jagged point of the rung here. I'll have to test to confirm, but it's used heavily in these." He held up his hands to show a pair of medical gloves on his hands that matched the material.

"Could it belong to any of us?" I asked.

"I doubt it. Only Robert and I have gone to the roof so far. We were the ones that lowered the body. He's still up there, but I just had him check his gloves. He doesn't' have any tears in his and neither do I."

"So, prints probably won't be found anywhere," said Marcus.

"Probably not. This guy is smart enough to wear gloves, but only the idiots don't take that precaution."

"Sounds like business as usual," I added.

Making a note of the gloves possibly used by our killer, I looked up wondering if Robert had found anything up top that could be incriminating. Glancing at Marcus, I stepped back smiling and gestured to the ladder, "After you."

"I haven't found any epithelial cells on the rope ends, but there were a few drops of blood on the ledge," said Robert as he gave us his report. He continued examining and taking photos of the ropes as he spoke to us. "Most likely it belongs to the victim, but Kathryn will test all of it back at the lab."

"Kathryn?" asked Delgado.

"She's another one of the forensics techs," I said, "but she specializes in blood samples. These guys gather everything physical and test it, but the blood goes to her."

Leaving Robert to his work, I looked around the area to see if anything had been missed. The forensics team was thorough, but we were all human. Any of us could miss something, which is why we worked in teams. In a corner along the northwest wall, I spotted a red smudge hidden behind a wooden crate. After setting it aside, I interrupted Robert's examination of the rope fragments. "Mr. Jones, we've got more for you over here," I said.

Marcus looked up at the sound of my voice and followed the tech over to me. Robert asked us if we could step to the side while he snapped some photos. Written on the wall in dried blood were the words 'Ex malo bonum'. Delgado's response to it surprised me.

"Good out of evil," he said. With a raised eyebrow, I tilted my head at him like a dog hearing a strange sound. "It's Latin. I studied it in college. It seems our killer is leaving us a message."

"Yeah, we find this at every scene," I said. "It's like a calling card. You don't find many people that read Latin."

"Yeah, it's a dying art. What I don't understand is what that message is. Is he trying to tell us that murder is a good thing?" I didn't have a response for him. To date we had assumed the killer meant that a bad person being stopped permanently was a good thing even though murder was evil, but there is no way to know for sure until the vigilante is caught. Until then, it's all speculation. The silence was ended with a camera snapping more photos.

"Look at the scholar over here," I joked. "Quite impressive. You're running along the same lines that we've been though. We believe he's sending us a message that he's one of the good guys, but he does bad things to make that good. We've found this at every scene since the beginning. It's so popular that everyone in the precinct knows the translation."

Allowing the forensics team to finish up, we left with what we had so far and took our questions to the morgue. Amy would be there cleaning the body by now, and hopefully she would have some answers for us.

Chapter 6

We descended into Madame Amy's Palace of Death, as our resident coroner liked to call it, at half past nine in the morning. Amy had a quirky sense of humor that you couldn't help but appreciate. It probably came in handy entertaining herself since she spent most of her day in the basement alone with nothing but assorted corpses to keep her company.

I remembered the first time I came to the morgue during training when an older man worked there. He wasn't far from retirement at the time and he'd had an odd sense of humor too. He liked to tell this story to new recruits about a time he was down there late at night and he heard scratching on one of the steel doors to the cold storage. He would reenact the story as he told it, approaching the doors as he tried to figure out where the sound was coming from. Bringing the trainee to one of the doors in question, he'd open it to show the body inside.

After pulling the tray out, his cohort on the table would suddenly sit straight up screaming at the top of their lungs. Every year at least one trainee would tumble backwards in fear, shouting profanities as he fell to the tile floor. It would always get a good laugh from everyone that was in on the joke. For the life of me, I couldn't recall his name, but I did take pride in that I was lucky enough not to be the one falling prey to his prank.

Stepping through the swinging doors of the death palace, I found Amy bent over a table looking over our dead body. Her back was to us from where we'd entered, and I could see the curvature of her hips through the pants that hugged her so tightly. That area just below her back was exquisite, and it was one of my favorite physical qualities on her.

Amy was very gifted in that department, and she was fully aware of the attention it drew from others. Her ass had been in my top three for many years, and it looked just as fantastic under the sheets. Clothing could sometimes play tricks on the eyes that fall apart once the skin is laid bare. What Amy had was not a trick, and the most recent pleasure I had to view it was just a few nights ago. She seemed to have a sixth sense when it came to catching men staring at her hindquarters though as she busted me again.

"Afternoon, gentlemen. I have some good news for you." As she walked around to the other side of the body, I noticed her autopsy sheet was already finished. Our John Doe was on his back, supported by the steel table with a white sheet covering his bottom half. His hair was still damp from Ms. Doyle washing the body, which allowed a clearer view to the cuts to the chest.

With surgical precision, the letters R-E-U-S were cut into his chest. We'd seen this before on the other bodies that have appeared during each Blood Week. It was the call sign of the vigilante and each victim was identified with it. As we stepped closer, Delgado's knowledge of the Latin language was further realized.

"Guilty," said Marcus.

"Your new partner comes well-equipped," said Amy. "It took us a while to figure that out the first time. It would've been nice to have you around. I've got more for you too." She grabbed a file off the table next to her and handed it to me. "Based on prints, your John Doe is actually one Justin Sullivan."

The name set me back a step. Opening the folder, I skimmed over the sheets of information within. "I know this asshole, or rather I know *of* him. He's a known rapist." Looking up from the file, "Justin liked to prey on blondes in the 17-21 age range. As I recall, he did some time, but got out a year or so ago. Although it was believed he was up to his old habits, we had trouble connecting him to any recent assaults."

"Nobody able to identify him?" asked Marcus.

"Not exactly. He started using roofies on them, as well as always using condoms. So, everything we may have found was always circumstantial, such as he had been seen at a bar where a woman was assaulted, but there was nothing that could prove he was connected any further. The victims' memories were clouded with rohypnol and the condoms prevented DNA evidence."

"Sounds like karma caught up with the piece of shit," interjected Marcus. Looking back to Amy, "Anything else you can tell us?"

"Yes, funny you mention roofies," she said looking my way. "Justin had a large dose of Flunitrazepam in his system; commonly known as rohypnol."

"Someone used his own strategies against him?" asked Marcus.

"Unless he dosed himself, that's what it looks like. I also found a micro-fracture on the right side of his skull from a recent blunt-force trauma, as well as bruising down his side. It looks like he may have fallen recently. But obviously it was the cut across his throat that made all the injuries permanent."

"With the drugs running through his system, I'm sure he was tripping all over the place," I said. "Anything else?"

"Nothing you don't already know from previous victims. Your weapon is a surgical blade like this one here." She held up one of the scalpels from her tray. "And I can confirm that time of death is sometime between 11pm and 1am."

"Is it possible that a relative of one of the victims is the killer?" asked Delgado. "Whomever carved guilty into his chest had to have known what he'd done."

"Usually I'd say no, since we didn't release the list of suspects to the victims, but the one he did jail time for would have seen him in the court room. The girl he raped on that case had a brother that we caught following us during the investigation and when we went to arrest Sullivan. I remember he went ballistic in the courtroom during the sentencing because Sullivan only got a year. His sister had committed suicide a week before the trial."

"Sounds like motive to me." Delgado pivoted on his heel to walk out, "Seems to me we have a suspect to question."

I glanced at Amy as I started to follow him, but stopped when I saw the dumbstruck look that stared back at me. "That's it? I give you a few tidbits about your dead guy and you're ready to go?" she asked playfully. She put a finger between her teeth and grinned devilishly. "I thought I might get more than just business. A lady likes a little fun now and then.

Checking back up the stairs, I spotted Delgado looking back at me with a grin that stretched from ear-to-ear. I opened my mouth to explain, but nothing came out. I stood there slack jawed and it was clear there wasn't a way to explain away the exchange I'd had with Amy. "I'll meet you in the parking garage," he said laughing as he continued up to the elevator.

With a sigh, I gave up on trying to create any charade that everything was platonic. With bold steps, I strode back to Amy and scooped her up in my arms. Breathing in her scent, my hands squeezed her ass as she responded by wrapping her legs around me and squeezing me in tight. Our lips met and it was pure electricity. I could have taken her right there on the lab table if there wasn't a dead body currently occupying it.

Pulling back slowly, I lowered her until her feet were back on the tile, assuring her that there was more to follow. But right now, I had work to do. Amy smiled and whispered, "I can't wait." Then she bit my earlobe before turning back to her work.

Chapter 7

We pulled up to the address on file for Greg Orton, the brother of Samantha Orton. Samantha was one Sullivan's numerous victims, but one of only two that were successfully pinned on him. As senior in high school with a small frame and long blonde hair, she had fallen into the demographic he'd chosen to prey on. She'd been on the cheerleading squad and had just been accepted to University of Kansas to the school of nursing.

Samantha was found in the park missing all her clothes with defensive wounds on her wrists. Eventually her dress, sandals, and purse were found in a trash can about thirty yards from her body with the cash missing. EMT's were called on scene and took her to Truman Medical Center for evaluation. There wasn't much physical harm to her body, but that emotional damage can be far worse than the physical scars. Since this happened before Justin started using condoms, the DNA led us straight to him.

Sadly, Samantha hadn't been able to find a semblance of peace after being violated in such a way. Weeks later she was found after slitting her own wrists. It left Greg as her only surviving family member when he found her in the bathtub too late to save her. After hearing what happened, most of the department secretly hoped Sullivan ended up dead in a gutter. It was a wish that, as of this morning, had come true.

The apartment building was in one of the worst parts of town. It was full of small studios from top to bottom and looked to be well past its hey-day. A number of windows were boarded over and the building appeared to be two steps away from being condemned. I wondered what the going rate for rent was with the slumlords of the area.

Opening my door, my nose was immediately violated with a horrid smell from the nearby sewer. The worst time to come down here was after a good rain. Sewers would begin to overflow and carry up an odor that could make anyone decide to give up breathing.

Looking up at the building I said, "I wouldn't get your hopes up about Orton."

"Why do you say that?" asked Marcus.

"It's not the first time we've investigated people with motive on the Blood Week murders. Every time it comes up, it's not our guy."

"I can see that, but how many of the others had timing match up?"

"What do you mean?" I asked.

"I looked at Samantha's case while you drove. Her trial was just over five years ago. With the Blood Week murders going on for the past five years, perhaps the others were all practice leading up to Justin Sullivan."

I had to admit that I hadn't noticed the time lines on the murders starting after Sullivan's trial. Strange that the new guy seemed to be so on top of things on his first day. The more I thought about it, Captain Hawthorne really found quite the detective. As we ascended the front steps, an older woman exited the building with a large hand bag. I quickly ran up to hold the door for her. Accepting her gratitude, we stepped in and climbed to the third floor to apartment 3F.

"Who is it?" a voice asked from inside after I knocked on the door.

"Mr. Orton? KCPD, we'd like to ask you some questions." No sooner had I finished my sentence, we heard footsteps scurrying across the apartment. "He's running", I said as I kicked the door in. We both entered, guns drawn, and swept the room. I spotted him outside the window as he started descending the fire escape.

"Marcus, chicken's out the window. Cut him off at the bottom while I..." Delgado was out the door and down two stairs before I'd finished my sentence. Swinging my leg over the window ledge, I stepped onto the black grating to follow him down.

I felt my heart pounding, matching the adrenaline pumping through my veins. No matter how many chases or high-intensity situations a cop gets into, it's always like the first time. The excitement is dipped in a thick batter of fear that combined together in a strange mixture of duty to the badge attached to my belt. I had a job to do.

Already down one level, I began descending from the second floor of the fire escape when the suspect reached the pavement. I was able to get past another floor before he picked a direction and started running. As Greg made a break for the front of the building, I jumped from the bottom level of the fire escape rather than take the ladder.

Hitting the concrete, I fell to a roll and ended up right back on my feet to continue the chase. I yelled "Freeze!", but the squirrel seemed in no mood to cease the flight. Greg had almost reached the front of the alley when he glanced behind him to check on the distance between us.

By the time his eyes returned forward, he'd exploded onto the sidewalk at the front of the apartments at the exact moment Delgado reached the alley. My partner came into view already off the ground, flying forward in mid-tackle of our runaway perp. The two men collided with the force of Marcus shoving Greg off his feet and onto the hard ground.

Once I caught up, Delgado was already cuffing him and beginning Miranda rights. "Greg Orton, you are under arrest. You have to right to remain silent..." This guy was good.

About an hour later, I stood in a dark room looking through a two-way mirror. I watched Mr. Orton, who sat at a steel table with handcuffs securing him to the bent pipe that curved from the center of the table. He had rips in his shirt where he'd been taken out like a running back trying to score.

Whether he was guilty of murder or not, he was definitely guilty of something with the way he ran. Calling out "KCPD" and seeing who fled helped find those with a reason to run.

When Captain Hawthorne arrived in the room, Delgado and I made our way into interrogation. I entered the room followed by Marcus who closed the door behind us.

"I didn't do anything!"

"Greg, if you didn't do anything, why did you run?" His face scrunched up as he tried to create an answer. Instead of letting him fabricate something, I decided to continue, "Where were you last night between ten and two this morning?"

"This morning? Why? What's this all about?"

"Just answer the question, Greg," responded Delgado.

"Umm, I was working."

"And where were you working, Greg?" I asked.

"At work, why are you treating me like this?"

This wasn't getting us anywhere, so instead of continuing this back and forth, I pulled open a file. "Do you remember Justin Sullivan?" Before I could finish the name, his face went from confused to angry contemplation.

"Of course, I remember that piece of shit. Why the fuck are you bringing up the son of a bitch who raped and murdered my sister?"

"I thought your sister committed suicide," said Marcus.

Greg fell silent and glared at my partner. Then very calmly he replied, "If not for that mother fucker touching my sister, she would still be here. Her death is his fault; he murdered her."

Trying to get him back on course, I did what I could to defuse where the conversation had steered. "Mr. Orton, what happened to your sister was unforgivable, but we need you to answer our questions. Justin Sullivan was found dead this morning, so I hope you understand why we need to question you."

"Wait, he's dead?"

"Yes," said Marcus.

"Good, I'm glad he's dead. I hope that mother fucker rots in hell!"

"I can't blame you for wanting him dead, but we still have to investigate this like any other homicide."

"Wait…I'm here because of what he did to my sister?!? That guy deserved everything he got and then some! I would've loved to be the man to kill him. I would have relished in it. Do you have pictures?"

"So, you're saying you didn't kill him?" asked Marcus.

"No, I already told you that I was working. But I sure would've liked to do it."

"If you let us know where you were working, we can corroborate your story," I said.

"I work overnight for the warehouse on Central; I was there until five this morning. My boss should still be there. You can check with him."

Writing down the information, I ripped off the sheet and handed it to Marcus who stepped out to check on it. "Even if you were working," I continued, "that doesn't tell me why you ran."

"I was scared."

"We identified ourselves as KCPD. What could you have been scared of?"

"You guys show up at my door and I had no idea why." I stared at him without saying a word, waiting for a better answer. "Ok fine. Look, there is a warrant out on me for a drug charge, ok? But I still had nothing to do with killing that fucker. Wish I would've been there when it happened though. I could've helped stomp his face into the curb." Just then, the door opened and Delgado peeked in nodding his head.

"Well Greg, looks like your alibi is solid. Some uniforms will be down shortly to take you to booking."

"Wait, I don't get to go home? You just said that I have an alibi. I didn't kill him."

"That was also before you ran from the police and admitted to your warrant for possession."

Stepping out of the room, I closed the door as Mr. Orton came to terms with the fact that he wasn't going anywhere. Just before the door latched, I heard him exclaim "You're a fucking assh—"

Sitting back at my desk with my feet propped up, I stared at our white board with the case information, which was void of anything substantial in this early stage. Justin Sullivan was strung up for the whole world to see, and nothing had popped up yet. That was until my phone vibrated on my desk, playing the theme from *Back to the Future*.

Marcus popped his head up and started laughing when he saw it was my phone. "Hey, don't judge me," I said. "It's a great movie." Smiling, he nodded in agreement while I slid my thumb across the screen to answer it. The news came in from the forensics lab that they'd gotten a hit on the semen from the condom we'd found in the alleyway outside of Java-Break.

Ending the call, I pocketed my phone. "Marcus, get your stuff; you'll never believe who that condom came back on."

Soon we were pulling up in front of the coffee shop for the second time that day. With the early-afternoon sun on its way back down the opposite side of the sky, I felt the gurgle in my stomach telling me I had missed lunch. I decided to get something as soon as we finished up here. The news from forensics was too good to wait until after a meal.

The sidewalk was still blocked off with police tape while a few field techs were packing away their gear. A large white van sat on the corner with its rear doors open where a high-pressure water sprayer was being used to clean the sidewalk. Seeing the clean-up crew getting the blood out of the sidewalk meant the police tape would probably be down by early evening, but our shop owner had some gaps to fill in before then.

Stepping under the yellow tape, Marcus and I entered the Java-Break where I could see Mr. Williams in the kitchen cleaning up through the cutout in the back wall. The bell chimed as we entered, which caused his eyes to flare at the possibility of customers.

"Detectives, you're back," he said coming back to the main lobby. "I'd ask if I could get you anything, but we've put everything away to begin prep for tomorrow morning. I'd be happy to have something ready for you first thing. I'm hoping we'll get some extra business to help with the lack thereof today."

"We're actually here in an official capacity," I said.

"Oh, what can I do for you?"

Marcus stepped forward first, "Mr. Williams, we found a used condom in the alley by your shop this morning. The DNA has led us back here today." The shop owner's face went blank as his eyes swelled in alarm.

"Judging by your reaction," I said, "am I correct that you already knew it was there?"

Mr. Williams looked around the room, and then glanced around in the kitchen through the wall window. Assured there wasn't anyone else around, he turned back to the detectives. "Can we take this discussion outside?" he whispered. Obliging him, we stepped out to the alley to avoid the water being sprayed on the sidewalk. Apparently, our kind little coffee shop owner left a little information out of his statement. Upon DNA analysis, the semen had come back as his own.

His DNA had been on file because of a ten-year-old case of a man that died in a work accident. Skin cells had been found under the man's nails, and it was initially believed that the death had been intentional. All the workers at a factory had been swabbed while searching for a match to skin cells, and Mr.

Williams had been one of those workers before opening his own business.

Nobody was implicated in the death at the factory after it was discovered that the epithelial cells were from him tripping on a pipe and scratching the hand of a coworker trying to catch him earlier that same day. His death in falling from the second level was ruled an accident in the end.

As with all deaths, the detectives on that case had done their due diligence in gathering DNA evidence. It was for this reason that today we were able to link the condom to Franklyn Williams, owner of the Java-Break.

"Look, my wife doesn't know about this, so please keep it between us."

"Our discretion depends on the information you have for us, Mr. Williams," I said.

"My wife and I haven't had sex in two years. There is only so much a man can take before he starts fishing in other ponds, if you know what I mean. Last night, I told my wife that I was going to go bowling with my brother, but I was actually here with one of my part-time cashiers. For the past three months we've been meeting regularly for sex, and last night I tossed the condom from the car window because I didn't want to walk in the rain to the trashcan."

On my notepad I wrote down the information he gave me. "What time were you finished cheating on your wife, Mr. Williams? Were you still here between eleven and one?"

Shaking his head, "I was back home by 9pm, and my wife can confirm that because she gave me an earful about being out so late. If you have to ask her though, will you be able to leave out the details of where I really was last night?"

Cheating on his spouse had no bearing on our investigation, so, regardless of my thoughts towards it I decided to keep it out of any questions with Mrs. Williams. I couldn't say if I agreed with his actions, but two years was a long time to go without sex. He'd waited much longer than I would have, or most men for that matter.

Once we confirmed his arrival time at home, and heard plenty about her husband being out late at that "damned bowling alley", we found ourselves back at square one.

On the ride back to the station, Delgado was the first to speak. "This vigilante seems really good at what he does. I mean, to have never left any tangible clues behind must say something about him, right? Five years running and nobody has identified him."

"Not to mention being able to go after hardened criminals without dying himself. That definitely has some skill involved."

"That, or a shit ton of luck," Marcus joked.

"I'll tell you what, once we get back I'll pull up the case files from past years so you can get caught up."

"Sounds good."

Back at the precinct, while my partner was brought up to speed, I put the final touches about the day's events in our report. Just as I finished, Captain Hawthorne called me into her office. "How was it out there today?"

"As usual, there weren't any clues to tie in a suspect."

"And Delgado?"

"Seems like a decent detective. He was a little short with Greg Orton today, but it was nothing too horrible. He's got a lot of good instincts, and a familiarity with the area I wasn't expecting. He's reading the police history on the Blood Week vigilante now."

"Okay, keep me informed on the case and be careful out there. We still have six days to go." Looking at the clock on the wall behind me, she continued "Looks like shift is over, how about you grab something to eat with that new partner of yours? Get to know him better since you have to trust each other with your lives." With a smile and a nod, I decided her advice wasn't a bad idea.

At Delgado's desk, I asked, "How're you doing with all this?"

"Not bad, I've read about half of it, so I'll have to finish the rest up tomorrow."

For the past few weeks, I'd had a craving for a restaurant in the Power & Light District. It was one of my favorite places to eat, and this seemed like the perfect excuse to indulge. "So, Marcus, do you like sushi?"

Chapter 8

The Drunken Fish was an upscale sushi bar in the downtown area that I enjoyed on a regular basis. Beyond the phenomenal food and views of the heart of Kansas City, the lack of children flocking in with the goal of getting trashed created a pleasant atmosphere. Although I was only in my thirties, I still looked at the early twenty-somethings as children. And I had no interest in watching them try to go shot-for-shot with each other. Funny, since the first word in this restaurant's name was drunken.

However, this sushi bar was more of a business-casual style of restaurant, so you weren't likely to find the kids Jaeger-bombing. While I hadn't always been a fan of sushi, my introduction to the world had been life-changing. My first experience with what a place was calling sushi had been a cheap California roll. That atrocity didn't spend much time in my mouth before being spit into a napkin. But once I was introduced to real sushi, I'd been a huge fan ever since.

I hadn't been to the Drunken Fish in a while. I'd been trying to find time to go, but hadn't been able to make it for a couple weeks. I was lucky that Marcus was willing to give it a try and it also allowed us to share a few drinks and possibly learn a few things about each other that weren't contained in a personnel file.

We met outside the restaurant at 7pm, which meant the night air was still a bit sticky, but it was at least starting to cool. Inside, Jeanette was standing behind the hostess table as we entered. She smiled when she saw me and stepped out to greet us.

"Mr. Saint, we haven't seen you for a while."

"And I've hated every moment we've been apart."

Her eyes sparkled as her smile deepened. "Well I hope we can live up to what you've come to expect of us. Could I interest you in your usual table?"

The bar was sectioned into four parts that were separated by red partitions and multiple floors. Near the main entrance were high-top tables with low lighting for a romantic atmosphere. The back had tables of standard height in front of the main bar. With the bright walls contrasting against the dark wood floors, it was upscale without the inflated costs.

In addition to the interior, there were two sections for outside dining. On the main floor was what could be called a balcony that overlooked the sidewalk outside. It was a raised patio that sat about four feet above the outside walkway. The best option for seating—and where I usually liked to dine—was the roof terrace. Another bar was surrounded by steel patio furniture, complete with umbrellas. But along the edges of the terrace were dark whickered furniture with red cushions that sat around tables with gas fire pits built in the center.

"You know, it's getting nicer outside by the minute. I'd love my usual table, Jeanette." As her eyes lingered on mine, she grabbed two menus from the hostess booth before asking us to follow. We ascended the stairs to the terrace and she sat us in a corner table where the fire was already lit. I came here so often that they always sat this table last just in case I came in. It was tremendous service to go along with the exquisite cuisine.

"Let me know if there is anything I can do to make your stay more pleasurable," she said as she handed me a menu. Her fingers brushed lightly against mine as she smiled. She handed the other menu to Marcus and left with a nod.

"Am I the only one noticing that?" asked Delgado.

"No," I laughed.

"Does she always flirt with you like that?"

"Usually, but I'm not going out with her again."

"Again?" Delgado set his menu down and leaned forward. "You dated the hostess?"

"I wouldn't call sex dating."

"Does Amy know about her?"

I shrugged. "She might," I said. "There hasn't been any talk about exclusivity. Besides, that's not really my style. I like to sample from all the buffet has to offer."

"So, you're saying that you get around a lot, huh?"

"Define a lot..." We both laughed.

Opening his menu, Delgado continued to ask about my dating life. "If you're the scoundrel I'm thinking you may be, are there others at the precinct you've sampled?"

"You should stick to the specialty rolls," I said, effectively changing the subject. "Just about everything here is fantastic, but you'll get to see how this place shines if you stick to those."

Along with the sushi, I convinced Delgado to get a bottle of sake with me. As he lifted his cup to take another sip, he paused and said, "I'm telling you, it's a dead-end investigation unless more evidence comes up." He downed his drink and poured more from the clay bottle between us. I couldn't help but agree with him about the evidence. Any leads we traced never seemed to turn up anything concrete on the vigilante killings.

"So, the whole point of this," he continued, "is to find out more about each other, right?"

"Yeah, I think it's important to know your partner beyond just the job." Through the course of dinner, many interesting facts had come to light. These were personal things that told me about the man beyond the detective.

He met his wife Rita on the job when she was a material witness on a robbery seven years ago. Sparks flew back and forth during her initial interview and once the case was closed, Marcus jumped at the chance to ask her out. It didn't sit well with his captain back in California at first, but it got better with time. Especially when the news of their coming daughter came eight months after they were married. She was named Victoria after Rita's mother.

With Rita's family being from Olathe, he'd spent a lot of time in the city over the years they'd been together. At times, he felt like he lived in two places with how often he'd been coming to Kansas City. I also learned that he liked to paint in his spare time, which was something I hadn't expected. He even had a few of his pieces shipping to Kansas City with plans to display them in his house.

"Wow," he said taking the last bite of his third Strawberry Cheesecake Makimono. It was New York cheesecake that was rolled and tempura fried before being topped with chocolate sauce, mixed nuts, powdered sugar and strawberries with whipped cream. "That just might be the greatest thing I've ever tasted." I'd recommended the desert to him as the finishing touch of the meal, but this was the first time I'd seen someone eat that many of them.

"I want to order another, but Rita would kill me. She's been trying to get me off all the sugar."

"Women want us to be the best we can be," I said.

"Yeah, but it's hard to give up things that taste that good. I'll call it a win by not ordering a fourth roll."

As the night winded down, I also learned that classical and Jazz music were staples in the Delgado household. Rita played the violin, Marcus the jazz trombone, and Victoria wanted to take up the clarinet when she got a bit older. I had to admit that Marcus had quite the musically cultured family. It was something we connected on since I too played jazz trombone in high school and throughout college. Though I hadn't played in almost a decade.

With the added alcohol flowing, Marcus returned to a topic he seemed truly interested in. "I'm sure if the right woman came along you'd be ready to settle down. Perhaps that right woman might be our lovely coroner? You two were quite cozy earlier."

Before I could find a way to brush the comment aside, my phone vibrated across the table while the voice of a white haired, time-traveling scientist yelled "1.21 GIGAWATTS!!!"

Delgado looked at my phone and then back at me before he burst out laughing. He pointed at my phone asking why that is the second time he'd heard reference to that movie coming from my phone. I said the only thing that I could think of to explain it away.

"I guess you guys aren't ready for that yet, but your kids are gonna love it." Laughing I added, "I know that my geek is showing quite a bit right now, but I'm just an avid movie lover. I switch up the sounds on my phone every few months, and right now I'm on a *Back to the Future* kick."

Grabbing my phone, I pulled up the text I'd just received to discover a message from Amy Doyle. "Speak of the devil" I said, showing Marcus who the message was from.

Tapping the box to open the picture attached to the text as I took another drink, I almost spit out the mouthful of sake over the table fire. Narrowly avoiding singeing my face, I was staring at a self-taken photo of Amy wearing red lingerie that squeezed tightly against her breasts as the fabric struggled to contain them. It came complete with a caption reading, 'This is what's waiting for you. Come over now.'

I didn't need a more blatant invitation than that. I grabbed the bill and told Marcus that I'd cover it this time around and he could get the next one. Leaving so abruptly wasn't the politest thing to do, but my reaction was clear enough to him as to where I was heading. I had an important package waiting for me, so I paid for the meal and responded to Amy that I was on the way.

Driving up to Amy's house, I pulled in the driveway and hopped out. Rushing past the cars, I continued up the walkway towards her front door while hitting the button on my key fob to lock the SUV. I didn't even have a chance to rap on it before the door opened.

Amy stepped into view in all her glory with the same outfit from her text, but now I had to pleasure of seeing the rest of it. Along with the top pressing tightly against her skin, she had a matching garter belt with straps holding up matching satin thigh highs that made her legs scream to be touched. The straps stretched over her naked thighs as the only fabric concealing the skin around her ass as the thong made sure to keep her completely exposed. Inviting me in, she closed the door behind me and wasted no time getting started.

I pushed her hard into the wall as I moved in, pressing my body against hers. Coming ever closer allowed our lips to meet. With my hand on the back of her neck, I tasted the strawberry of her lip-gloss. Her mouth parted and invited my tongue to dance with hers. Slowly, my focus traveled down past her cheeks and paused just above the collar bone.

As I bit her neck, her head tilted back as she let out a whispered moan. I released the clasps on her top allowing her chest to fall free. As the top fell to the floor, my hands began to massage her breasts and she began pulling on my hair. My hands caressed her thighs before jerking her legs up around my waist so I could carry her into the bedroom.

Laying her on the bed, my lips kissed slowly down her neck past her shoulders and continued down her chest while my hands slid back up her thighs. By the time my mouth reached her navel, my thumbs had pushed up under the strands of her thong and began pulling her panties down. I didn't stop until they had passed her toes and I could drop them to the floor.

Standing up, she pushed me into a chair and climbed into my lap. Lightly licking my neck with intermittent kisses, Amy unbuttoned my shirt and slid it down my shoulders until she pulled it off my arms and tossed it into the corner of the room. Her hands rubbed down my chest to the belt buckle of my pants where she undid the clasp. With a hard pull, the belt was ripped from the loops. She unfastened my pants before standing both of us up and pulling them off. I kicked away my shoes as she did so to hasten the process.

Stepping forward and grabbing her ass, I lifted her up and wrapped her legs around me once more. Letting our nude bodies come into contact, I carried her towards the bed and placed myself on top of her warm skin. Our chests rose and fell against each other, breathing deeply in anticipation of a night of hot sweat.

Chapter 9

The sun had set on the city sending most of its citizens in for the night. The news had heavily covered the events at the coffee shop on East 12th Street that day. Little coverage was provided for anything else. It was as if there wasn't anything else news worthy in the entire city.

The investigation had uncovered a few leads, but they had fizzled out leaving the detectives on the case hitting a brick wall. Normally there was the argument that it had only been about 24 hours since Sullivan's death, but the city knew better. The first night of Blood Week had come and gone, and the setting of the sun began the countdown to another body.

The beginning of the second day meant there would be increased police traffic on the streets. Criminals battled with bouts of insomnia knowing there was a higher likelihood of cops in their neighborhoods, not to mention a killer that liked to prey on them as well. It was hard to sleep while looking over your shoulder for a hunter. The stress of it could make a person choose to sleep with the lights on. Shadows had a funny way of playing with your vision.

That isn't to say that everyone reacted to Blood Week this way. Some liked to play the odds since it was unlikely to be targeted against the large number of bodies in the city. Unlike the casinos, this time the odds were in your favor. One such gambler was waiting for a delivery pickup.

On the corner of 18th and Troost, a man sat in his car with the windows down, smelling the KC air. There was a hint of mold on the wind from the surrounding buildings. Many of them were in desperate need of repair, but not a lot of money was flowing into the neighborhood, so buildings began to decay. The street lamps gave the neighborhood an ominous yellow glow making the kid on a bike riding towards the car feel uneasy.

Over the shoulders of his blue t-shirt was a backpack filled with items that he hoped to stay hidden. As he pedaled past a black car parked near the edge of the intersection, he gave the man inside a nod. The driver watched as the boy working for him sped by with one of the many packages he had in route. He, and others, were like his very own postal service.

Turning his head towards the sidewalk, he spotted a newspaper in a nearby trashcan that could offer some entertainment to pass the time, so he stepped out of the vehicle to retrieve it. He read the headline *Killer Still at Large* as he flipped through the pages of the Monday edition of the *Kansas City Star*. Underneath was a small blurb about the death of Justin Sullivan. He was a convicted rapist and had been strung up with his throat slit.

As this was an active investigation, there wasn't much information beyond that. There wasn't a mention of the vigilante's calling card of cutting 'REUS' into the victim's flesh or writing 'Ex malo bonum' in their blood. This information had never been released to the public, but that didn't stop news outlets from connecting the dots to show that Kansas City had a vigilante in their midst.

The man pulled out the funny pages and tossed the rest back in the trash before returning to his car. The reader catching up on the latest antics *Garfield* and his love of lasagna was Danny King. Originally from Independence, he moved to Kansas City when he got deeper into his start-up business. He was an entrepreneur, of sorts, deep into the local drug trade.

Danny King—otherwise known as Big King—started out as a drug mule for G-Rule. He carried cocaine, weed, or meth in a backpack to addresses all over Independence. Dropping out of school at fourteen, he started running drugs full-time. In his eyes, there was more money in carrying a backpack of narcotics than having it full of books. King had decided early on that school didn't make sense when there was paper to be made in the real world.

Moving up through the ranks, he was eventually transporting cash payments back from the drop-off points too. On one such occasion, he was attacked as a rival gang tried to steal the money he was transporting. He successfully protected the parcel and ended up earning quite the reputation in the process.

The story spread that two men tried to take the backpack at knife point, but King pulled out a pistol and shot one of them as the other ran off. He gained respect that garnered him upward momentum in the organization. After running backpacks for two years, he started dealing at sixteen. This meant getting his own delivery boys like the kid on the bike.

King started small, but after four years he had pushed his way into the big time. Moving to Kansas City, he took over a ten-block territory that allowed him a large network of drug mules that ranged from ages twelve to fourteen. He used them to shelter himself by never having the drugs in his possession.

With the added enticement of getting a small cut of the sale, the kids were hooked in as his employees. Only death or prison ever lost him a staff member. Cash spoke volumes in the area of persuasion, and he had plenty of it to speak with. King tried to cover every inch of his supply chain from manufacturing to delivery to avoid the inflated costs of purchasing from a larger dealer. Instead, he made anything he could on his own, and the two he produced regularly were meth and marijuana. It was common for customers to ask for a bag of M&M's when they purchased to get an assorted bag of both.

Danny had three houses growing pot and two more cooking meth under his umbrella, but he still kept a close eye on everything. However, no matter how meticulous Danny was, problems still surfaced during production. The siren of a fire engine echoing in the distance signaled one of these setbacks.

Its wails were accompanied by police cars rushing to a small building that had caught fire. Accidents happened from time-to-time in this business, but King didn't enjoy the loss of revenue. He discovered from a call moments ago that the sirens were heading to a meth lab where one of his cooks forgot his competence.

Toxic fumes were venting from a batch of Meth, still cooking, when one of the new cooks chose to take a smoke break without stepping outside of the kitchen. The cigarette lit the fumes which blew him and the product sky high. Normally King would have put two slugs in the asshole for costing him money, but the explosion took care of everything for him. Big King was the kind of leader that sent a message to anyone that fucked with his cash flow.

King sat in his Dodge Charger Super Bee that he purchased outright last month. It was a birthday gift to himself, paid for in cash, which was easy to come by since this was backbone of his entire business. There was plenty of paper to make in the drug trade, and business was good in his section of the city.

He looked up from reading his funnies every so often to keep an eye out for two more couriers he was expecting. He didn't like to sit around wasting time, and they were running a bit late for their appointment with him. Although that meant they would be running behind on their deliveries tonight, he always allowed for small things that could delay deliveries by up to 15 minutes. However, if you were later than that, Big King's temper would make an appearance. Right now, only six minutes had passed.

He wasn't really in the mood to sit around waiting for these kids with the loss of a kitchen weighing on him. Time was money and he needed to locate a new place to cook. Just then, he spotted the first of the delivery boys pulling up on his bike.

After exiting the car, Danny looked around to make sure nobody was around. The street was clear of any possible onlookers, so he leaned back in the car and pressed the button that popped the trunk. In the rear compartment were two large backpacks; one green and one red. Unzipping the small pouch on the back of the green bag, King pulled out a folded piece of paper and handed the pack to the boy who quickly put his arms through the loops and tightened everything to his back.

"Here's tonight's delivery address," said King as he handed him the slip of paper. "You need to make up some time."

"I will, Big King."

"Get on then." With a nod, the boy took the slip and read the address before riding off. In the time it took for the kid to pedal out of sight, King saw the second delivery boy coming up.

Following the same protocol with the red pack, he watched this one disappear down the street as well before sliding back into his Super Bee. He rolled the newspaper into a ball and tossed it out the passenger window. It completely missed the trashcan and bounced down the sidewalk propelled by a gust of wind.

Now that he'd finished handing out work for his troops, King hastened his exit from the area. Turning the car's ignition, he smiled as it gave off a deafening, guttural roar like a beast waking from hibernation. Revving the engine sent vibrations through his seat and echoed down the city block. Throwing it in first, Big King mashed the pedal and peeled down the street leaving plumes of white smoke behind him.

Arriving at his apartment complex a few miles away, Danny whipped the Charger into a parallel parking spot and cut the engine. Although King had an alarm and a GPS tracker on his car, most would still be afraid of parking such a nice car in this neighborhood. However, this piece of machinery didn't belong to just anybody; it belonged to Big King, and everyone in this part of town knew it.

After exiting the car, King hit the locks and activated the alarm as he walked to the building's front door. Although people knew this was his car, King wasn't stupid enough to not take precautions. If the alarm ever went off, it would simply be warning him that it was time to put a bullet in someone.

As he opened the door leading into the lobby, he noticed a man sitting on the sidewalk with his back against the building. The man wore a pair of jeans that didn't appear to have been washed in this decade and a dark sweatshirt with a hood. He had a backpack next to him which, based on his appearance, must have contained all his worldly possessions. He sat there sipping from a large bottle wrapped in brown paper.

While this man hadn't done anything to King, it didn't mean he wanted a beggar stinking up his front door. Being homeless was a disgrace in his mind, and he didn't want their kind around here. Stepping up to the man, Big King kicked him in his hip. It wasn't hard enough to severely injure him, but it definitely informed the beggar who the alpha was in this conversation.

"Get off my stoop you homeless piece of shit." The man glanced up at King before returning his attention to the liquor bottle, which Danny didn't take kindly to. Pulling out his gun, he pointed it at the squatter's head and kicked him hard enough to knock him to his side.

"Did you hear me, asshole? Get moving before I introduce this here bullet to the inside of your skull!" This got his attention as the drunk quickly gathered his belongings and ran off.

"That's right, when Big King says jump you ask how high, mother fucker."

Proud of himself, King waited for the man to round the corner before entering the building with a swagger. Walking down a hallway of green tile with yellow splotches of faded paint, he reached the elevator doors. Hitting the button to call for the car, he stood back to wait when there was a chirp from the phone in his pocket. Pulling it out, he read a text from one of his customers informing him the delivery boy just left. Confirmation of shipment meant more money in Big King's pockets.

About this time, the elevator doors opened with a loud screech of metal in dire need of some WD-40. Inside, he pushed the button for the sixth floor and listened to the noise again as the doors closed. The elevator was in worse shape than the hallway with stained plaid carpet completely ripped up in the back corner. Above this missing piece was a faux brass hand rail that was covered in rust and dents. One piece hung to the floor at a forty-five-degree angle. In all, you had to really trust the elevator to have stepped foot into it. The bell dinged and Danny cringed slightly to the doors opening again for him to exit.

Walking towards his door, he noticed the lone fluorescent lamp by the stairwell flicker before dying completely. He heard footsteps in the stairwell, which made him chuckle since they were now walking in darkness. Unlocking his door, he stepped in and closed the door behind him.

Inside, he pulled out his handgun and placed it on the dinner table next to a square piece of mirrored glass. Danny grabbed the remote and turned on the TV to a reality show that he was addicted to. From in the fridge, he pulled out a plastic ring that held together three beers and a plate with a few slices of pepperoni pizza that he put in the microwave.

As the pizza was nuked, he pulled a can of beer from the plastic rings and tossed the other two onto the counter. The can hissed as he opened it and took a few swigs as he waited for a warm dinner. The timer went off and he removed the plate, setting it and his beer on the table.

He walked down the hall to the bathroom to take a piss. It wasn't until he drank a bit of the beer that he realized how badly he needed to relieve himself. Standing in front of the toilet with one hand on the wall, he leaned forward to let it flow. Just as he was finishing up, a small creak came from the living room that grabbed his attention.

"Hello?" Danny said, peeking around the corner of the bathroom door. On the kitchen counter was his cat eating from a leftover bowl of cereal. "Dumb fucking cat," he said, angry that it had startled him.

King walked back to the kitchen and shoved the animal off the counter before pouring some cat food for him. After putting the bag of food back in the cabinet, he opened a drawer and pulled out a tiny box that he carried back to the table with his dinner. He took a few bites of pizza and laughed at the TV when a guy that had gotten too drunk had to be carried into his room. After he finished the first pepperoni slice, he opened the box from the drawer and pulled out a rolled up hundred-dollar bill, a razor blade, and a bag of white powder.

King poured the cocaine onto the mirrored glass and started sliding the razor along it. The blade clicked and clacked against the mirror as he worked the powder into three parallel lines. Taking the hundred-dollar bill, he leaned in close and snorted the lines one after the other. Sitting back in his chair to enjoy the high he was about to achieve, he took another bite of pizza. As he swallowed the delicious pepperoni, a hand covered his mouth and jerked his head to the side as he felt a sharp sting on his neck.

King's eyes started to flutter as he came out of the strangest high he'd ever experienced.

His mouth felt dry, and he felt stiff all through his arms and chest. He wondered if the bumps he took had been cut with something tainted. Opening his eyes completely, he lifted his head and came to the realization that he couldn't move his arms because his hands were tied behind the chair he sat in and the dry sensation in his mouth was from the gag stuffed in it. The last thing he realized was that he wasn't alone.

The homeless man that he had chased off was standing in front of him wielding a silver blade the size of his index finger. King hadn't seen the man's face while on the sidewalk, but the skin that was beneath the clothing didn't carry the same layers of filth. He stared wide-eyed and slack-jawed as the realization hit him who the man was that stood in his living room.

"Finally! You, sir, are quite the sleeper. I thought I was going to have to resort to smelling salts like last night, but it appears that you've finally decided to join the party." King shook against his binds trying to find a way out of his fate.

"Don't waste your time because you aren't going to free yourself." The man grabbed another chair from around the dining table and placed it backwards in front of King before sitting down and resting his arms on the back of the chair.

"You have made quite the name for yourself, Big King," he said pointing the blade at him. "Not a problem on its own. I mean, isn't becoming rich and famous the American dream? However, I feel that I have to object to how you gained this notoriety."

King's cheeks and jaw twitched as tears started forming in his eyes. The man took notice to the change, "It's a bit late for that, don't you think?" The chair the man sat in creaked as he scooted closer to Danny. Leaning in enough to whisper, he said "You're right. I'm exactly who you think I am and you've made it onto my list."

While unconscious, King's shirt had been removed and the cold blade against the bare skin of his chest made him notice. The sensation went quickly from shock to utter terror as he watched the blade resting there. He'd heard the stories of how the vigilante tortured and mutilated his victims, but he never thought he'd witness it personally.

"You use innocent children to spread narcotics around the city. What you do to entice them into your world offends me. When you add in all the lives you've stolen away from others, it's a surprise it took you this long to have me as a guest in your home." The man said this as he pet the cat that was rubbing against his leg.

"I do have a question for you though," he continued. "Are you a fan of dead languages? I've always had a great fondness for Latin. Do you know any Latin?"

Danny grunted as he struggled against his bonds. "I'll take that as a no. I'd like to share some with you if you don't mind." King struggled with every ounce of strength he could muster, but it was no use.

The blade pressed harder until it cut into Danny's flesh. His muffled screams of agony did nothing to halt the knife as he slid across his flesh. He felt like a bottle of soda being shaken as the torment and pain built with no way of being released out of his bonds.

The homeless man from the sidewalk carved four letters into Danny's chest; R-E-U-S. With his work finished, he stood up from the chair and stepped behind King. Placing the blade to his throat, he delivered judgment.

"Instead of helping the youth of our city, you use them for illegitimate means. You reap rewards off the pain, suffering, and even death of others." After a short pause the man continued, "No longer will this be allowed to continue." Plunging the sharp steel deep into King's neck, he dragged it from left to right and released a red torrent that gushed over Big King's lap. "Qui tacet consentire videtur."

Chapter 10

Standing in the hallway of another slumlord-owned apartment building was not how I wanted to start my morning. Receiving the call so early that I hadn't had my morning coffee had me on edge. I'd even noticed myself being cross with a few of the techs, which had them walking on eggshells in my presence. I could be a different person sometimes without my caffeine fix, but I doubted many of them would hold it against me for too long. We all had our bad days after all.

Thinking of that wonderful black liquid, like a narcotic, dancing across my taste buds to give me my much-needed fix was somewhat ironic with the landscape before me. Waiting for the forensics team to finish up, I stood in the hall, staring into the open door of an apartment on the sixth floor. Inside, a man, clearly having a worse morning than myself, sat bound to a chair. While I was being cranky about a lack of sleep and not having my coffee, this guy's morning had me beat hands down.

From the hall I could see his wrists duct taped to the back of his chair and wad of cloth taped into his mouth. The victim's chair was facing the door almost as if to greet anyone passing by. *Good morning fellow tenants!* On the table beside him was paraphernalia indicating a fondness for cocaine, but that wasn't the worst of his day. The occupant's throat was slit and under all the dried blood was that word indicating another Blood Week victim.

"Looks like our man strikes again." I turned to see Marcus standing next to me holding a coffee in each hand, one outstretched towards me. "From what the lab coats told me, you're in dire need of this," he said with a chuckle. "Did you really threaten to shoot one of them?"

"That's why we're issued weapons, right? Thanks," I said taking the cup. As it reached my lips, that delicious fix I'd been yearning for trickled onto my pallet and kicked me into gear. I savored the flavors that tickled my taste buds while injecting the caffeine my body had been depleted of.

"You look like you were up all night," said Delgado. "Should we all be thanking our lady coroner for your mood this morning? She must have shown you quite the time last night."

"You don't know the half of it, but a gentleman doesn't kiss and tell. I will just say that you can trust me on the fact that she is equipped with a plethora of skills."

"Fair enough, I didn't get much sleep either," he said in deference.

"Did our newbie find a little action too?"

"We'll just say I found something to pleasantly pass the time," he said with a smile.

"Off topic question; do you play poker?" I hosted a poker night every couple weeks for a few detectives and some street cops. We also did a large poker tournament twice a year where anybody at the precinct could attend. I usually rented out a place and had it catered with a percentage of the night's take. It wasn't too bad on the nights I won because I'd bring in enough to pay for the entire night. When I lost, I'd have some out-of-pocket expenses to pay for everything, but I didn't mind because I liked doing something nice for my brothers and sisters in blue.

However, the poker night I was hosting in a few days was one of our smaller occasions. We took turns hosting, and this week it was at my place. I figured this was another time I could get to know my new partner. It also meant that Marcus could get to know a few of the guys outside of the workplace.

"I've been known to. Why?"

"We've got a small game at my place Wednesday night if you want to join. It's a $50 buy in for chips."

"I think I can make it, but I'll have to run it by Rita."

"Well, if the wife approves it, let's hope it wasn't like the last game we had. Simmons went on a hot streak and ran the table pretty quick. The night was over in less than two hours."

"Simmons...he's the older guy carrying a few extra pounds around, right?"

"Yeah, that's him. He can be a card shark when he's not distracted. I'll write down my address when we get back and keep an extra seat saved for you."

"Sounds good," he said. "In the meantime, we have a witness over there that saw someone fleeing the scene early this morning."

Falling in stride with my partner, we left the doorway of our victim to speak to a short elderly woman a few doors down. Her silver hair cut a few inches above the shoulder was bright against her coffee skin. It dangled just above the fluffed fabric of the auburn robe that covered most of her baby blue nightgown. On her feet were matching slippers that saved her from the cold tile floor of the hallway. She dabbed her face with a handkerchief that was wet with tears as we approached.

"Ma'am, my name is Alexander Saint and this is my partner Marcus Delgado; we're the detectives working this case. It's Ms. Saunders, is it?" She nodded in between sniffles. "I understand that you were the one that found the body?" She nodded again. "Can you tell me how well you knew the victim?"

"Well enough to know that whoever did this has got balls. That's Danny King in there and he's a big shot in this neighborhood." Saying the victim's name seemed to puff out the woman's chest.

"You mean Big King?" I asked. "I've heard of him, he's a dealer in this neighborhood."

"That is police propaganda," she said in defiance. "Danny assured me that you have never proven anything because there is nothing to prove. You were just attacking a good boy out of hatred."

"Are you saying that you didn't know about his drug dealing?" asked Marcus.

"Drug dealing?" she shouted, incredulous. "He was a good Christian boy that wasn't involved in anything of the sort. Daniel was always incredibly nice to me and made sure the landlord took care of things whenever I had a problem."

"So, you knew Mr. King well then?" Delgado asked.

"Well enough. He always told me that I reminded him of his Grandma." She wiped another tear from her eye before continuing, "I'm up at 4am every morning to drop my trash by the door for the morning pickup. When I did it today, I saw a young man come running out of his apartment. Since the door was left open, I walked over to tell him that my heater was on the fritz again. I always told him because Mr. Grotter never listens to me."

"Mr. Grotter?" I asked.

"He's the super in the building. Daniel always made sure he took care of things for me. Before that poor boy came along, nothing ever got done around here."

"Ms. Saunders, after you saw the boy running from the apartment, what happened?" I asked.

"Oh, well I looked in on him to get my heater fixed and found him tied to that chair covered in blood." Reliving the events caused her eyes to flood over again. She whimpered as she wiped at her nose.

"Can you describe the man you saw coming out of King's apartment?" asked Marcus.

"He was a white boy with dark hair. I don't think he could have been older than sixteen. I didn't see much of him when he ran out because my vision isn't what it used to be. You understand." I nodded.

"After I saw poor Danny there in all that blood, I called 911. Now you're here asking me questions," she said with anger growing in her voice. "How about you get to work and find the fucker who did this?" I stifled back a laugh. It wasn't the place to find humor, but when a senior citizen started cursing it always caught me off guard. There is always this image in my head of the older generation being proper, but in reality, they are just as human as the rest of us.

Clearing my throat to hide my laughter, I pulled a card out of my pocket and handed it to her. "We'll do everything we can, ma'am. But if you think of anything else about what you saw, please call me." Taking the card, she nodded and went back in her apartment blowing her nose into the handkerchief.

"Hard to believe someone getting so worked up over a man like Danny King," said Marcus. "If I hadn't seen it with my own eyes, I wouldn't have believed it." Seeing Delgado's eyes dart up, I turned to see that forensics had finished their work around King's body. We could now begin working the room, so I chugged the rest of my coffee and gave the empty cup to a uniform and asked him to toss it in my car. I wouldn't want my trash getting mixed up with anything found at the crime scene.

Marcus and I were each handed a pair of fresh gloves as we entered to make our first sweep of the scene. First thing I noticed was one of the lab techs working on a wall in the kitchen. Red streaks spelled out "Ex malo bonum", which we already knew was Latin for Good out of Evil from all the previous crime scenes. If the killer held true to his history, we'd also find that it was written in the victim's own blood.

"I'd say that Latin and sharp blades are our killers M.O." said Marcus.

"Going on five years now," I added.

"So, what exactly is the deal with all the Latin? We've never figured that part out." I turned to see the question coming from Captain Hawthorne standing in the doorway.

Delgado was the first to chime in, "Well, what do most people think of when you bring up Latin? For me, it's always the Catholic Church coming to mind."

"Please don't tell me your theory is that the church is behind these murders," I laughed. "We'll put an APB out on the pope as soon as we get back to the precinct. I'll have Simmons put a call into the arch bishop to see what he knows."

"What are you thinking Marcus?" asked Hawthorne.

"Well, captain, what I mean is that you don't hear Latin in common practice very often. The first place that came to my mind was the Catholic Church. Don't they still do service in Latin at some locations?"

"I believe so," she said. "What's your point?"

"Could it be a religious action on the part of our killer? Obviously not acting on behest of the actual church, so you can hold the APB on the Pope," he said looking at me. "But maybe he thinks he's doing something helpful. Is it possible that our killer thinks he is using the Judgment of God and acting as his hand in punishing these men?"

Picking up on what my partner was getting at, I chimed in with "Do you mean our killer thinks he is like the archangel Michael or something?"

"I hadn't thought of it exactly like that, but perhaps. How else do you explain the Latin? He is marking the corrupt before offering up the ultimate judgment on their souls."

The Captain looked a little puzzled, "You'll have to help me since I'm not up to date on my Catholic Mythology."

Helping her out, Marcus told her, "Michael is an archangel in the bible who was like a warrior of God. In the Book of Revelation, he led the armies of heaven against the Satan in a battle of good vs. evil. He helped cast Lucifer and anybody that followed him into hell. I know it's a lot of faith-based ideas, but it fits what we know so far, doesn't it? This modern-day archangel feels these men have committed evil acts in God's eyes and he's punishing them for it."

"Lex talionis," I said. Both Delgado and Stacey looked at me. "It means the law of retaliation; it's like an eye for an eye." The blank stares continued so I smiled and added, "After all these murders, I've learned some Latin as well."

"Yeah, the law of retaliation; that sounds exactly like what could be going on here. They took a life so our killer is taking theirs," said Marcus with enthusiasm.

"So, you think that our killer is doing this based on his religious beliefs? I'm not sure you have enough evidence to support that theory," I stated. "Are there other reasons he could be using Latin?" Captain Hawthorne shot me a look.

"Yeah," said Delgado. "I guess you're right, but it does fit."

"Regardless," Captain Hawthorne interjected, "follow whatever leads you think are sound and let me know what you find."

"We'll keep at it Captain and see what develops," I said.

"Okay guys, keep me informed," she said, leaving the apartment and heading back down the hall.

Once she was far enough down the hall I turned to Marcus, "So does that mean you're going to start calling him the Catholic Avenger?"

"That sounds like it'd be catchy in a comic book, but I don't want to paint this guy as a hero."

Somewhat stunned, I looked back at my partner. "Are you saying you've decided you're not a fan of our vigilante?" Before I could get a response, we were interrupted.

"I've got a partial over here!" exclaimed a tech who'd been working the blood stains on the kitchen wall. "It's at the bottom of the X."

Both of us rushed to his side and peered down at where he indicated. I was shocked because we'd never found a shred of evidence on our killer. The entire department had grown accustomed to playing janitor duty. We simply cleaned up the mess, but suddenly it seemed we had a legitimate clue. I told him to have the lab process it through the system immediately. If there was an actual lead on this murder, then there was work to do.

The rest of the scene was expected, so we left the apartment for the precinct. A few hours later, we received word there was a match on our partial. It pointed to a seventeen-year-old boy named Bradley Thompson who'd spent time in Juvenile Hall for possession. According to his file, he'd been working as one of Big King's suspected mules for a few years, and had recently been released after another stint inside juvie to cover for Big King. It was yet another time that the employee took the heat for the employer. It was enough to aggravate anyone with a badge, but it's possible that Thompson had served his last sentence for King.

Released two months ago, his counselor had had high hopes that Bradley would keep his nose clean. While his nose may be clean, it appeared that his hands weren't. Pulling in front of the address that his parole officer had on file, Delgado and I exited my SUV to approach his doorstep.

The neighborhood was populated with single-floor, cookie-cutter homes on the west side of the street and various two-floored models on the east. Standing on Thompson's front porch, I could see five other homes that had been boarded up when repossessed. It was a deterrent to squatters, but I could see two that I'm sure had already been infiltrated. The dilapidation of the neighborhood was depressing, but that wasn't our reason for visiting.

Bradley's home, being on the west side, didn't have a driveway, so we had parked on the street. A long row of concrete steps led to the covered porch that had brick pillars on either side. The house had wood siding that had been painted white to contrast with the pillars. The porch was screened in to keep out bugs, but it was unsuccessful since the screen door was missing. The entrance had a plain white door with a half-moon window near the top. A black cast-iron security door was attached over it that was commonplace in the neighborhood.

Marcus rang the doorbell with no response. After the third ring, a woman finally answered, "What the hell do you want?"

"Ma'am, I am Detective Delgado and this is my partner Detective Saint. We're looking for Bradley Thompson. Are you his mother?"

"Yeah, what are you people accusing him of now?"

"He is a person of interest in one of our investigations. Is he home?"

As Marcus focused on Ms. Thompson, I noticed a boy hiding behind a row of shrubs along the edge of the property. His eyes watched us unblinkingly. Glancing at the photo we had and back at the boy, I turned towards him. "Bradley Thompson?"

Without hesitation, Bradley turned and bolted away in full sprint. Delgado turned his head in time to see his back running away. "Damn it," he said, "can't anybody just cooperate instead of turning this into a marathon?"

"Everybody runs," I said, bounding down the steps towards the sidewalk. Running to catch up, the two of us sprinted around the corner in pursuit of our suspect. He came back into view when we saw him hopping a fence into a backyard about five houses down. Getting to the chain link just in time to see the runner hop the back, privacy fence, we both followed after him. The fence at the rear of the property hadn't been as easy to scale as it was over five feet high, but I had worked my way up and rolled over the top.

As I landed, I spotted Bradley trying to make it across a busy street in a personal game of *Frogger*. With Marcus not far behind me, I ran into the street to catch him just as a semi nearly smashed me as it rumbled by. The horn blared as it passed, causing Thompson to look back and see us still on his tail. He was already on the other side and took off down an alley. It took a moment, with vehicles passing us at over 40MPH, but we finally entered the alley where we lost sight of him.

At the other end, another street to cross that had slowed Bradley down. That is where I found him struggling to find a way to cross over. "Watch where you're going, asshole," someone yelled as their car passed him. Without slowing, we both exploded out of the alley just as Bradley threw a hail mary and ran full bore across the four lanes of traffic. With luck on his side, he made it across and disappeared over another privacy fence.

Pulling out my badge and holding it up as I stepped into traffic, I was able to get vehicles to come to a stop for us to cross. On the other side of the street, we scaled the fence where we'd last seen him and found two directions he could have gone. We stood in another alley that went straight through to a different row of houses, but halfway down was a left turn into the parking lot by the market.

With two choices, I ran towards the next neighborhood while Marcus went to the market. When I got to the row of houses, I looked in all directions and didn't see any sign of Thompson. I strained my eyes trying to find the smallest bit of movement that I could attribute to a fleeing suspect. Taking a gamble, I turned left and continued up through the homes in hopes of getting lucky.

At the next cross street, I was joined by Delgado who had continued over from the marketplace. As he approached me trying to catch his breath, he shook his head. We stood there another few minutes looking around, but it was pointless. We lost him.

After exhausting our resources on finding Mr. Thompson, we released the information to the press to see if the Tips Hotline would be able to get us a lead on his location. Marcus and I sat with Captain Hawthorne and a few others at the precinct watching the evening news broadcast. We were waiting to see the story on Bradley so we could be ready if any calls came in immediately after the story ran. The plan was to give it an hour before we all went home.

While we waited, we had sandwiches delivered from the deli a few blocks down. Although we were all there to work, that didn't mean we had to skip dinner. I hadn't eaten much the entire day, so I was starving. The food arrived just before the TV went to commercial. "Our next story is about a man the police need your help in finding," said the anchor. "Have you seen Bradley Thompson? We'll have more on this after the break."

During the commercials, Hawthorne dished out the sandwiches and I brought in some sodas from the break room fridge. I placed them all on my desk so everyone could grab what they wanted as I sat down and peeled the paper back on my sub. It was warm in my hands and the smell consumed me before I could finish opening it. Inside was parmesan chicken with marinara sauce, mozzarella, and oregano on wheat bread. I was like a ravenous animal as my teeth sank into the sandwich. The bite was getting washed down with a root beer when I heard the broadcast return with the story on Thompson.

"Police need your help in finding Bradley Thompson. He is a seventeen-year-old white male with shoulder length brown hair that escaped custody this afternoon. Mr. Thompson is a suspect in the death of Danny King who was found in his apartment early this morning suspected to have been murdered by the Blood Week killer."

"Could Mr. Thompson be the man behind these murders? That is what police need your help to find out. If you have seen Thompson please call the Tips Hotline at--" The anchor suddenly stopped talking to the camera as he listened to his earpiece.

"Wait...what?" he said, clearly trying to sort out new information coming to him. There was a short pause as the anchor listened further to the voice speaking through his ear bud.

"Uhh this just in, Bradley Thompson has just called into our station and would like to say something to the police. Bradley, you're on live..." I nearly choked on my sandwich and coughed a few times to clear my throat. We all placed our food aside to catch every word of the broadcast.

"Yes, my name is Bradley Thompson. I want to say that I didn't kill Big King, and I have nothing to do with the Blood Week stuff. I've never killed anybody."

"Bradley, we're told you ran from the police today. If you aren't the killer, why did you run?"

"I ran because...well...it didn't have anything to do with Big King. He was already dead when I found him. I didn't kill him, but I saw the man who did."

Chapter 11

"Call the news station now!" said Hawthorne. "Get the number for Bradley's call so we can trace." As one of the other detectives called the station to acquire the number, the rest of us continued watching.

The anchor continued, "Mr. Thompson, can you tell us who you saw?"

"Hell no! I'm not going to get myself killed by snitching. All I wanted to say was that I ain't the one that did it." There was sharp static that came over the line followed by silence.

"Mr. Thompson, are you still there?" The anchor asked again, but there was nobody on the line with him. "Ladies and gentlemen, it appears that Mr. Thompson is no longer on with us. As always, we bring you breaking news here first. We'll have more after--" I turned away from the television and walked to the detective that had been on the phone with the network.

"Great, thanks," he said as I came up next to her. She saw me approach as she hung up the phone, "Saint, we've got his number. It's a cell phone."

"Perfect, check with the cell provider and see if we can get a GPS location on the signal." She didn't have to be told how to do her job since she had already picked up the receiver to begin dialing. If we got a trace on Bradley's cell, the truth about the vigilante might finally come to light.

With the GPS from the phone provider, the signal led us to two-story yellow house. We parked two blocks down and positioned a lookout across from the house to confirm Bradley was inside. I wasn't expecting a struggle but we didn't want to lose him a second time; once was bad enough. To make sure we didn't make the same mistake twice, we had Detectives Edward Pinick and Richard Bronson backing us up.

Pinick was a short fellow with thick brown hair that curled naturally, so he liked to keep it as short as possible. He was of thick stock just like his partner, except Bronson easily had two feet on Pinick. The pair had been partners for nearly a decade at that point, and each of them were rarely seen without the other.

Fifteen minutes before we moved on the house, the four of us went over how we wanted to breach. Pinick would enter the rear with Bronson while Delgado and I would take the front. Our lookout would continue watching the house for any exits through windows. The warrant arrived ten minutes before we planned to breach.

To make sure everyone was on time, we all programmed our watches. "Okay," I said, "sync on 9:35 in three-two-one." Multiple watches beeped simultaneously. "Gentlemen, we breach at 9:45 on the nose...happy hunting." All parties separated and headed to their entry points.

Leaving the squad car down the street with a uniformed officer avoided alerting anyone to our presence as we ran towards the house. The unmarked that had been keeping an eye on the house was still close enough to assist if we needed a vehicle for pursuit. A few doors from our target, I noticed the nearby street lamps were out, making it easier for us to slip by undetected. We didn't want any mistakes since it would be difficult to live down the kid escaping us more than once.

Creeping up the front driveway, Pinick and Bronson separated from us to head towards the back of the house. When Delgado and I reached the front door, we waited for the other team to reach their entry point. My heart was pounding in my chest like it did every time I was in a situation like this. All the planning in the world couldn't prevent something from going wrong. And once you were in position, all the things that could happen got the adrenaline flowing. The anticipation excited the nerves, which made it that much more important to stay focused.

I wanted everyone on my team to make it out alive, but we had no way of knowing what was on the other side of the doors. Would everything go according to plan? Would the suspects have weapons, and would I have to fire mine? These questions always ran through my head as the seconds ticked by. Even the most seasoned veteran couldn't escape the worry of what could be.

We all wore bulletproof vests, but there were still plenty of body parts exposed. A stray bullet could penetrate you in the arms or legs and still leave you with a good chance of living to tell the tale. But my head was exposed too, and ringing that bell would be the end of the fight. Surveillance gave us the information we had to work with, and our plan was to be executed with speed to keep the likelihood of incidents low, but there was always a chance. Checking my watch, I looked at Delgado and an unsaid conversation passed between the two of us. It didn't need to be verbalized because we were ready. We breached in five…four…three…two…one…"KCPD!"

Delgado kicked the door open and entered with me hot on his tail. We cleared the first room and turned down the hall that led towards the next. Following the plan, we laid out, we quickly swept the house to find three occupants that didn't know what hit them. One moment they were all on a couch in front of the television, and the next they were on the ground with guns pointed towards their heads. Luck was on our side this time as Pinick put Bradley Thompson in handcuffs.

Slapping a pair of bracelets on him, "You're under arrest for the murder of Danny King." He read Thompson his rights and escorted him out of the house to the flashing lights as he professed his innocence. The vehicle down the street had been pulled to the house by the officer that had waited in the driver's seat. Taking Thompson to the end of the driveway, Pinick opened the rear door of the first black and white he came across.

Putting his hand on Bradley's head, he helped guide him into the back seat, "You'll have your chance to tell us your story once we get you downtown Mr. Thompson." Pinick shut the door as the boy continued screaming of his innocence. Ignoring him, Pinick got in the passenger seat to head towards the precinct. Bronson rode back in the unmarked car with Delgado and myself. The consensus was that we had our man.

Back at the station, Bradley was handcuffed to the table in the interrogation room. He'd been left to wait for over half an hour, so his throat and long since grown tired of screaming. No sense in wasting the energy when nobody was ready to listen. Instead, he now sat quietly picking at the back of his left hand. There was a scrape he got from a metal trash can lid when running from us the first time that had scabbed over. I contemplated how to handle his questioning as I watched him through the glass, but I knew he was adamant about proving he didn't kill King.

Once the room was set up with audio running, Marcus and I stepped in to begin the interrogation. "About time," said Thompson. "I'm telling you I didn't kill him. I found him that way!"

Each of us pulled out a chair opposite Bradley and sat down. I set a notepad on the table and wrote his name and the date at the top of the legal pad. "You gotta believe me," he continued. "I had nothing to do with it."

"Is that so?" Marcus asked. "Perhaps you can provide us with your version of events. Why didn't you call 911? Were you too busy trying to think up an alibi?"

"I can tell you exactly what happened that night; I was working."

"Where were you working?" I asked. "If you let us know, we can call your boss to verify your employment."

"You can't," he said. He went back to picking at his hand.

"Why not?"

"Because I was working for Big King, ok? I got a bag from him around ten. I was given an address and a time to deliver it."

"What was in the bag?" asked Marcus.

"I can't tell you that."

"Why is that?"

"Does a mailman open your mail before dropping it at your house?"

"Fair enough," I said. "Where did you deliver it?"

"I can't tell you that either."

"You don't seem to be giving us anything to show you aren't the one that killed King," said Delgado. "You can't tell us where you went or what you were delivering. How can any of this prove that you are innocent?"

"If I tell you where I went, the people there will know I snitched on them."

"How are you snitching? You don't know what was in the bag."

"Maybe not," he said, "but everyone knows what Big King was into."

The kid had a point. All of us knew that there were narcotics in the bag, but Bradley didn't want to admit to transporting it since that would put a felony on his record. What he didn't seem to understand is that he could say it all he wanted, but nothing would really stick without any evidence of a crime. Right now, he needed to focus more on giving us something that pointed away from his connection to the death of Big King.

"How about we skip the exact address," I said. "Can you tell us where you met King for the bag, and what area you took it too?"

Bradley gave us the corner where he got the bag, and indicated to a neighborhood about an hour away from King's place. "I then had another bag they gave me to take back to King," he said. "On the way back, I stopped at that 24-hour diner near Westport to get some eggs and waffles. Big King always gives us a little extra cash to get a bite on late deliveries. He was cool like that." Apparently, kindness to old ladies and teenagers in his employ made up for everything else.

"I got done and left for Danny's around 1:30, and it took me over an hour to get there since it was all uphill. It was some time around four when I got there. After I locked up my bike, I went upstairs and found King already dead."

"Did you see anybody else there?" I asked.

"No—wait...I did bump into some guy in the hallway outside King's place. With all the burnt-out bulbs, I didn't see him until I ran into the guy. He said excuse me, so I knew it wasn't Big King because he wouldn't like someone running into him."

"Sounds about right," said Delgado.

"Please continue," I added to keep Bradley talking.

"Yeah, so the lights were off inside the apartment."

"How can you be sure of that?" I asked.

"Because the fucking door was open, man. I called out a few times, but I didn't hear anything so I walked in to turn on the lights. I've been there a few times so I knew where the switch was, but I felt something wet on the wall near the switch. It wasn't until the lights came on that I saw all the blood."

Bradley continued that he stepped back from the wall, puzzled about what he was seeing. It wasn't until he bumped into the chair where Big King was strapped down with blood spilling from his throat that he realized what was happening.

Feeling a retching in his stomach, Bradley made a mad dash to the bathroom with his hands over his mouth to contain what was coming. Sliding across the tile on his knees, he lifted the lid and threw up the waffles he'd eaten earlier. As he flushed the toilet, he realized that King's death meant he had the chance to make the biggest score of his life. He knew King kept a duffel bag full of cash from the week's score in the bedroom closet until he deposited it on Wednesday afternoon. This meant there was nearly a week's worth of dealings in that bag.

Without another thought, Bradley ransacked the closet until he found the bag of cash. It wouldn't be missed now that Big King was out of the picture. Nobody would even know that it had been there. With the duffel bag strap over his shoulder, he rushed out of the apartment as fast as his feet could carry him. Bursting forth into the hallway, he mentioned that he nearly ran over an old lady that shouted profanities at him.

"When I got down the stairs," said Bradley, "I heard that woman start screaming. That's when I figured she found Big King. But all I cared about was all the money I'd just made."

Marcus asked a follow up, "Can you give us a description of the man you saw?"

"Hell yeah, I can," he said with renewed excitement. Asking about the description of the man he ran into meant there were more suspects than just him, and that was news worth celebrating.

"Okay, so what did he look like?"

"First off, I don't want to go back to juvie. You get me immunity on the drug charge and anything on me running from you, and I'll talk."

"Quite the demand from someone who is still our prime suspect. Your alibi hasn't even checked out yet, and you think you can run the show? The sooner you give us the information we want, the sooner we'll be done here."

"I've been around the block enough to know that if I don't get immunity on those charges, I'm going to get locked up either way. You get that taken care of and I'll squeal like a pig. Until then, I'm done talking."

"That will take a little while," I said to close the discussion. "First, we're going to check on your story with the diner and we'll get back with you, so you should get comfortable."

Chapter 12

"Were you working on Monday between midnight and 3am?" Standing in the diner on Main Street across from the movie theater, Simmons questioned a server about our prime suspect. The waitress confirmed that she had been there all night. "Did you see this boy here around that time?" He held out a photo of Bradley Thompson and her eyebrows shot up with instant recognition.

"Yeah, I remember this kid. He was here between like one and two that morning; I remember thinking how young he looked to be out so late. As I recall, he came in and left on a bike that he chained up out front."

This was the conversation that Simmons relayed to me over the phone. He'd been in the area, so I requested that he canvass the diner for us. As Bradley's luck would have it, a witness corroborated his whereabouts, which meant he couldn't have been at King's during time of death. I thanked Simmons for checking and ended the call.

"I guess that's it on Thompson," I said.

"What do you mean?" asked Pinick from his desk that sat behind mine. Turning towards him, I explained to him and Delgado that walked up how Bradley's location had been confirmed. "Wait, the waitress said he left on his bike a little after 2PM, right?"

I nodded, but I could see on Pinick's face that something about that was eating at him. "That doesn't' alibi him out," he said.

"How so?"

"Just because he left on his bike around that time, doesn't confirm he was on it the entire way. He could have easily ridden away from the diner a bit before getting into a car.

King's place is only like a twenty-minute drive from there. He could have easily made it there in your window."

I felt like a detective fresh off the streets with that bomb drop. "Shit," I said, "you're absolutely right. If we can't confirm everything he said about riding back to King's on the bike, then he's still our prime suspect."

"He could have easily still killed King then," said Marcus. "The breakfast story could just be a way to get out our scope, but how do we confirm one way or the other?"

As we pondered on the question, Pinick's brow wrinkled and his eyes stared out the ceiling until his lips suddenly spread wide in a huge grin. "Traffic cams!" He clapped his hands in praise of his idea as he leaned forward as if to tell the two of us a secret.

"There are a few that run along the road to King's place," he said. "We can check them to see if Bradley is seen on any of them." It was a good idea that showed me why I liked having Edward Pinick on our team. It was a simple idea that was exactly what we needed.

I called into traffic to get the footage from that morning, and to our benefit there wouldn't be many commuters due to it being in the middle of the night. We could simply fast forward through the footage until someone passed by. Since it was well past our shift and it was his idea, we passed the reigns over to Pinick and Bronson to do the legwork. Their response was that they'd love to, but I could feel the sarcasm oozing off their excitement. Nobody liked scrubbing camera footage.

In the break room Pinick prepared two cups of coffee; one with creamer and two sugars and one black that he carried through the bullpen. He passed a few officers filling out paperwork from an arrest they made where he overheard the radio on a late-night talk show. The topic of the day was on the Blood Week murders. "Killing is killing," said the caller. "It doesn't matter if you only kill other murderers; you're still a killer."

The talk-show host responded that there had been mixed reviews about the vigilante, and he then questioned what the police were doing about it. "More than you are, schmuck," Pinick said as he passed. Another caller came on to praise the work of the vigilante. He even went so far as to state he was willing to sign up for the fight if the vigilante needed a sidekick.

A pat on the back startled him enough that he nearly dropped one of the cups. "Sorry, didn't mean to scare you," Simmons laughed. "I wanted to make sure you're coming to poker night. I feel another hot streak coming on. I can just take your donations now if you want to make it easier on yourself."

"Yeah, yeah enjoy it now because I'll be taking it back from you with interest soon enough." Simmons smiled and started walking away before Pinick stopped him. "Hey, do me a favor and have them shut that crap on the radio off." While everyone had a right to feel however they liked about the situation, he didn't care for listening to badmouthing about the force if he could do something to avoid it. It was even worse hearing that babble flying around in the office.

Saying he'd take care of it, Simmons walked right over to the radio and changed the channel. With coffees in each hand, Pinick walked into the IT room and handed the straight black cup to Bronson. They needed a pick-me-up if they expected to make it through the traffic reels that had come in without passing out.

"Thanks, the pizza should be here soon. We have ten traffic cams along the route that Thompson took back to King's apartment. Your half of the DVDs is stacked by the other player." Pinick hadn't expected nearly that many cameras, so he sighed heavily at the amount of time this was going to take them. Sitting down at the second monitor, he slipped the first DVD into the system and started its playback.

The majority of what he saw was an unchanging picture of an intersection at night through two hours of video. Luckily, they played them back at four times normal speed so each video only took a half hour or so to view. Every so often he would have to roll the video back and slow it down when something had come into view. One of these times afforded them some entertainment to break of the monotony.

On the screen was a man who was exceeding the limits of alcohol that the human body could handle trying to walk up a hill. He was bent over at the waist doing everything he could to keep his balance. After a few steps, it looked like someone changed the pitch of the hill on him as he suddenly tipped to the right and started jogging sideways. The man tried to stop himself but it was a parked car that finally helped him do so. Slamming into the vehicle at full speed, he fell onto it and set off its car alarm.

Pinick let a loud laugh slip out causing Bronson to jump. "Pause your video and look at this guy," said Pinick. Bronson rolled his chair over to join him, and they spent the remaining fifteen minutes of his drunken stupor laughing and sipping from their cups. Once the poor sap finally made it up the hill and out of frame, they each continued searching their separate film reels.

Half way through his third round of footage, Bronson came across a couple having sex in a car parked on the street. He sped through that section to avoid any jokes from the peanut gallery next to him. Near the end of that disc, something useful finally made an appearance. "There he is," he said. "Thompson passed this camera at 11:17 that night. He couldn't have been our killer." Pinick pulled up beside him and confirmed his findings. "Looks like Saint will be requesting that immunity deal."

Early the following morning, while waiting for Bradley's deal to come back from the judge, I stepped outside for a breath of fresh air. Small groups of pedestrians walked along the sidewalk entranced by their own worlds; most had their noses in a mobile device. A couple passed conversing about their day while sounds of nearby traffic occasionally drowned them out. All of them scurried along on the way to their destinations in the constant hustle of downtown Kansas City.

The wind carried sounds of heavy machinery, like dump trucks and a skid steer with a jackhammer, from the construction going on off Twelfth Street. No matter what time of year it was, there was constant construction happening. Eventually, I had stopped paying much attention to it. Detours from closed streets and heavy traffic from closed lanes was a byproduct of living in any major city, and it got worse the closer you got to the heart of the it.

Returning inside, a few of us decided to finish off what was left of pizzas that Pinick and Bronson had ordered in for the overnight shift. The remaining boxes contained a selection of cheese or supreme. It's funny how those were always that last two pies to be eaten. The thought of vegetables on a pizza made me queasy, so I settled for a slice of plain cheese when I saw Captain Hawthorne out of the corner of my eye. She jolted up from her desk chair like she'd just sat on a tack and slammed her phone onto the receiver.

Storming into the bullpen with the ferocity of lion attacking a gazelle, she immediately gathered everyone's attention. "Get that TV turned on," she ordered. "Channel 4 news received a letter from our killer that they're airing now." I was out of the break room heading for the TV before she could finish her sentence. Maybe it was after working with her for so long or perhaps that you just learned to think in terms of chess—ten moves ahead—that I didn't need to wait for her instructions to end. Pressing the power button on the side of the flat screen, it flashed to life just as the report was starting.

"...from the man that police have been searching for. We received it by messenger a mere fifteen minutes ago and weren't immediately sure if it was authentic. However, upon opening the envelope we found a Polaroid of the most recent body meant to verify that this is real. As such, we here at Channel 4 are bringing it to you first. Before airing this breaking news, our producers notified local police about the letter to assist in their investigation. I want to emphasize that these words are that of the Blood Week killer, and aren't to be used to reflect the thoughts of this news station."

Those that condemn do not understand that I am the force holding back that which is infesting this city. Thou shall not kill is a motto all should hold near and dear in their lives, so this is not something I do lightly. Call it divinity, sanctity, or the works of insanity, there are consequences that we all must answer to.

Stealing innocence will not be tolerated. Police do what the law allows, but those that skirt their capabilities will find me on their doorsteps. It is through secrecy that I clear the filth, and while some say that I will burn for my actions that won't stop my blade from exacting vengeance for the weak.

Eventually, judgment comes for us all and I will be the jury of your execution until my day comes. I am the purveyor of death for the corrupt. Qui tacet consentire videtur.

"We spoke with a local university professor in the language department about that last line," said the man reporting once he'd finished reading the letter. "I apologize for the pronunciation but we've been told that the final words are in Latin, which translates to 'he who is silent is taken to agree.' We can only assume at what message the killer is trying to convey, but the rest is quite clear. Criminals beware. We'll have more on this story as it dev..."

I hit the mute button as I turned to Stacey, "Are they getting us that letter to print it?"

"Yes, the copy they read wasn't the actual letter. They promised to put the original aside and use a copy for broadcast. I couldn't keep them from reading it, but I was at least able to get them to agree to some protocol for evidence." Hawthorne scanned the room until she found who she was looking for. "Simmons?" Her stern voice snapped him to attention as he stood up and awaited orders. "I have the station holding the package and letter for us. I need you to get down there and pick it up."

"On it," he said, grabbing his can of cola and hurrying towards the elevator with his usual waddle. He pressed the button on the wall, but the doors had already started to open where thin woman in a charcoal suit stepped out. Her dark hair was pulled back tight and carried a sheen as it reflected the light around her from too much hairspray.

She walked directly to Hawthorne's office with a manila folder tucked under her left arm. Eyeing the captain in the bullpen, she proceeded up to her and held out the folder. "I have an immunity deal from Judge Steel for Bradley Thompson." Joining up with Stacey by her office as she escorted the courier through the door, we signed for custody of the envelope and the woman left.

I signaled for Delgado to join me in interrogation as I brought it over for the kid to sign. On the way, I pulled it out and scanned through it. The judge agreed to let Bradley walk on the two charges we had him for in exchange for the stolen duffel of cash, the location where he made his delivery that night, and a description of the man he passed in the hallway of Big King's apartment building.

When I opened the door, I found the boy sucking down a bottle of root beer while holding a final piece of crust from the two pizza slices we gave him. He'd been put down in holding overnight, but when word came that his deal was on its way, he was brought back up to spill his guts. I figured that he would be more amiable after signing the papers if he'd also been afforded a full stomach. From the look of fulfillment on his face, I assumed I was correct.

"Your deal just came in," I said. Pinick and Delgado followed me in and stood near the door as I sat across from Bradley.

"About time," he mumbled, shoving the pizza crust into his mouth. I slid the paper his direction and placed a pen near the top. Reading through the page he looked up to me, "No problem." He grabbed the pen and signed it while telling me the money was under his bed at his Mom's. He also provided the address of his final delivery for King, which I wrote on a legal pad before tearing off the sheet and handing it to Pinick to pass on to the narcotics squad.

"Now, onto what we came here for." Delgado pulled up a chair to set beside me as I continued. "You said you had a description of the suspect?"

Thompson ran through what he saw of the man exiting King's apartment. "He was roughly your size and build," he said, gesturing towards me. "His jeans were faded and he had a dark blue hoodie."

"What did his face look like?"

"I don't know exactly. He had his hood pulled up so I couldn't really see his face, but I did see a *Guns N' Roses* symbol on the back of the back-pack he had. It was black and I think—"

"Wait!" The voice startled all of us as Richard Bronson barreled in the door. His eyes were wide with excitement as he tried to catch his breath. He must have run from the adjoining room behind the mirror to interrupt us. "Are you sure this is the man you saw exiting the apartment?" he asked. When Thompson confirmed, Bronson turned to me. "Alex, you need come with me. I have something to show you."

Bronson led us back to the room with the traffic cam footage and started tossing DVD's around until he found the one he wanted. Shoving it into the player tray, he rushed through the video, searching for what had him so excited. When he found it, he pressed pause and spun around in his chair to face us with the widest grin I'd ever seen on the man. Delgado and I stepped around him to see what had him riled up, and the recognition was immediate when our eyes caught what was displayed on the screen. I now understood what had Bronson in such a rush.

"Holy shit," said Marcus. "We've got a picture of him!"

Chapter 13

The image captured by the street camera was exactly as Bradley Thompson described. Two blocks from King's apartment, he was caught walking past a camera being used to study traffic flow in the area. However, the image of the GNR fan was a bit grainy since the recording device wasn't an HD camera. Regardless, you could still make out a man wearing jeans, a plain dark colored hoodie, and carrying a black backpack with a red smudge on the back.

"Looks like the guy wasn't kind enough to show us his face," said Delgado. "He still has that hood pulled up."

"Put a few copies of the suspect on a jump drive for me," I said. "I'll get the photos down to the lab to clean it up. Maybe they can enhance the details like that mark on the backpack."

"Will do," said Bronson.

"In the meantime, what are we going to do with Mr. Thompson?" asked Delgado.

"Keep him in holding until we hear back from narcotics. I want to make sure the rest of his side of the bargain is being held up before we let him go. Once they've collected the money and busted the buyer, we'll release him."

"Done," interrupted Bronson. "Here's the screen shots." He handed me the portable hard drive that was smaller than my thumb. With the photos in hand, I left for the elevator. Once I got it down to one of the lab technicians, perhaps they could work some magic and give us something better to look at.

When I passed by the interrogation room, the image of Bradley through the small window in the door gave me pause. During my tenure on the KCPD, I'd seen people do a lot of weird things when they were thought to be alone. But many forget that while you're alone, it doesn't mean someone can't still see you. Some of the stories that had passed via the grapevine through the force were shocking. One guy had thought the alone time was the perfect reason to rub one out. A detective out in Overland Park had accidentally interrupted the show and had been ribbed by his mates as a peeping tom for weeks.

The perp had been found with meat in hand, cranking away as if trying to finish before anybody came back. With his pants around his ankles and the back of his chair leaning against the wall, his hand flew up and down like he was trying to get the last of the ketchup out. With his eyes tightly squeezed and his grit-teeth moaning, he didn't even realize he was no longer alone. Worse, he seemed more annoyed than embarrassed when the detective cleared his throat to announce his presence. His pants had to be forced back on and each hand cuffed to opposite ends of the table.

Bradley Thompson was setting up to be the latest story to pass along. The kid had removed both his shoes and socks to sit barefoot at the long silver table to make it easier to bite his nails. And as someone might ask why the removal of footwear would be required, it wasn't his fingernails that he chose to chew on. Thompson had his left heel resting on his knee while he was hunched over chewing on the big toenail.

Since I had to get the photo to one of the lab techs, I let Bradley continue chewing on his tootsies and continued towards the elevator. Inside the car, I selected the floor for the lab and started my descent. Just as the doors opened on the basement floor, I bumped into Kathryn Morrison waiting to head upstairs. She was one of the many technicians from the lab, but she specialized in DNA analysis. In her hand was a folder the more than likely had information on an active investigation that she was taking up to one of the detectives.

"Mr. Saint," she said coyly. "What happened to our date last week?" She puffed out her bottom lip and shifted her weight onto her right leg like a pouting child. She couldn't hold the look long though as she giggled slightly. Her eyes narrowed as she smiled, causing them to sparkle. The blood rushing to her reddening cheeks showed her shyness through the flirtation.

Grinning back at her, "I'm so sorry, Kat. Something came up at the last minute, but I'm free for a few hours this evening."

She stepped in close to me to keep any passersby from hearing. Her shoulder-length locks were as bright as the sun and pulled back in a tight ponytail. And Lord knows I love a ponytail. "What I want may take all the time you have," she whispered. Her eyes flicked for a second to my crotch before looking back up at me. Standing about a head shorter than me, the way she looked up at me was begging me to take her on the floor immediately.

"Oh, I know all too well how long it takes to calm your kitten." Kat and I had had many adventures betwixt the sheets that it was nearly a weekly ritual minus last week's cancellation.

"Well, I expect a night of sweat this time, Mr. Saint," she said. I smelled the citrus of her perfume as she leaned even closer and pressed the elevator button behind me. She stared deeply into my eyes, "Mama needs to be satisfied," and snapped her teeth together like a lioness showing her vicious side before stepping around me to wait for the elevator.

"I'll cook you dinner at my place tonight," I said walking backwards down the hall. "How does six o'clock sound?"

"As long as you take me to the Blue Room afterwards," she called back to me without turning around.

"Done."

As her elevator arrived, I turned down the bend in the hallway and listened to my heels clacking against the tile all the way to the double doors that led to a large room full of forensic investigators. Rows of computers and equipment allowed for anything we needed as long as there was someone on duty who knew how to use them. Some of the machines were so sophisticated that it took special training to even know how to power the damn thing on.

In the back was the media center where I found a blue lab coat with its back to me. Hunched over a circuit board, he had a soldering iron in his hand that popped and sizzled as he worked. I cleared my throat to get his attention and the sudden noise in a previously empty room startled him. His head shot up, banging against a shelf above him.

"Oh shit," I said as I reached out to him. "Are you ok?"

Turning around, he vigorously rubbed the back of his head as he looked up at me. The friction caused his red hair to stand on end, leaving an awkward bulge at the back. "Morning, Saint," said Eric Masters; resident expert of all things media and computer related. Eric was my go-to guy whenever I needed something like an image recalibration done quickly.

"I'm ok," he said. "I just didn't know you were standing there." After another quick rub of his head, he did his best to flatten the hair back down and straightened his lab coat. "What can I do for you?"

"We found a few images of a man believed to be connected to Blood Week on some cameras near Big King's apartment." I handed him the flash drive, "I wanted to know if you could clean them up or enhance them to give us something better to look at."

"Let's take a looksee," Eric said, sliding his chair over to a nearby computer and slipping the drive into one of the many ports. When the folders popped up on the screen, he clicked through the files to open the image or the man with the backpack. Eric took a moment to study his new project to know what he had to work with. Like I'd seen many times, his lips pursed into a slight frown as part of his concentration face. This always emphasized the freckles on his face for some reason. When he was finished, he pushed his black, plastic-framed glasses back up the ridge of his nose. This was the indication that he had finished his once over and was ready to report.

"Shouldn't be a problem, but I'm not sure how clean it will be from such a low-resolution camera." Standing up, he grabbed the drive to move to another computer that had specialized software for the task. He towered over me as he passed by and sat at another terminal. "Give me about an hour and I'll have something for you."

"Thanks, Eric. Also, if you could get a close up on the red mark on the side of his backpack, it would be helpful."

"Will do. I'll call you when I'm finished."

Thanking Eric again for his help, I left the media center to go back upstairs. On the way to the elevator, I spotted Detective Simmons holding an envelope and a sheet of paper inside an evidence bag as he spoke with another forensics technician. It was the note from the vigilante that had been read over the news. He'd returned with the original copy and was discussing having it processed with the tech.

Noticing me pass by, Simmons flashed the bag to me like it was first prize at the science fair. He was very good at his job, but he could be a bit quirky in his old age. Although he wasn't far from retirement, sometimes his actions were much more childlike than his aged appearance would give him credit for. Pushing sixty, Simmons loved the job but I knew he was secretly ready for retirement. I returned a thumbs-up and continued out the double doors to hail an elevator.

Back on homicide's floor, my phone started playing a song that would make any movie nerd want to take that DeLorean back in time. Answering, I found Travis Gibbons who ran the narcotics strike team on the other end. This was the kind of guy who was all business at work, but came across as the surfer bro that dabbled in drugs himself when not in uniform. He wanted to fill me in on what happened with the raid on the address provided by Bradley Thompson, who still sat in the interrogation room.

"For starters," he said, "the money was right where the boy said it was. His mother was hesitant to let us in until she could read through the warrant, but we recovered the bag without incident. As for the bust on the drop-off location, that's another story. They were much more unwilling to have us enter than Ms. Thompson." Immediately, I envisioned an assault on the building and was worried that one of ours may have been injured.

"We breached the home to find four assailants on the premises; guns were drawn." It seemed my fears were about to be validated. "Fire was exchanged from both parties injuring two and killing another. The last man gave up after his associates went down."

"Were any of ours hit?"

"Luckily, no. We came out all clear. The one who surrendered himself is in custody, while the others are being escorted to the hospital. I've notified the coroner's office of the DB heading their way."

"Good to hear all of ours are ok. I'll release Mr. Thompson, since his part of the deal is finished, and let you wrap up on your end."

I informed Stacey of the update I received, and got the go ahead to release Bradley from custody. I let him call his mother from my desk since he lived across town and we couldn't just shove him out the front door and wish him the best of luck. "What the hell, Mom?" he said after what had been a ten-minute argument. "Fine." His exasperated sigh showed that he had lost whatever they had fought about as he offered the phone to me. "She wants to talk to you."

Taking the receiver, "Ms. Thompson? How can I help you?"

"Can you get one of your officers to drive him back here? I'm not coming out to get him. After the shit he put me through, I am not in the right state to worry about driving there."

After a bit of discussion with Bradleys' mother, I decided it was best to just get her off the phone. "We're not really a chauffeur service, ma'am, but I'll see what I can do." She thanked me and I hung up the line.

"Someone's in trouble," I said in a mocking tone. I knew I sounded like an adolescent making fun of a schoolmate being called to the principal's office, but it seemed to fit the situation.

Looking around the bullpen to see who I could convince to take a babysitting run, I noticed Officer Oswald Kitna—or Okie Dokie as he's known—grabbing a coffee in the break room. "Wait here," I said to Bradley as I went to talk to Kitna. The boy grumbled a bit, but sat in the chair beside my desk and waited.

"How are you holding up after finding Justin Sullivan's body the other day?" I asked as I stepped up next to him to prepare my own cup of java.

"Better now. I'm not used to that kind of stuff, ya know?"

"Glad to hear it. It does get easier with time." Glancing back at my desk, I watched as Bradley grabbed an entertainment magazine from Pinick's desk and flipped through it. "Do you have time to do me a favor?" I asked, turning back to Kitna.

"Sure. I'll be coming off shift soon but I've got some time. What do you need?"

"That boy at my desk over there," I said, pointing. "Can you run him uptown to his Mom's place?"

Dokie looked at Thompson, "That your rabbit from yesterday?"

"Heard about that did you?" He nodded and quickly took a sip of his coffee to try and hide the smile that formed on his lips. "Listen, newbie, you'll have plenty of your own rabbits over the next few years. You can count on that," I said with a grin and a friendly shove on his shoulder.

"Fair enough. Tell you what, to make up for it I'll run the boy home, but he's sitting behind the cage."

"I wouldn't have it any other way," I said chuckling. Being taken home in the back of a squad car might be just what the boy's neighbors need to see to set him right.

Walking with Dokie back to my desk, I reached down and snatched the magazine from Bradley's hands. "That's not yours," I said with the voice of a parent berating their child. Tossing it back onto Detective Pinick's desk, I continued. "You'll be happy to know that you're done here. This is Officer Kitna and he'll be escorting you home. A parting word of advice though, stay out of trouble this time and if a police officer wants to talk to you, don't run again." I emphasized the last bit to imply an 'or else'.

Watching his head bow slightly, he looked at the floor and said "Yes, sir."

He stood up and followed Kitna down the hall, clearly happy to be leaving the police station. I waited by the door and watched as the elevator doors opened for them. Out of embarrassment, he never looked back at me. Perhaps he'd think twice about his actions and try to lead a better life. But time on the force had the pessimist in me doubting it. Returning to my desk, I hustled through the paperwork on Thompson's release.

Right as I was signing my John Hancock on the final sheet of paper, my computer chimed with an email. As I reached for the mouse, I heard the chirp of a cell phone a few desks down and saw Simmons who had returned from the tech lab reaching for his pocket. Opening my email page, I found a message from Eric with the finished work on the photographs. I was about to open the jpegs he sent when I saw Simmons stand from his desk out of the corner of my eye and waddle towards me as he finished his call.

"They've finished the work on the letter."

"Already?" I asked. "You just dropped it down there." It was strange to have forensics finish with an analysis so quickly, but the news Simmons received explained why. They didn't find any DNA on the seal of the envelope, nor were there any prints on the letter other than that of the producer at the news station that had opened it.

"From what they tell me," he said, "the paper is standard white stock that you can pick up from any office supply store."

"Well, that looks to be a dead end then. What about the delivery? Was there anything we could use to track where it came from?"

"No, it was delivered by bike messenger. After checking with the company, we found that they didn't have any deliveries around the news station. Ends up that a man stopped the messenger on the street and gave him $200 to deliver the letter."

"Did you speak with the messenger?" I asked.

"Yeah, he said he was so focused on the money he'd been given that he never even looked at the guy's face. All he saw was an address and a couple Benjamins. We even asked if he could remember what intersection he was at when he was given the letter, but he didn't remember. All he could tell us was that he was somewhere on 22nd. I gave him my card in case anything came back to him."

"Ok, let me know if anything develops with the bike messenger. Eric, in the lab, just emailed me the photos he enhanced of our guy with the backpack."

Simmons stepped around to view my monitor as I opened the attachments. What we found didn't reveal much more than we were able to see before enhancement. Eric had said it probably wouldn't be much due to the low sophistication of the camera that took the image, and he was right. Mr. Masters was able to reveal that the man had a lighter skin tone by the cleaning done around the hands and chin. The red mark on the bag had also gone through corrections as it now showed the *Guns N' Roses* logo more clearly. This all lined up with Bradley's testimony, but it didn't give us much more to go on.

"Too bad," said Simmons as he went back to his own desk. I copied the files onto the precinct database so others could access them and emailed Captain Hawthorne and Marcus to let them know that they were available. They'd want to take a look as well.

Filing the paperwork on Bradley Thompson's release, I grabbed my things to head out. I had a dinner date with a kitty Kat that was anxious to purr for me. As I threw on the jacket over the pressed shirt and tie, I turned to leave but was interrupted.

"Another body's been found," announced Hawthorne. "Saint, find your partner because you guys are up."

Fuck, there goes my plans again.

Chapter 14

Surrounding the 12th Street Bridge were old brick buildings that housed factories in the fifties. They ranged from four to six stories tall and while many were abandoned, most had started to be repurposed over the years. A few that were tall enough to peek over the bridge, were now used as haunted houses during the Fall. It had been several years since I'd been to one of them, but the Beast and Edge of Hell were the most recognized haunted houses in the city.

Although tickets were starting to sell to these attractions, I wasn't in the area for entertainment. The freight elevator I stood in made creaks and groans as it rose towards the sixth floor of one of the unused buildings. The walls of the brick chute could be seen passing by through the slats of the wooden framed walls of the car, which made me feel like I could almost see the history held in the stone. It was like sounds of the industrial revolution were reaching out to be heard.

With a final screech and a jolt as the car came to a stop, the street cop we rode up with lifted the doors at the front for us to exit. Under orders from Captain Hawthorne, Delgado and I were on the case as leads with backup from Detectives Pinick and Bronson. My partner and I were only on duty for another half hour, so would have normally left new business for our brothers in blue, but this case had special rules since I was the senior detective on it. With that in mind, it made sense that the Captain wanted us to get a preliminary of the scene before turning it over to the late shift. For them, not 45 minutes on duty and they were already at a murder scene.

The room we stepped into was huge. Without any dividing walls, it ran the entire expanse of the building. Bronson whistled as we walked through the space. "Place is huge," he said. "It must be a few thousand square feet."

"And look at that view," added his partner. I glanced out the window and saw outside the brick walls of the old factory was a gorgeous view of the downtown skyline of Kansas City, MO. This floor wasn't as high up as the balcony in my apartment due to being in the valley of the West Bottoms that surrounded 12th Street, but the view was better. Since the Walnut building was in the middle of downtown, I was given a limited view of the city around me. But from here, you could truly see how breathtaking the city could be.

The evening lights were just starting to peek out with the setting sun on places like the Town Pavillion and the Sheraton Hotel. Even the new One Kansas City Place was there as the tallest building in the city. While it may not be as great a view as the balcony at City Hall, where I often found myself, it was a scene with everything I loved about my home. It made me wonder if this building could be turned into condominiums to take advantage of the sight. It almost made one want to become a real-estate developer.

The interior walls entirely made of red brick wasn't something you found in newer construction. It imbued the building with a feeling of nostalgia that would make this a place that drew in high prices from potential tenants. If you threw in some new hardwood floors and divided the space up into individual apartments that kept elements of the original structure, a developer could make a killing. But first, the killing that was already here would have to be dealt with.

In the center of the room, a black male in baggy jeans and a wife-beater tank top soaked with blood was duct taped to a chair. The dark stains were spilled down his chest like a bucket of burgundy paint. Kneeling next to him, Amy Doyle was hard at work on determining TOD and COD. As we approached her posterior, Pinick got the ball rolling, "What do we have, Ms. Doyle?"

"Oh, hey Edward. D.B. was tortured before death-"

"No shit," interrupted Bronson. "Guy looks gruesome."

"Seen worse," said Amy. "Anyway, I found a wallet on him that had an ID inside." Pulling it from an evidence bag, she handed it to Pinick. "License says his name is Shane Jackson."

"Judging from the tats, he was a Ryder," said Bronson while examining the victim's arms.

"Ryder?" asked Marcus.

"The 12th Street Ryders. They're a gang that are constantly warring over this neighborhood with Los Colabos. Bet you can't guess what ethnicity they are."

Skipping over Bronson's attempt at humor, Edward returned us to the job, "Anything you can tell us that could lead us to a suspect?"

"You actually think I'll have something more than usual this time?" she asked. As we stared at her, she realized we hadn't noticed yet. Helping the boys catch up, she pointed with her pen towards the ceiling. Smeared in blood above us was 'Ex malo bonum.'

"Well that explains why Hawthorne insisted we come," I said to Delgado. This body was another to add to the growing list of deaths associated with Blood Week.

"I have to admit that this took planning," said Pinick.

"What do you mean?" Bronson asked.

"Do you see a ladder or anything anywhere? How the fuck did he get up there?"

"Good point," I said. "You two may want to see if there is something sitting around that we aren't noticing on how he did that." The two of them took a quick tour of the room from stem to stern. Turning back to Amy, "What can you tell us about the torture?"

"Based on what I've seen, I could probably walk you through what happened from start to finish." Waiting with pads ready, we listened to her recant a story based on Shane Jackson's wounds.

At some point late last night, Jackson was struck across the back of the head with enough force to knock him unconscious and brought here. Amy then told us the colorful tale as told by our latest dead body.

"Mr. Jackson? Oh, Mr. Jackson…?" The man bound to the chair started to stir, but slowly. His eyes started to flutter at the sound of his name as he groaned, trying to shake away the cobwebs. "There you are, Mr. Jackson. I was starting to get worried. How was your nap? Pleasant dreams I assume?"

"What," he started. "What happened?"

"That is what is known as blunt-force trauma to the head," the man said. "It probably stings like a mother right now, but I assure you the pain won't last long."

Shane's vision returned to him as he looked around the large room. It smelled musty like it hadn't been inhabited for a long time. It was dark outside, and only a few flickering bulbs illuminated the floor around him. Beyond the area under the lights, everything was black. He couldn't tell how far the room went in each direction, but it sounded quite large the way sounds played off surrounding surfaces. He looked down at the floor and saw wood that was rotting and torn up in places. "Where am I?" he asked.

"Don't worry, Mr. Big Shot. You're still in Ryder territory. There's nothing to worry about because nobody would dare mess with someone like you on your own turf, right?" He laughed as if the idea was the most hysterical thing he'd heard in years, and Shane was the only one that didn't get the joke.

Annoyed, Shane tried to stand and finally noticed the tape securing him to his chair. "What the fuck?" He shook against the restraints, grunting loudly as he did so. Eventually he screamed at the top of his lungs with frustration at his failure to free himself. Taking deep breaths, his eyes focused on me from beneath his brows as his nostrils flared.

"Who are you?" he asked through clenched teeth.

"Wow," the man hidden in shadows said. "Such grit in your voice. It's almost as if you feel like you're the predator in our little pairing."

The blood in his veins boiled at the man's audacity. "I SAID WHO THE FUCK ARE YOU!?" He struggled slightly as if he could break the bonds with brute strength and attack his captor, but it seemed that he'd never been informed that you actually have to hit the gym to get big muscles.

Shane Jackson wasn't stick thin, but he also wasn't aspiring to be the next Schwarzenegger. He was of average height and build and—like most thugs today—assumed brandishing a pistol made you powerful. What the trash like this didn't get was that although a gun could do a lot of damage, it didn't match the power of the mind. This is why the street thugs would never reach the status of those running said streets.

"Temper…temper, Mr. Jackson. Have you ever considered the thought of taking anger management classes? I feel that you could benefit from them greatly."

"Fuck you, asshole! You better let me up before me and my boys fuck your sissy ass up!"

"Your boys? YOUR BOYS?!?" he asked, incredulous. "Oh wait, do you mean those guys who don't have the slightest clue where we are. The ones rolling to Collabos territory right now because of a note they found indicating they had a hand in this? Are those the 'boys' you speak of?"

The guest-of-honor for the evening opened his mouth to curse again, but then thought better of it. Instead, his kidnapper's words sunk past Shane's pigheadedness as he came to terms with where the power lied in this conversation. Squinting as he peered into the blackness before him, he tried to find the face to go with the voice. Instead of stepping into the light for him to see me, the man continued.

"We don't want any interruptions. You and I have plans for tonight, so I sent them on a little errand to the Collabos side of town."

"I'm gonna kill you, mutha fucka. Untie me you piece of shit, or you gonna die!"

"Well which one is it, Mr. Jackson? Are you going to kill me, or let me go? To kill me, I have to untie you, but then you say you're going to do so if I don't untie you? You can see the confusion you're creating, yes?"

"Fuck you, Collabos scum!"

"Damn it," he said with a sigh. "And here I thought you'd been listening. I'm not in one of these factions you're always fighting with. I just made it look like them so we could be alone." The man walked around him, but always just at the edge of the light so Shane couldn't see him.

"While we're on the subject of your inability to make sense of things, could I ask you a serious question?" His footsteps clapped against the hardwood and fell dead on the expansive room. "Why is it that individuals such as yourself think that chest-puffing and unearned bravado like that will get you anywhere?"

Reaching Jackson's right side, the man turned around to walk another semicircle before him. This time he came farther into the light so the lower portion of his body started to appear. Shane's eyes fixated on his exact position as the speech continued. "If I'm not mistaken—and feel free to correct me if I am—the ranting has not magically made your bonds come free. Nor has it struck fear into my heart or allowed you to start working on that threat of killing me. No, if I were to spit conjecture, I think that you've got it all wrong."

The shadows surrounding the man gave way like a dark sheet yanked away when he stepped right in front of Jackson. Leaning down face-to-face with him, the man smiled maniacally. "I think that it is, in fact, I who's gonna kill you...mutha fucka."

Rising back up with more pep in his voice, he returned to the matter at hand. "But first, I have a little treat for the 12th Street's number one enforcer. In case you forgot, I believe that's you," he said, pointing at his captive.

Shane Jackson had been with the Ryders for nearly eight years and had gained a reputation as the man happy to kill anyone the Ryders painted a target on. Without the brutish force for honorable battle, he used handguns to kidnap people and then beat them within an inch of their life to get what the Ryders wanted. If the person didn't do what was expected of them, they were rewarded with three bullets. One in each kneecap and another to the head. Eventually word got out, and people did what the Ryders wanted.

"You see, I know all about your reputation and I thought it was cruel that you weren't buying the product you sold."

"What are you talking about?" Shane asked softly.

"What I mean is I think you deserve a taste of your own medicine." Dragging a backpack from the shadows, the man placed it in the center of the yellow spotlight three feet in front of Shane. Kneeling over it, he unzipped the pack and pulled out a pair of brass knuckles that shined in the light. "Recognize these?" The knuckles belonged to Jackson.

The man slid them onto his fingers, admiring how comfortable they were. Taking a boxer's stance, he bounced around throwing a few air jabs. Shane's muscles tightened as he tried to move away, but his bonds weren't giving him an inch.

"You ain't gonna get away with this," said Jackson. "My boys'll find yo punk ass and show you all about pain, bitch."

"There's that unearned bravado again. You know, you should really show more respect to your fellow man. But if you'd done that, I wouldn't be here, would I?"

"Wait," he said with his brows furrowed. An idea suddenly struck Jackson. "You're him, aren't you?"

"Ding, ding, ding," the man shouted. "Let's show him what he's won, Johnny!" The fist flashed faster than Shane's eyes could see as the brass jewelry connected first with the side of his face and again with his ribs.

"He has bruising covering a large portion of his upper torso and face," reported Amy. We listened as she examined the dead body. "Jackson was beaten severely with something that—based on the shape of the discoloration—is most likely the brass knuckles forensics found. They've already bagged them to test the blood residue."

Bronson asked, "What about his legs?" He was referring to the large hole in each of them around the knees that had stained the pants with blood.

"His legs," she said, "was when the savagery went a step further."

Bound to the chair, Shane Jackson moaned in pain. Blood trickled from his lips and formed a small puddle in his lap as his eyes lulled back-and-forth. His face was covered with contusions that were beginning to darken from repeated strikes. The pain overloaded his senses to where he knew of nothing else. As he started to pass out, his head suddenly snapped back as his captor cracked smelling salts beneath his nose.

"I don't think so, Mr. Jackson. We aren't through yet because we're only up to the second round." Shane heard the clang of the brass hitting the floor as the man tossed them aside. Flexing his fingers and rubbing his hands together, he stepped closer to Shane.

"Those things aren't that comfortable after all, but I suppose it was worse for you. Even worse was trying to get them over these damn gloves," he said, pulling at the blue nitrile and letting it snap against his skin. "Still, I think it's time we move onto the next item of business. Is that ok with you?" Shane made a gurgling sound as he coughed up blood.

"Please, no more," he moaned.

"Come on, Mr. Jackson. We had a wonderful curtain and now the audience is demanding the third act. Intermission is over. We can't just stop the show if we want a good review. How would they know how the story ends?"

"Just kill me already…please."

"All in good time," the man said. Digging in the backpack on the floor once again, he pulled out a silver pistol with a large suppressor screwed into the barrel. He stood up and let the weapon rest at his side as he surveyed Jackson's wounds.

"No more," Jackson whispered. "Make it stop. I'm sorry for what I did."

"I'm grateful to hear your remorse, Mr. Jackson." The man stepped forward and rested the business end of the pistol on Shane's right knee. "It's always good to get right with the universe before it all ends, but I'm not done yet." Pointing the barrel straight down, he fired a single round through his kneecap that exploded from the back of his calf with the same brutality Shane had inflicted on his victims.

He screamed with a renewed feeling of fire tearing through his flesh. Worse than any pain he'd experienced in his entire life, pieces of meat and bone splattered onto the floor beneath his chair as the bullet seared through him.

"We're half way there my friend," said the man with the gun as he moved the barrel to its next target. As the explosion rang forth once more, Shane shuddered through waves of excruciating pain as both his knees were destroyed.

"Someone blew out both his kneecaps?" Delgado asked.

"Yep," replied Amy. "The bullets were found imbedded in the floor. Forensics dug them out, but they haven't found the weapon yet."

With timing so perfect that it seemed planned, a voice on the other side of the room cried out, "Found it."

"Spoke too soon, Ms. Doyle," I joked. Her nose wrinkled as she made a face at me. "Anything else we should know?" I asked her, getting back to business.

"Just that after all Jackson went through, he was finished off with our man's signature move."

After what seemed like an eternity to Shane, screaming alone in the spotlight, the man returned from the darkness. "It's been fun, Mr.

Jackson. I hope you've enjoyed experiencing what your victims went through, but it's time to end this in spectacular fashion."

"No more," he whispered.

"Shane Jackson," the man said ignoring him. "You are here because you made it your life's work to inflict pain on the people of this city. People guilty of nothing more than your coveting were tortured and murdered."

The man stood alongside Jackson and let the cold steel of a surgical blade slide along his forearm and up his bicep until it came to rest on his chest. Shane felt the harshness in his throat from repeated screams as he once more bellowed while the scalpel cut into his flesh.

The man continued working as he carved out four letters as a brand for the guilty. "You have been arrested time and time again with plenty of chances to make better choices." He finished cutting into Jackson's chest and took a position behind his chair as he continued.

"However, it has become clear to me that you are incapable of change. You chose this path that brought our lives together, but this is where it ends." With Jackson longing for an end to the pain, the man was happy to oblige. "Qui tacet consentire videtur"

"The final cut along the throat was what did him in," said Amy as she indicated to the point that stained the victim's shirt with all the blood."

"He even has 'REUS' like the others," added Delgado.

"I think we have enough here to let you guys take over," I said to Pinick and Bronson. "Let me know what else you find in the morning."

"Will do," said Pinick as he mockingly saluted. Smiling and flipping him off, Delgado and I left the rest in their capable hands. We'd already been on overtime for an hour now, and Hawthorne wasn't about to pay us more, so we had to hand over the reins for the night. Besides, now I still had time for my date with Kathryn.

Chapter 15

I entered the Corrello's Market at 13th & Main in the Power & Light District. I did most of my grocery shopping here because it was a convenient location less than a half mile from my apartment building, and the owners spared no expense in making the inside contemporary and beautiful. The family owned many grocery locations around the city, but this felt like the flag ship of the fleet. Stepping through the rotating doors was like stepping into a grocery-filled showroom.

There was designer lighting from the shelving to the ceiling that also highlighted the rich-wooden displays and hardwood floors throughout. Corrello's Market was more than just another grocery store; it was practically art. Past the cashiers near the front was a deli that served fresh food daily, such as standard sandwiches or salads, but there was also braised chicken, spareribs, or even sushi.

If the splendor of the building and convenient location wasn't enough to keep me coming here, there was also how much they did for the community. Each year they partnered with a local radio station and donated thousands of dollars in food to people needing a hand up around the holidays. I tried to shop at local businesses that helped the community they serve. It was the least I could do for the kindness they shared.

I initially heard about their community efforts through a rock station that got the city involved to help those in need. The station and the morning DJ got the listeners involved and the way they helped people they didn't know always touched me.

Walking around the different sections of food, I grabbed some chicken, green beans, and a bag of red potatoes. My thoughts were that garlic herb chicken with grilled red skin potatoes and green beans sounded like the start of a wonderful dinner. But I was still missing something to make the meal complete, so I continued to the southwest corner of the store where there was an entire section of various wines both local and foreign. After sorting through various bottles, I decided to go with a red from *Pirtle Winery*; local stock from Weston, MO.

As I placed the bottle in my cart, I noticed a young teen boy loitering around the section of alcohol. His eyes kept darting towards the front and down the adjoining aisles as he stood in the back corner. Keeping his hat pulled low on his brow, I watched him pace along the back wall as I crossed to an aisle behind him. I kept my eye on him as the boy tucked a vodka bottle in his shirt and start walking back towards the exit. Before he could get to the front doors, the boy had to walk past me, and I reached out and grabbed his arm just as he started to.

"Are you sure you want to do that, son?"

"I don't know what you're talking about," he said. But as he did so, he shifted to keep the pocket with the pint of vodka as far away from me as possible. His eyes also seemed to have the ability to look everywhere but back into mine.

"Yes, you do. That might bring you a lot of trouble if you go through with it." The boy continued trying to play dumb as he questioned what I was talking about, but I pressed him again and, after a moment of silence passed between us, he dropped his head in shame. As his eyes stared down, they caught a flash of tin at my waist where my badge rested on my belt.

"Oh, god," he said, shaking. "I'm so sorry, sir. Please don't take me to jail. I promise it will never happen again." He stared back at me, on the verge of crying in the middle of the store, as he continued holding his arm near me. I looked around to make sure nobody was watching because I didn't want to cause a scene.

"Tell you what," I said once I felt sufficiently inconspicuous, "you put that back where you found it, and I'll buy you a soda." The boy stared at me looking for any possibility of deceit. It seemed to take him a moment to realize that the cop who'd caught him red-handed was giving him the option to make a better choice that night and avoid trouble. "Do we have a deal?"

Nodding his head, he walked back to the shelf and placed the bottle back where it belonged and followed me to the registers. True to my word, he picked out a Coke that I purchased along with the rest of my groceries. Outside, I handed over the soda, "Try to make better life choices in the future, ok? You never know who might be watching."

"Yes, sir. Thank you, sir. I will." With a smile that still seemed unable to accept the lifeline he was just given, the boy walked away with what I hoped was a better idea of what the world could be like. With the boy on his way, I started the short journey back to my apartment with my purchases that would soon be transformed into a delicious dinner for Ms. Kathryn Morrison.

The sun had finally finished setting when I arrived at the entrance to my building. What had once been bits of pink and orange painting the evening sky was now bespeckled with tiny dots of light in the night that covered the city. Through the brass-trimmed revolving doors, I passed over salmon tile with a white diamond all edged with black marble. I passed Chester at the dark mahogany concierge desk just inside the lobby on the way towards the elevators. Giving him a nod when I passed, he wished me a good evening to which I did the same. Through the doors at the back of the lobby, I pressed the button on the wall to call the elevator and, once inside, I pushed the number five to get to my floor.

Upstairs, I finished slicing the potatoes and adding herbs and spices to the chicken before putting them both in the oven. Stepping out to the balcony, I sipped on an iced tea while watching the city below. My mind wandered around until it paused on the facts so far about the Blood Week vigilante. The image from the street camera that Bradley Thompson had put us on could put the vigilante one step closer to being apprehended. His face wasn't clear in any of the photos, but he'd eventually slip up again, which meant it might not be too long until his identity was revealed. Hiding would be difficult after he was brought out of the shadows. I finished the last of my tea before stepping back inside.

While the food was still baking, I went to the bedroom and opened the safe hidden behind the autumn painting. Once it was open, I un-holstered my weapon and cleared the magazine and chamber of rounds before placing it inside. I also unclipped my badge and returned it to the hole in the wall before closing the safe door and repositioning the canvas over it. Undressing, I put my suit aside to be dry cleaned and hopped in the shower to get cleaned up before Kathryn arrived.

As I stood under the warm water hitting the back of my neck, my mind kept returning to the case. I wondered how long the vigilante could continue his work unscathed. After five years of success, could this be the year that he is finally unmasked? The idea kept rolling through my mind as I washed and continued as I dried off. I did what I could to file it in the back of my mind, so I could focus on the evening as I donned a fresh, button-up shirt and grey slacks. Slipping on a pair of fun dress socks that looked like a shark was eating my foot, I finished with my favorite pair of brown wingtips with matching belt.

Foregoing the blazer of my suit for the moment, I put on an apron to check on the chicken and scalloped potatoes. Checking the meat with a thermometer, it required about fifteen more minutes, but the potatoes were ready to cool. After pulling the dish and placing them to the side, I grabbed a pot out of the cupboard and started warming the green beans. While the food finished up, I filled a wine bucket with ice and placed the bottle in with the cubes. Normally wine was served at room temperature, but I knew that Kat preferred hers chilled. The buzzer on the oven went off a short time later, so I removed the chicken and placed it alongside the potatoes.

The room was permeated by the scent of garlic and herbs as I pulled out two plates from the cabinet. On each of them I placed a single chicken breast and surrounded them with scalloped potatoes and green beans. After placing a pair of wineglasses next to the chilling bottle, I carried the plates of food to the dining area. Just as I set them on the table, I heard a knock at my door. After a quick survey of the table ensuring it was complete, I answered the door to find an angelic vision of a woman wearing an ankle-length blue dress with slits up to her thighs.

As Kathryn stood leaning on one leg, her bent knee spread one slit open, exposing her milky flesh. Her thighs were begging to be caressed all the way down to her four-inch black heels. Her blond hair was down, but pulled back over her ears, which allowed the smokiness around her eyes to accentuate her gaze.

"Wow," I said, looking up and down the hallway and back to her. "You better get in here before my date shows up, she might be jealous."

Kathryn smiled and smacked my arm just as she noticed the words written across the chest of my apron. "Kiss the cook huh? Sounds like a wonderful idea to me." Leaning up on her toes, our lips met in what felt like only an instant. It was funny how women could always leave you wanting more.

Inviting her in, I led her to the table where I pulled out her chair before pouring a glass of wine for each of us. I sat in the chair opposite hers and we clinked our glasses together as the start to our evening. We each took a sip; our eyes never leaving the others. "I must say how beautiful you look tonight, Kat."

"Well, I thought about showing up in yoga pants and a hoodie, but I wasn't sure if that was classy enough."

"I'm sure you'd look great in anything or nothing; dealer's choice really."

"All in good time, Mr. Saint." She bit her tongue and winked at me before taking her first bite of chicken. Immediately her attention became distracted from the banter. "Mmmm. This is delicious," she said with her mouth still full.

"I'm glad you like it. It was actually a recipe of my mother's." The mention of my parents was unexpected, putting a momentary damper on the evening.

"The anniversary was a few days ago, wasn't it?" I nodded. "Amy mentioned it to me. Honestly, I didn't know about what had happened to them. I'm sorry to hear about your loss."

"It was a long time ago," I said with a wave of the hand.

"Still, I can understand how it feels. I lost my Dad pretty early on too. I was only 12 when he died."

"What happened to him?"

"Let's just say that he didn't run in the best of circles. Nothing worth mentioning over such a wonderful meal." She took another bite as she looked around the apartment. It was clear that she wanted to talk about the deaths in her family about as much as I did.

"Well, I'm sorry we missed last week," I said. "You know how busy things can get at the precinct."

"Don't I know it," she laughed. "I have been swamped with DNA swabs over the past few weeks. I don't remember the last time I had to run so many profiles for so many detectives. Sometimes it's hard keeping them all straight."

"Who were you running information up for this morning?" She tilted her head and furrowed her brows in confusion. "The file I saw you with at the elevator?"

"Oh, that actually wasn't for a case. I'm actually applying for a loan to see about buying a house."

"Really? That's great."

"Yeah, I figured it was about time that I started doing some adulating, ya know?" We both laughed as we continued our evening.

Our conversations continued on topics that ranged from work to upcoming events; all of which was intermixed with flirtatious and often sexual remarks. Dinner seemed to finish quickly with thoughts of pressing our bodies together at the forefront of both our minds. Although the plan was to go dancing at the Blue Room that night, her legs peeking out of her dress had other ideas.

Lifting her up and setting her on the kitchen's island, she wrapped her legs around me as our hands explored the other. I pulled at the clasp at the back of her neck, allowing her dress to fall to her waist and expose her breasts. Before I could examine them closer, she pushed me back and hopped of the counter. Doing so allowed her dress to fall completely to the floor and reveal what had been in hiding. The view of Kathryn's exposed flesh made me feel like a voyeur as her totally nude body caused a tightening of my pants. Without a moment to waste, I picked her up and cradled her in my arms as I whisked her away to my bed.

Chapter 16

A blade of light crept across the streets of Kansas City, as the sun rose over the skyscrapers downtown and fought back the darkness. It pierced through the cracks in window curtains to greet humanity with its morning glow. But as those rays snuck past my drapes in search of my face, it peeked through my eyelids to wake me like a dog needing walked. It didn't care that I wasn't ready to wake because if it was up, then I should be too. Trying to fight off the morning after a long night, I pulled the comforter above my head, but it seemed the world was banding together to revoke my sleeping license.

The alarm blared with that buzzing sound that made me want to introduce it to my gun. Since shooting the alarm clock still required getting out of bed to retrieve my weapon from the safe, I resorted to other means for silence. My palm slapped the electronic nuisance to cease the ear-rattling sound. Although I wanted nothing more than to tell the world to fuck off for a few hours, the time on the clock confirmed its vocal nonsense was valid. My whopping two hours of sleep had come to an end, so I rolled out of bed with a groan.

If I didn't know better, I'd swear that my head had just hit the pillow seconds before the buzzing woke me. Sitting on the edge of the mattress, I rubbed at my face to force back to urge to roll up a human burrito with the comforter as the tortilla and me as the filling. Although the comfort of my California King put up a convincing argument, duty called. My shift would be starting soon so a cold shower and a jolt of caffeine was a requirement to keep my body motivated this morning.

My night of dancing at the jazz club went much later than originally anticipated. Although, the dancing was not on our feet and the jazz was only over my stereo. Ms. Morrison and I made the walls ashamed of what they'd witnessed last night.

Afterwards, I was wide awake and didn't pass out until a couple hours ago. She had crashed immediately, so I left her alone in the bed to let her get some sleep.

Twisting around, I looked at her laying on the other side of the bed. With how I'd tossed the covers back, her back was exposed low enough to hint at the cusp of her backside. Her bright blonde hair was like fire on the dark grey pillowcase. My evening with her had burnt the candle at both ends to say the least. The longer I sat there, the more the urge for a morning delight followed by more sleep begged. No matter how pleasing it sounded, I didn't want to be late for work. As I stood to go take a shower, I felt Kat's hand grab mine and pull me back.

Tilting her head towards me, she pulled me down to taste her lips. At my touch, she pressed her chest into mine. Flashes of the sexually charged night went through my mind as our escapades had moved to the kitchen, table, and even the balcony for a time. It was voyeurism at its finest. For now, though, it was time to get ready for work.

"I should go," I said between kisses. "I have to clean up for my shift."

"Are you sure you have to leave?" she moaned. "I can make it worth your while." With her arms wrapped around me, I pulled back and saw the sexiest little smirk.

"Tell you what, how about you join me in the shower. You can make it worth my while and get me clean at the same time."

Without responding, Kathryn released me and hopped out the bed as she headed off towards the bathroom. Her naked body bobbed from side-to-side with each step until she paused at the doorway. Brushing the strands of hair from her face as she peered back at me, she winked and disappeared into the bathroom. As I heard water begin splashing against the shower tiles, she peeked back around the corner and smiled, "Coming?"

I didn't have to be asked twice as I hopped out of the bed like it was on fire and the shower was the only thing that could put out the flames. The glass was steaming over from the heat of the already occupied shower. Stepping in to join her, I interlaced my fingers in the wet strands of hair behind her head and pressed my lips to her neck. I tasted the warm droplets sliding down her skin as my tongue traced a line towards her chin. Pressing her against the walls, I ran my other hand down the back of her thigh before wrapping it over my hip. This was the best way to get clean.

After the shower, I turned on the radio while getting dressed. All thoughts of more sleep were gone as the shower had left me fully refreshed. As I gathered my suit for the day, the latest rock played over the station. It reminded me of a concert I'd gone to a few months back at Liberty Memorial. Each year they held the largest single-day rock festival in the country on the grounds of the WWI monument. It was a giant party that brought in over fifteen bands to kick off the summer. I'd gone a few times, but I wasn't sure if I'd be there next year or not.

Before I'd settled on a suit, Kat peeked her head into my walk-in closet and picked one for me. "You should wear your sexy suit," she said. When I didn't know which one she considered to be 'sexy', she pulled it off the rack for me. Obliging the lady, I sat out the navy one she liked on the bed and finished drying off. Since she also had to work today, she chose to leave after having chosen my attire. I walked her to the door and kissed her goodbye before going back to the bedroom to get dressed.

When I finished, I was craving a morning pick-me-up more substantial that the shower escapades. I decided to get a shot of caffeine from *Scooter's Coffee House* since it was only a block down Walnut. When I got there, I selected a mocha which was in my head moments later. Having also picked up one for Delgado, I hopped in the Tahoe and nearly spilled one down my leg. Luckily it hit the pavement instead of my slacks, but the drops that landed on my finger burnt like hell.

I used one of the napkins I'd been given to dab away the spilled coffee while cursing the accident. Tossing the cup into a nearby trashcan, I quickly ordered a replacement before hopping back into the vehicle. With two full cups in stow, I pulled away from the curb to drive towards the precinct when my cell rang. Marcus informed me they'd found another body.

"Wait, where?" I asked when he tried to give me the location. When he told me again, I realized it was in the opposite direction so I flipped a bitch on 9th and headed to meet him. "I'll be there in twenty."

Chapter 17

Turning off Mission Road into the Reinhardt Estates, I found myself out of my jurisdiction. Fairway was on the Kansas side of the metro, and was well outside of KCMO. Located on the other side of the river, I was familiar with the neighborhood situated a few blocks from the Kansas City Country Club. It was a ritzy part of town that I'd been to a few times with my parents. I hadn't spent much time in the area since then, but houses and sections of streets were reminiscent of my childhood.

My destination was clear without the need to continue following GPS due to the overabundance of black and whites lining the curb. It was as if a large neon sign was pointing at the house to notify everyone that something had gone down. Off the main drag, the rubberneckers were relegated to people that lived nearby. This meant it wasn't as bad as on the highway where I'd spend twenty minutes trying to make it the quarter mile to an auto accident. I definitely didn't miss the beat-cop days.

Finding a spot had been difficult until Delgado saw me approaching and flagged me over to a spot he'd saved across from the address he'd sent me. After parking and exiting the Tahoe, I pushed my way through the parade of news vans and neighbors with their phones recording the mayhem up to the yellow tape where Marcus waited. With him expecting me, I didn't have to flash tin to someone I didn't know to get past the tape.

"We're a little out of our element, don't you think?" I asked Delgado as he held the line up for me to pass under.

"I know, but this was brought to my attention to address anyway."

"Why is that?"

"Probably best you just come check it out." I gave a shrug and he turned to lead me in. Now that I was past the circus in the street, I started to admire the house and surrounding neighborhood as I followed Marcus up the drive. I preferred the cityscape of skyscrapers to the suburbs, but if I ever decided to make a change, this would be a nice area to relocate. There was slim chance it would ever happen with how much I loved the city, but that didn't mean this area didn't have its merits.

For starters, under normal circumstances the traffic couldn't be beat. The streets never slept downtown, so that was the most glaring difference. Beyond that was the open spaces both inside and out that you didn't get elsewhere. Perhaps if I had a family at some point, places like these would make more sense. The thought of settling down made a certain brunette with a passion for forensic pathology flash through my mind. It was unexpected since I never really considered the future in that way. At least not consciously.

With my past though, family life didn't seem like something I was destined for. Before my mind could wander farther into that realm of uncertainty, we reached the front door to the large brick home. Delgado held open the large white door with four windows peeking into the open-concept entry, allowing me to step past him.

"So, we're having a bit of a crossing of jurisdictions today," he said as we entered. "Let me show you why." Gesturing with his hand towards the other end of the home, I followed him through a crowd of cops down the hall to the master bedroom. Stepping through the doorway, I surveyed the room and realized that this master suite was probably a third of the size of my entire apartment. While it didn't have the views of my loft, the space was nothing to scoff at.

On the large bed centered on the back wall was a man in his early 50's wearing nothing but a pair of boxers with blue and green squares. The covers strewn about on the floor were soaked with blood and so was the fitted sheet covering the mattress where the body lay. Although this was clearly a murder scene, it still didn't explain why Marcus had brought me out to Fairway, so I turned back to him with a questioning shrug.

Realizing that I wasn't going to figure this one out on my own, he pointed at the man on the bed. I looked over him a bit closer and was about to throw in the towel to ask what the hell I was doing here when I finally saw it. On his chest in tiny letters were R-E-U-S; one of the vigilante's calling cards. It would seem that the victim was part of our case; jurisdiction be damned.

"This is a Blood Week murder? But he always sticks to the city limits. What would have brought him out here?"

"It would seem he's branched out into new hunting territories," Delgado said.

"Strange that he's never done that before. Do we have a TOD yet?" I asked.

"Time of death is 12:37AM," said a raspy voice from the bed. I looked over and all I saw was the body, so I looked back at Marcus with a raised eyebrow.

"Mr. Raymond, resident pathologist for this side of the border," he whispered back.

"I'm not just a pathologist," said the stick-thin man that rose up from the other side of the bed with an evidence bag containing a few hairs. "I'm also certified in fingerprint analysis, forensic ballistics, and an accomplished pianist."

"I apologize for not reviewing your entire resume while we're here," I said, "but are those hairs a possible lead on who killed the vic?"

"Don't think so; look liked cat hairs. There is an orange tabby running around here somewhere, which is why my sinuses are in a tizzy. Regardless, I'll test to be sure."

"Among your expertise, can you fill me in on how you have such an exact time of death? I'm used to getting a time range, but you've made a specific delegation before even doing an autopsy."

Raymond indicated the area behind him that showed signs of a struggle and then lifted a rectangular desk clock that was contained in another wrapping of clear plastic. "During the struggle, this analog clock was knocked off the night stand and busted. The last time it indicated was 12:37AM when it struck the floor."

"How can you be sure the clock wasn't previously broken?"

"This isn't my first rodeo, detective. The clock also has a date indicator from last night. So, it's a safe assumption to say the death was around 12:37 this morning or last night depending on how you look at the day change."

"Each of the other victims was knocked out," I said, turning back to Delgado. "What makes this one so different?"

"Maybe Mr. Matthews saw him coming and put up a fight?" he said. Again, I raised an eyebrow. "Oh, the victim is Joseph Matthews."

"Oh shit, this is Judge Matthews? I know him."

"And yet you didn't recognize him," said Mr. Raymond in a noticeably condescending tone.

"Rather I know of him," I responded. "Judge Matthews is a retired Kansas City District Judge. If this is who we're dealing with, we need to get the captain involved."

Returning to the precinct to get all our ducks in a row, I'd informed Hawthorne privately of the ID on the body that took us on a trip to Kansas. "You mean the guy from your parent's case?" she asked.

"One and the same," I said. Judge Matthews had served on the trial involving my parent's death, which is why I knew the name. "I don't feel this will affect my work, but I wanted to make you aware."

"I trust you, Alex. Get your team working on how this is linked to the vigilante."

With a curt nod, I re-entered the bullpen to start throwing the ball around. Detective Richard Bronson was the first to speak up. "I guess the theory of him only killing criminals is blown."

"That's assuming there aren't skeletons in the judge's closet we aren't aware of," said Marcus. "The killer seems to always know something we don't or have a way of digging deeper into his victim's backgrounds. For all we know Matthews has done some despicably criminal things we don't know about."

"Seems unlikely from everything I've heard about him," I said. "According to stories told, he's a great man that devoted his life to the law."

"But aren't the squeaky-clean records always the ones that are hiding something?" asked Bronson.

"Not necessarily," responded Delgado. "But it seems out of left field if the judge wasn't dirty."

"I can vouch for him," said Pinick coming to the Judge's defense. "I've had dealings with him a few times in the past. He's a good guy."

"I'd have to agree with Edward. Also, how do we explain the other problems linking it to Blood Week?" All three men waited patiently for me to elaborate. "Didn't anybody notice the walls? "

"You're right," said Marcus. "Ex malo bonum wasn't written anywhere, but the murder was also in the suburbs this time. It's possible he was interrupted before the ritual could be finished. The body was found by the housekeeper this morning, so she could have unknowingly chased the killer away."

"I suppose it's possible," said Pinick, "but the theory seems a bit weak. The vigilante has always been so methodical.

Do we really want to believe he wouldn't know the housekeeper's schedule?"

"I agree," said Bronson. "However, can we ignore the evidence that does fit just because other items are missing and some of us heard good things about Matthews?" Delgado nodded towards Bronson in acknowledgement of validating his point about the Blood Week connection.

"No, we can't," I said. "Let's run with the connection to the vigilante for now and see where the evidence leads us."

Over the next hour, more information rolled in on Judge Matthews as Fairway P.D. turned over the evidence processed on scene to us. Cooperation between precincts from both sides of the river was common in KC. Since the metro crossed between Kansas and Missouri, mutual respect and cooperation was essential. That didn't mean there wasn't ever jockeying over jurisdiction. It was known to happen, but the concept of working together for the greater good usually won out in that battle.

In the evidence was a dark hair found on Matthews that didn't belong to him. His hair had gone white over the years and his wife was blonde, so forensics was testing it to see if the owner was in the system. That meant Kathryn would be pulling DNA from follicles, if there were any, before another would compare the hair to any from other cases. Additionally, it appeared Judge Matthews may have been tortured prior to death. This fact corroborated Delgado's initial push that it was connected to Blood Week, and he was all too happy to point that fact out.

With not much more to go on, Pinick and Bronson started working on a list of suspects based on a personal vendetta against Matthews. Being a judge for over 25 years meant there was a long list of criminals that could be disgruntled over his rulings. While they dug through the mud for leads, our attention was pulled elsewhere when another body was found.

"Fuck me!" Delgado covered his mouth and turned away, trying not to vomit. "His dick," he said between dry heaves, "it's in the fucking cup." Seeing what was left for us, I couldn't blame him for the queasiness. In an alley off the corner of 9th and Central, a man was cuffed to a pipe that ran up the side of the largest of the surrounding buildings with a clear mutilation to his state of manhood. "How the hell could someone do that to a man?"

"This isn't the first story of a man getting his dick cut off," I said. "At least this guy didn't live to see the day without it."

The alley was off a one-way street that had little traffic at night, but the parking lot across from it was widely used during the day. For this reason, the body was spotted and called in as soon as the sun had risen high enough to cast light into the alley. Surrounded by large buildings and the narrowness of the alley meant it was midday before anyone noticed. On top of that, you had to be directly across the street to even see the body from the parking lot. It was well hidden, but still open enough to eventually be discovered. This time it was by a woman that worked nearby.

The victim's cuffed wrists supported his weight like a prize fish posed for a photo by the fisherman. Found completely naked, the John Doe had gone through major surgery during the night as his penis and testicles had been removed. The severed bits floated in a clear solution in the mason jar at his feet. Other than the castration, the only other wounds to the body were R-E-U-S carved into his chest and the sliced jugular vein that probably added to the large pool of blood on the pavement.

"Can you believe this shit?" asked Marcus, still trying to calm his nerves. His hand motioned across his chest in the cross for protection from what happened to the victim. "Who cuts off a man's junk?" He stared at the jar on the ground with his hand over his own crotch like it might be torn off just by proximity.

"Maybe a woman he screwed over one too many times?" Amy Doyle laughed at her remark as she finished up her preliminary examination. "We can be spiteful like that," she said, looking up at me with a smirk. Men should know to keep their women happy if they want to be happy too. Piss us off and..." She gestured towards the mason jar.

I couldn't help but think this could be a jab at me. Men could be dense at times, but she had laid it on thick. She knew about my private life with the other women because I never kept those things from her, but she'd been hinting at a level of exclusivity together. I'd thought about it on and off over the past few months, but I never found myself able to pull the trigger. Things about my life weighed heavily on me, and I wouldn't want to put her in a position where I didn't live up to what she'd built in her mind. On top of that, I still fancied myself a lady's man. Was I even ready to give that all up?

As I'd come accustomed to when she started hinting, I deflected. "Better take this lesson to heart Marcus. Happy wife equals happy life."

"Noted," he said with a grimace.

"Your worst nightmare here," said Amy as she toyed with Marcus, "had his genitals removed with a fine blade; most likely a scalpel. Obviously, they ended up in this jar here, and most of the blood around him came from that amputation. The chest was done first, and it's safe to assume that the neck came after surgery. Chest...cock...neck," she said making a slicing move with her head at each point.

"This takes torture to a whole new level," I stated, staring at the man. "Did anybody find a wallet or ID around?"

"I did, sir," said a voice to my right.

"Okie Dokie!" I exclaimed as the officer walked up to me with the wallet in his hand. A few days ago, the newbie had worked his first DB, but lately the guy was becoming a natural. I supposed that working Blood Week could do that to someone.

"I don't think the killer wanted us to waste any time searching for identification because it was found at his feet by the jar," he said, handing it over to me. Afterwards he hovered like something was on his mind.

"Spit it out, Kitna. What's the question?"

"Detective, isn't this out of character for the vigilante?"

"What do you mean?" I asked.

"According to the file, he only kills one person a day. But I heard there was another over in Kansas this morning."

"That's a very good question, but one that I can't really answer right now. However, I think we'll let forensics do their job and then we'll start on ours."

"Yes, sir," he said before returning to his duties.

"We should probably head out," I said to Delgado. "For starters, you can't stop holding your dick, and we'll have more to go on when the techs have finished up."

"Sounds good," he said. "Want to grab something to eat on the way back?"

"I'm surprised you're hungry after your reaction to the mason jar."

"It's fucking gross. I'll give you that, but I was at Judge Matthew's place so early this morning that I missed breakfast. Now it's past lunch and I'm starving. So, I'm thinking we can hit up the diner for something."

With a nod, we left forensics to finish gathering evidence for us to work. But if it was like the other Blood Week murders, there wouldn't be anything there for us.

"Simmons, I'm serious. They said his dick was cut off and put in a jar at his feet." The buzz had reached the bullpen before we got back although it had only taken us about 45 minutes with the twenty-minute diversion to eat. We'd arrived just in time for the peanut gallery's rendition of the scene. Seeing us enter, Simmons turned from his conversation to report while the dick-chopping dialogue continued without him.

"I ran the name from the license and got a hit," he said. "Joey Tenackle has, or rather had, a record in Jefferson City Corrections for—you're not going to believe this—child molestation. That prick touched little kids, Alex."

"That explains why his was cut off," I replied.

"He should have lost a lot more than his life," said Marcus. "It's bad enough these guys are out there killing each other, but you don't fuck with a child." Not a single officer in the precinct would argue with him on that point. No matter what is going on in this world, you don't mess with kids.

"I'll toss this in the file and have someone notify next of kin," I said. "Chock it up to lack of evidence, but I don't see us having much to go on with this being another Blood Week victim."

"Yeah," said Delgado. "Move onto something more important is my vote."

The rest of my day was filled with the paperwork on the recent dead bodies, which did little to keep my mind of the filth of the child molester. I agreed with Marcus, he deserved a lot more than death, but death was better than nothing. Once I'd finished up my filing, it was time to call it a day. Paperwork had a habit of eating away the hours.

Before I left, I stopped by Delgado's desk. "I wanted to remind you about poker tonight," I said. "It's going to be a lot of fun and we'll have plenty of beer if you think you can join."

"Looking forward to it," he replied.

Chapter 18

With my shift over, I went home to prepare for the evening's festivities. Since I lived a few blocks away from the precinct, it didn't take long to make it home. The air coming through the open driver's window was sticky and warm, but it was still cooler than a week ago. Another month and the leaves would start turning and jackets would become common attire. It was my favorite season because the temperature would be mild instead of the extremes brought by summer and winter.

Exiting the Tahoe in the parking garage at the Walnut building, I ran through the checklist of items I needed for the night. At the top of the list was winning my money back from last month. It wasn't that I needed it, but I liked winning just as much as the next guy. And if lady luck was truly on my side, she would return the money I'd lost with interest. Poker night was always fun, but walking away the winner was the icing on the cake.

The game started around 7PM, so I wanted to make sure the fridge was stocked before then. I usually carried a variety of pale ales, stouts, lagers, and wheat beers. In addition, we would usually sample something new that wasn't as easy to get our hands on. The search for new and exciting beers was an endless one, but it had introduced us to quite a few brands not normally stocked in Kansas City. Of these, the favorites were darker beers such as *Duck-Rabbit Milk Stout* and the *Hofbräuhaus Dunkel*. Not as easy to acquire as a *Bud-Light* since they weren't distributed in this market meant we didn't get to have them often.

If I really wanted something different, I'd have a friend in Dublin send some *Guinness* to me under the radar since it wasn't exactly legal to ship. What was brewed fresh in Ireland didn't have the same flavors as what we found in the American

Liquor stores. It paid to have contacts in other markets, which was the same way I got *Duck-Rabbit* out of North Carolina. On the plus side, *Hofbräuhaus Dunkel* had recently started to be stocked by some local stores, but it wasn't the same as it was in Munich.

That left all the micro-breweries in the area that offered great beer as well. More readily available than the imports, they became the usual suspects found in my kitchen. Whether from the local KC favorite *Boulevard Brewery* or up-and-coming *Border City Brewing Company*, the need for good beer at a poker game was essential.

Checking the situation with current stock, I found plenty of beer waiting to be tapped. There wasn't a need to make a run, which meant the only thing left to make a night of beer and poker with the guys complete was buffalo wings. I called ahead to the Wing King and placed a large order for mild, spicy, garlic, and honey BBQ. Their food was fantastic and messy, so I requested extra napkins too. Before I went to pick up the order, I slid the poker table into the living room from the spare bedroom. It was stained hard wood with a thick center leg that twisted until branching out in four stabilizing feet. The green felt on the top was encased in stained wood with cup inserts carved into it and room to sit six people. With the table and chairs squared away, I went to pick up the party wings.

At twenty to seven, I returned with food that I set on the counter and walked over to the stereo on the back wall. Feeling a little old school tonight, I selected the sounds of one Mr. Frank Sinatra to pass the time. Nothing could set the mood better than good ol' Frank. As the melody of *Swinging on A Star* began to flow through the apartment, I snapped my fingers to the beat and sang along as I danced through the kitchen.

"Would you like to swing on a star? Carry moonbeams home in a jar? And be better off than you are? Or would you rather be a mule?" Stepping to the beat, I spun around in the kitchen as the words flowed through my soul. I danced all through the apartment as I carried items from the kitchen to the table like bowls, celery stalks, and a large bottle of ranch dressing. If I had a time machine, I'd go back in time to witness him live; preferably in a lounge setting. His music made men feel like men. Frank passed the time so effortlessly that I nearly missed the knock at the door. It took a second round of raps for me to realize someone was there.

When I answered the door, I found that Bronson, Pinick, and Delgado had all arrived at the same time. "Come on in guys." Since tonight counted as a weekend day for Bronson and Pinick, they weren't covering their normal late shift.

Bronson's ears perked up as he entered and heard the sounds coming over the stereo, "Frank? Nice."

I pointed at Bronson, acknowledging a man of good taste. Closing the door behind them, "I heard from Simmons and he'll be here soon."

The four of us crowded around the kitchen counter to make our wing selections and toss them into our bowls. As each of us carried our food and a cold one from the fridge to the table, we started to dig in when another knock came from the door. Simmons walked in with the swagger of a man hoping to clean us all out. "Am I too late to walk away with all your money?"

"We were actually just settling in," I said. "Grab some grub and we'll start the first hand."

After making his own dish and grabbing a drink, he joined us as Pinick reached for the deck and took the first round as dealer. "All right, gentlemen, we're going to start out with Texas Hold'em."

As he started dealing out the cards, he began telling us about a recent long weekend he took to St. Louis. He liked to tell stories, which came out even more when he was playing poker. It was how he kept himself from focusing too much on the cards and giving off any tells. I was onto him, but it's not like it helped me to figure out when he was bluffing. While in St. Louis, he'd visited the *Budweiser* Brewery with some friends and saw a Cardinals game. He couldn't say enough about their ballpark.

"I mean it's located right in the middle of downtown," he said. "It was only a couple blocks from the hotel so we just walked there. I could even see it from my room window. And the seats we had...man were they good. They were in the club level so we could go inside and get food and everything. It was fantastic."

"Fuck their stadium and the whole team," said Bronson. He was an adamant Royals fan, and that meant hating their rivals.

Ignoring his partner, Pinick continued his story. "The hotel was also right by the arch. I didn't get to go inside it, but I had a great view of it from my room window." Before coming back home, he mentioned that his friend took him to a bar district called The Landing where he played pool and hit on girls he had absolutely no chance with, but that wasn't going to stop him from trying. Everybody laughed at the idea of portly Pinick hitting on college girls half his age.

Simmons followed that up by jumping into work-related discussions that eventually led to our current case. We all pondered on the vigilante's connection to the judge as we played the next hand. If he hadn't killed Matthews for causes that we were used to seeing during Blood Week, then what were we missing about it?

Speculation on this ranged from the judge cutting the killer off in traffic to jealousy of the aging Matthew's good looks. He may have been of retirement age, but he was what the ladies would call a Silver Fox. More laughter followed at the outrageous motives. At this point, the alcohol had been flowing for nearly two hours. Needless to say, none of the conversation was being taken seriously anymore.

As he laughed, Simmons started spinning around in his chair with his head looking over his shoulder. Trying to look at the back, he fidgeted with the back support above where it connected to the chair. "Alex, did you know this chair is loose on the back? It's half coming apart."

Straining my neck to see beyond the table, "Really? I hadn't noticed. Oh well, I'll fix it later. For now, who needs another beer?" Standing up, I took drink orders as the gracious host and got everybody their next round. When I returned to the table, the conversation on the case had continued, so I played along. "Did you hear about the murder weapon?"

"Yeah, that was odd," said Delgado. "It wasn't a scalpel or anything this time. From what Amy could tell, it was some kind of hunting knife."

"I hadn't heard that," said Pinick. "Did she give you anything else to go on?"

"Not to me," I said, "but didn't she tell you something about the DB?" I said, gesturing to Marcus.

"Yeah, there wasn't any evidence that he was ever knocked out or tied up."

"Explains why there was a struggle," said Pinick.

"But it doesn't explain why he doesn't fit in with the other victims," added Bronson.

"Perhaps he's changing his MO?" offered Simmons.

"We won't know until more evidence comes in," said Marcus. "Speaking of more evidence, did anything come back on that hair found on the body?"

"I haven't heard anything yet," I said. "I told them to email me when they had some results, but that's enough shop talk. I was actually hoping to ask you something, Marcus." He turned towards me with an eyebrow raised. "Why did you transfer to Kansas City? There wasn't anything listed in your file."

He sat for a moment, making no move to answer the question that hung in the air. He took a drink and shifted in his chair as if the conversation would move away from the topic of he waited long enough. After another sip of his beer, he took a deep breath, "Honestly, I don't want to go into all the gritty details, but I'll give you the cliff notes. I was the subject of an Internal Affairs investigation on excessive force with a rapist I arrested. I was cleared of wrong doing because he was just trying to get off by making the claims against me. Afterwards, my captain didn't seem to trust me anymore. I got tired of the looks and snide, under-the-breath accusations so I transferred here."

It didn't take long for the next question to drop, and it was Simmons who said it. "Did you do it?"

"No."

"Too bad. Anybody that lays his hands on a woman like that deserves to have ten guys beating the little shit to death. Maybe he could be gang raped with a crowbar."

"Wow," said Bronson. "I really don't know how to respond to that."

"The correct response," began Simmons, "is 'I know a guy with a crowbar'."

"I hear that," commented Pinick as they clinked their bottles together.

The night's pot moved back and forth between us just as the conversations did, but eventually it was only Pinick and I left in the game while the others watched. It came down to a game of five-card draw. I looked at him and wondered what he could possibly have. Just then, he went all in and stood up to get himself another beer. With the remainder of his chips in a pile at the center of the table and only his back visible to me, I couldn't tell if he was holding anything real. Reviewing my cards, a pair of jacks and three sixes looked back at me. I figured a boat could probably take him. In fact, the move to get a beer was more than likely covering up any tells that he was bluffing.

"Call," I said, laying my cards face up on the table as he sat back down with his beverage.

"Damn it, Saint! I got a flush and you still beat me." He looked at the cards on the table and grimaced. "If I'd had your six of clubs I would've had a straight flush too." Leaning back in his chair, he chugged at his beer with arms crossed.

I raised my bottle to him and smiled, "Better luck next time, pal." I then downed the rest of it and tossed the empty bottle in the trash. Reaching under the table, I pulled out the steel case containing each player's buy-in money and shoved the bills into my pocket before filling it with the chips and cards.

With the game over, we cleaned everything up and put the poker table back in the spare room. It was much easier returning it with the help. Considering the amount of alcohol consumed, I called a cab to pick up my guests from the lobby as we each finished the last of our beers. As I bundled the trash to carry to the chute, the building's concierge called to inform me the taxi had arrived.

Wishing my comrades a safe journey home, and accepting their congratulations on my winning tonight, I walked them out so I could carry the trash down the hall to drop down the chute to the dumpster in the basement. The guys took an elevator down to their waiting cab and were gone when I returned from garbage duty.

Back in my apartment, I went set up the brewer to make coffee in the morning and realized I was out of beans. Waking up without a morning cup was damn near impossible lately, and I didn't want to be sharp with anyone like the other day, so I decided to take my winnings down to the market to purchase a bag of coffee beans. It was convenient how close I was to groceries when things like this popped up.

Outside on the sidewalk, I watched guys in their early twenties stumbling from the nearby bars back towards the parking garage. The fist-bumping drunkards were rambling about how "hot those bitches were tonight." Luckily one of them appeared to have his wits about him, so I assumed he must be the designated driver. I was happy to see that they'd chosen to be responsible.

At the store I found the black beans I liked and also grabbed a chocolate bar at checkout. Normally I purchased grounds, but every occasionally, I liked to go with beans that I could grind myself for extra freshness. I opened the chocolate bar on the way home and had just taken my first bite when my phone vibrated. "Saint," I answered.

"Hey, Alex, it's Eric. Sorry I didn't get a chance to call you earlier, but we had a bit of a meltdown with the servers and I've been up to my elbows in that shit all night."

"Don't worry about it. I complete understand. Get everything fixed?"

"Yeah, thank god it's all working now. Anyway, I wanted to let you know we got a hit on that hair from Judge Matthews."

"Shouldn't Kathryn be the one calling me on this?"

"Normally yes, but the servers going down had affected her machine, so she couldn't pull up the data. She'd asked that the second I have access to everything that I call you."

"Makes sense, so what do you have for me?"

"We got an ID on the hair, and I've been told that you'll never believe who it came back on. A BOLO was released for him and Captain Hawthorne had me place the file on your desk for the morning."

"Glad to hear it. I'll look at it first thing."

"One more thing," said Eric. "Did you hear about the blood room?"

"No, what is that?"

"The late shift got a tip about a murder, but when they got there they found a room covered in blood without a body. It was surreal."

Finished with his gossip, Eric said his farewells and I returned my phone to my pocket just as I reached the lobby of 909 Walnut. When I saw who was working the desk that night, I stopped to make small talk. "Evening, Sammy. How's the wife?"

"Much better, Mr. Saint. She spent a couple days in bed, but it seems like she's getting over it now. Hopefully she'll be back at work the day after tomorrow."

"I'm happy to hear it. Anything else interesting happening tonight?"

"Not really. Some weird looking guy in a Hawaiian shirt is visiting Nora on your floor, but it's been pretty quiet other than that."

In her seventies, it seemed odd for her to have a visitor so late. "Is everything ok with Nora?"

"As far as I know; he said he was just checking in on her."

"Ah, well be sure to give your wife my best."

"Will do, Mr. Saint."

Back on my floor, I went to unlock my door when I realized I never locked it when I'd left. It's funny how a little alcohol can make you forget the little details. After I entered, I set the coffee beans on the counter while I fetched the grinder from the cabinet. After filling it and turning on the blades to chop it up into a fine powder, I started unbuttoning my shirt and walked to the bedroom. The room was dark and there was a strange odor lingering in the air that made me stop in my tracks. The smell had a tinge of rusted metal to it, and after a moment I realized that I recognized it.

Flicking the light switch, I found where the smell was coming from. On the wall near the door was a stain of blood that had been smeared on the wall that read 'I Am Him.' In the same instant that I read the words, there was a sharp pain at the back of my head that threw me to the floor as I passed out.

Chapter 19

My head pounded like my brain had been attempting to escape my skull through brute force. I opened my eyes to blurry surroundings that took a moment to come into focus that was better but murky. My senses were groggy but awake, although it seemed the rest of my body wasn't cooperating yet. The brain was telling everything else to move, but the minions refused to respond. This was not the first time I'd had an instance of the brain waking before the rest of the body. It was a peculiar feeling that could be frightening, but it usually only lasted seconds.

The first time I'd experienced this sort of grogginess was after surgery to repair a broken wrist. In a brief moment of rage, I punched a wall to release my frustration after a bust gone bad. The last laugh went to the wall though. After the anger had subsided, I noticed an odd protrusion pushing up against the skin on the back of my hand. Ends up that I'd punched a stud that snapped my right ring metacarpal out of place near the wrist. Surgery placing pins in my hand reset the bone and it eventually healed. However, the actions cost me five visits to the department shrink.

After the surgery though, I'd come out of the anesthesia mentally before I did physically. This meant I could make out the sounds of the people around me as I lay on the hospital bed, but I was unable to move or speak. Honestly, I was terrified for the few seconds I rested in this state, but it didn't last long until the rest of me caught up. Although there were similarities to last time, I realized that I hadn't been to the hospital recently. As the back of my skull throbbed, I tried to remember what I'd done to feel this way.

My mind cleared soon enough with the passing seconds, but the pain remained with me. In front of me was the kitchen and I tried to stand again to get a glass of water, but I still couldn't move. Nothing from my body was obeying commands, but it didn't feel like it did after surgery. Looking down, I finally realized that it wasn't the haze of early wake from anesthesia that had my body frozen in place but the rope that wrapped across my legs, arms and chest. Shoving my weight forward caused me to rock onto the balls of my feet and then slam back down on the four legs of the chair, which shot pain through my skull that rang in my eardrums.

The sound of my shuffling alerted the intruder in my apartment that I was awake. I heard movement behind me and when I went to ask who they were, I felt the tightness around my mouth formed by duct tape. The strip of sticky goo kept my lips and cheeks frozen in place, so screaming for help was out of the question.

It was all coming back to me as I sat there in my living room. When I'd come back home, my door had been unlocked. My first assumption was that I'd forgotten to latch the door, but now I wasn't so sure. The houseguest I could hear behind me and off to the left had been here when I returned. It was their actions that had knocked me unconscious. My first thoughts were to open dialogue; see what they wanted. But that was difficult with the sticky situation over my mouth.

Again, my guest was reminded of my presence as I made muffled noises in hopes of bringing them back to me. I needed to know what the hell was going on. Closing a door behind me, the intruder moved some things around before walking up behind me. As they did, my vision suddenly went dark as a hood was yanked over my head. I heard as he went into my kitchen and I jumped when a loud clap sounded that was most likely something dropping on the tile floor. The footsteps became less pronounced as he returned to the carpet of the living area and started dragging something through the room.

The object sounded heavy as it dragged for a second and was followed by quick footsteps and dragging again. The sounds passed along my right side until it dissipated into the bedroom behind me. I heard a muffled thud through the wall as the item was dropped to the floor. I uselessly strained against my bindings again, but all the strength I could muster didn't make a difference. I wasn't sure what was in store for me, but curiosity killed more often than not.

The footsteps were back as they came straight at me. I felt a hand grab the back of chair before tilting me back at an angle to drag me across the carpet towards the bedroom. In contrast to my thoughts of escape, I hoped this guy wasn't ruining my carpet by dragging the weighted legs of this chair across it. Turning me to go another direction, I could feel the person struggling with my weight and the awkwardness of the chair. He cursed openly as he struggled to move me around. That's when I realized I was definitely going to be forced to replace the carpet.

My seated prison wiggled back and forth as I was shimmied through the door with one of the legs banging against the jamb. Another jerk to the side, and this time it was my knee connecting with it that felt like a screwdriver being pounded into the bone. My pain came out as a muffled moan through the gag.

"You're fine," said my captor as he finally acknowledged my state of consciousness. "I thought you'd be out longer but that's okay." If nothing else, I now knew the gender of my midnight visitor. "Questions will be answered soon enough, but first I have something to show you."

The hood was gripped from the top and yanked free, taking strands of hair from my scalp along with it. Sitting in the master bedroom, I was again seeing the blood the intruder had smeared across my walls. It still said, 'I Am Him', but that wasn't the only thing I could now see. Off to my right was a rolled-up rug that must have been what he'd been dragging through the apartment. Strangely enough, it was placed on a layer of plastic sheeting near the foot of the bed. I tried to peer around to see my assailant, but I couldn't move enough to see his face.

"So, what do you think, Detective Saint?" I let out a few grunts to remind him of something important; my mouth was still covered in tape. "Oh, shit, I forgot." He gripped a corner of the sticky strip and ripped it from my face. It stung like a mother fucker. "That's better. So, what do you think?"

"Well, for starters," I said, "ouch. Secondly, what do I think of what? The rug you brought me or the fact that you don't feel you need to be invited into my home? I could also mention the creepy, dominatrix vibe you're giving off by tying me to this chair." My comment was rebutted with a balled fist arching down over my right shoulder and connecting with my stomach. I coughed uncontrollably at the unexpected gut punch.

"You'll want to watch that," he said. "I don't care for smart talk." Could have fooled me, I thought. "I meant what you thought of my plan to offer you up to the police as the Blood Week killer."

The man stepped from behind the chair into my field of vision. With the hopes of surviving this encounter, I etched his face into my memory. I wanted to have perfect recall of every piece of him. He was Caucasian, about 5'10" with thinning cinnamon hair that I could see over the top of the hockey mask he wore. With an average build and gait, he wore dark skinny jeans with a white tank top under a flowery Hawaiian shirt. I remembered the description of this guy from Sammy in the lobby. Looks like the visitor wasn't checking up on Nora after all.

Sporting socks and sandals to complete his ensemble, I wondered what women thought when they saw him. There were a lot of fashion don'ts happening in front of me; so much so that I wasn't sure what I should say first. When I give his description to the authorities, should I start with the fashion police? Maybe Joan Rivers could weigh in on it too.

With the mask, I couldn't see any facial features, but I could make out bits of stubble through the holes in it. From the corner of my eye, I also spotted a large hunting knife straight out of *Crocodile Dundee* on my bed. "So..." I started slowly, "why would anything you're doing make Blood Week be associated with me?"

The man in the *Jason Voorhees* meets *Ace Ventura* nightmare costume took a few steps closer to the rug on the floor. Leaning over, he started to unroll it, and as he did so I suddenly decided to call him Jason Ventura. It was at least something until I had a legal name to work with. When the rug reached the end of its spool, it opened completely and spit out at my feet.

"You, Mr. Saint, are going to be revealed as the very killer you and your pals have been looking for. The one carving letters into people."

"So, it's no longer Detective, huh? Okay, I guess we can forgo the formalities, Mr. Ventura." The man tilted his head in confusion, but I continued before he had time to inquire about the name. "Why would anybody believe that I had anything to do with that," I said looking at the dead body. "I'm the *detective* investigating these murders, and I'm pretty sure the police will take my word over yours."

"That's a fair and simple question. You've been at every crime scene since the beginning, right? This gave you the perfect cover, but when you went to kill the poor gentleman on the floor, he fought back and you were stabbed by that very blade." He pointed at the knife laying on the bed.

"You still lack evidence other than the body you've brought with you. Who is he by the way?"

"Don't worry about it."

"Fine, then all you're going to end up with after this half-baked plan of yours is a long stay at a state-funded retreat. That's prison if you aren't keeping up."

"I'm not going to jail," he said with a grumble.

"Prison, not jail, but that's just semantics I suppose."

"My 'evidence'," he growled, "was pulled from the other scene you worked today. You know the knife that killed Judge Matthews?"

"Yeah...it wasn't the same as the other Blood Week murders. It was some sort of hunting knife."

Jason Ventura looked again at the blade laying on my bed. "And while you were sleeping, I was sure to get your prints all over it. Seems like you're going to be the perfect patsy."

"And why is that," I asked. I did my best to keep the man talking. I didn't like where his plan was taking aspects of my living through this day, so the more he talked, the longer I had to find a way out.

"I saw you at the Matthews house, so I Googled you."

"Yeah, that sounds like a good enough reason." Looking at the body, I again asked, "Who is he?"

"I think you mean who *was* he, right?" I stared back at him, unflinching at his attempt at humor. "Fine. He was just a man who crossed me, okay? That's all you need to know."

I was about to respond when I noticed the bucket on the floor. I'd seen it before I was clocked on the head, but I'd forgotten until that moment. The blood was put on the wall before he dragged in the body. The inner walls of the white bucket were coated in blood that I assumed must have come from the man that crossed him.

"I must say, I like what you've done with the place. I've been feeling that the walls could use a mural of some sort. The red really captures the room. Are you a freelance artist? I'm thinking I could get you to do more in the rest of the place."

"Fuck you," he said. "It sure got your full attention. Aren't you supposed to be some sort of hot-shot cop? How is it I could break in and catch you off guard?"

"You know what, you're right, but why don't we just call it an evening? You've had a long day with all your murdering and I could really use some sleep after the evening I've had. What do you say we just pick this back up tomorrow afternoon? Better yet, why don't you untie me, exit the premises, and we'll leave it at that. Sound good?"

"Yeah, right." Jason Ventura shifted my chair around to pull me back to the living room. Apparently, that was the end of the conversation. This time around I pulled my knees in to avoid any unwanted collisions with the door jamb. As he worked me back into the other room, I could hear the heavy breaths under the hockey mask.

Plopping me down next to the kitchen island, he returned to his work in the bedroom. Biting my lip, I looked around the room for a means of escape when it nearly slapped me in the side of the head. On the counter next to me was the block of steak knives sitting inches from my head. Salvation was within reach, but it chose to toy with me instead. The blades were right there, but my hands were tied around the back of the chair. I was unable to grab a knife to cut myself free.

I stomped my feet in frustration, or what constituted a stomp in my current predicament. It was really more like a toe tap. As I shook, I felt something shift behind me. Suddenly I remembered something that Simmons had complained about earlier that evening. As the night played through my mind, a flash of hope warmed me like a tall cup of coffee.

Immediately, I began twisting my right hand around until my fingers could grip the nut that held the back of the chair to the bottom. As the tips of my fingers struggled to grip at it, I strained against the binds until I felt it turn. I was in the same chair with the loose back that Simmons had complained about! I twisted my fingers around again and again, moving the nut millimeters at a time. With each passing second, the space between the seat and the poles along the back widened.

But before I widened it enough, I heard Ventura coming back into the living room. I kept working at the chair, but with less vigor so I didn't alert him to my movements. As he came up beside me, it was clear he had no fear that I was a threat when he placed the hunting knife on the counter next to the block of steak knives. Without a care, he started raiding my fridge for a late-night snack.

He pulled out a beer and I stared at him in disbelief as he opened the bottle and chugged it down. Who the hell was this guy? I understand confidence, but this man was clearly an idiot. While he'd worn gloves the entire time in my apartment that I'd seen, he apparently didn't realize that saliva had DNA. If I escaped, that bottle would be the first step to identifying him.

He noticed my disbelieving gaze and seemed to read my thoughts. "Mmmph," he mumbled while swallowing. "Don't worry detective, the bottle will be leaving with me. I wouldn't want anything left behind that would give doubt to the little story I've cooked up. I just needed a drink before we finish things up."

"Well, by all means," I said, "make yourself at home. You've already been doing that anyway."

As he tilted his head back to finish the rest of the bottle, I pulled up on the back of the seat and tugged hard at the rope. To my surprise, a large portion came free, but the rest had snagged on the bolt and was still secured around the back of the chair. With time running out, I wiggled at the nut again to free myself. It was coming off, but very slowly.

Ventura tossed his empty beer bottle into a shoulder bag by the front door and strolled back over to me. Gripping the hunting knife, he smiled from behind the mask. "Now to finish this."

Standing beside me, he placed the edge of the blade against my throat. The sharp steel was cool on my skin and felt like I was about to get a shave from a barber. I'd always thought about getting a straight-razor shave, but this one would be much closer than I would like to permit. As I saw the end drawing near, my sarcasm faltered in exchange for panic. The resolve I'd kept stiff until that moment was crumbling as the pressure against my neck deepened.

Mere centimeters from being free, all I heard was "Goodbye, Detective Saint."

Chapter 20

With ropes confining me to the chair and a large knife at my throat, I was closer to freedom than when this ordeal began. They say that your life flashes before your eyes when coming face-to-face with death, but the visions of my past never manifested. I felt the steel against my neck and pondered if I was experiencing my final breaths, but the only images in my mind was of what would happen next. The sharp blade would split through my flesh with ease, and the life of Alexander Saint would end with a splash.

Whether that was what fate laid out for me or not didn't matter. I wasn't the sort to lay back and accept things as they appear. While a predator would seem the victor when his prey was bound and seconds from death, even the flap of a butterfly's wings could alter the state of events. Seconds from releasing a crimson waterfall onto my carpet, *Ace Ventura* in a hockey mask lifted his elbow as he started to drag the knife across my throat. I felt the puncture in my skin, but never gave up the fight. In my last stand, I jerked my wrists violently against the ropes caught along the bolt on the back of the chair. I twisted and yanked hard enough that the bolt snapped forward and freed the rope.

This sudden release of the bolt that secured the back to the rest of the chair caused me to top backwards against my would-be murderer. The change forced him off balance, causing him to stumble backwards with his arms in the air to catch his balance. The pressure of the blade had left my skin with the equivalent of a shave that had come too close as I tumbled backwards to the carpet.

Continuing the momentum of my surprise, I pushed up with my legs as I fell and furiously connected the swinging fist of my free arm with his jaw. The change of events left him in a combination of shock, anger, and pain as he crashed into the granite countertop before crumbling to the floor. A loud clang followed as his knife came free and slid across the kitchen tile like a hockey puck.

Without stopping, I caught myself against the counter and pulled a cooking knife from the wood block and expeditiously cut at the rope around my chest. It came free with ease and the back of the chair slipped from my shoulders giving me more range of motion. I twisted forward to continue my grasp at freedom with the binding around my ankles. The back of the chair was still attached to my left wrist, but my upper torso was at least mobile. I knew that I would need my legs to truly put up a fight. As I did so, I could hear my Hawaiian-shirted friend regaining his composure as he scrambled across the floor for his knife.

I had one leg free as I looked over my head to see him retrieving his blade and rubbing at his cheek as he stood up from the tile floor. With one leg still secured with the thick twine, I didn't have the ability to choose a better defensive stance as he lunged for me. Focusing on using the kitchen knife for escape, it occurred to me too late that I could also use it for attack purposes. He connected with me like a linebacker hoping to take the star quarterback out of the big game permanently.

In my seated position, the forced shoved me over onto my chest before the two of us rolled over in the scuffle onto our backs. The motion twisted my ankle against the bottom half of the chair I was still tied to and I cried out in pain. From the throbbing pain pulsing through my calf, the tackle had come close to breaking my leg. His blitz gave him the added benefit of causing me to lose my knife in the tumble, but luckily, he lost his again too.

Although neither of us had a weapon, he still had the advantage with my ankle tied to the heavy chair. From where I laid on the floor, I could see the masked man scrambling across the carpet to reacquire the hunting knife. Watching where he was moving, I realized he was going for my kitchen knife this time. Regardless of what blade he chose, my position on the floor wasn't much of a defense against death. Even partially free from the chair, I was still susceptible to jugular penetration my kitchen instrument.

With the chair laying on its side, I attempted to slide the rope down the leg and over the wheel, but my attacker was coming back before I'd been able to do so. Kicking at his right knee, he doubled over and grasped at it while I was able to use the brief moment to yank the rope down and free myself of the chair. Both of us rose back up simultaneously as he came at me with the knife. I realized in the instant he sprang at me that the back of the chair was still tied to my left wrist, so I flipped it around to use as a shield.

The makeshift tool worked as each time he swiped or jabbed with the knife, I would catch his hand between the bars that formed what had been the back of a poker chair. Simmons issues with the wobbly chair was now my salvation as it kept the attacker at bay. As I parried his attacks, I slowly took steps around him until I had rotated the two of us and put my back to the door to the master bedroom. If I could make it in there, I could move the advantage to my side of the arena. In the bedroom was my gun.

As my dance partner became tired of the two-step, he decided to go after the hands holding the shield. With my fingers wrapped around the sides, they became tempting targets for his attacks. His blade slashed towards my hands, which made it more difficult to continue protecting myself. Catching the blade between two of the bars, I twisted the chair rapidly counter clockwise, taking his arm and the rest of him with it. The move forced him off balance as he leaned backwards like a man doing the limbo. With his weakened footing, I shoved the chair towards him and he tumbled to the floor. Pouncing on him, I punched him hard in the face before twisting the rope around his knife and shoving against his arm until the binding snapped in two. Completely free of the chair, I pushed off him and bolted for the master bedroom.

Rounding the corner, my fingers gripped at the door jamb to slow me enough to turn without crashing across the king bed in the middle of the room. As I ran towards my upper-hand, I could hear groaning from the living room. I knew he wouldn't be down for long, so I needed to wrap my fingers around the grip of my weapon quickly. Reaching the painting on the wall the wall of a beautiful day in autumn, I didn't waste any time admiring it. Yanking back on the painting so rough that I imagined nearly tearing it from the wall, I placed my thumb on the scan plate behind it.

The safe popped open just as my intruder entered the room in full sprint. His eyes were bloodshot and full of rage as he charged for me. The linebacker had another sack in mind, but this time his prey wasn't so defenseless. Sidestepping his lunge, I used his momentum against him as he slammed into the wall behind me. Narrowly avoiding the blade in his hand, I ripped open the safe and reached for my service weapon. The moment I felt the textured grip between my thumb and forefinger, an arm had wrapped around my hip and yanked me to the floor.

When I landed on the carpet, the gun flew from my hand and landed a few feet away. I was forced onto my stomach by the man who had more fight than I expected as we grappled beneath the safe. I swung my elbow around and connected with the corner of his throat, which caused him to stagger off me choking through raspy attempts to suck in air.

I took this chance to flip onto my back and kick him in the kidney, which forced him backwards into the bed. Reeling back, I swung my leg at him again, but this time I aimed for his face. My foot knocked off his mask as it snapped his head back.

He dropped to the side while I sprang to my feet and made a beeline for my pistol.

I found it under the opposite edge of the bed and once again wrapped my fingers around the hilt before spinning around to aim it at my attacker's last location, but he was gone. Where he had once been, I found only empty carpet. Before I could ask the question, I heard him running through the living room. Rolling onto my knees, I sprang to my feet in pursuit. Bursting into the kitchen, I saw the front door open and heard running footsteps echoing in the hallway.

When I arrived at my front door, I pressed against the edge and looked towards the south end of the hall and found nothing. Hearing the chime of the elevator doors opening, I spun to the other side and peered down to see him waiting for the lift rather than going for the stairs. Stepping into the hallway, I aimed my weapon at him and shouted, "FREEZE!"

As the elevator doors opened, he jumped in rather than obey my orders. I made a mad dash for the elevator, hoping to get there before it closed. Reaching the lift, I paused at the edge of the lift doors before springing out at him. As I did so, his hand flew out and reminded me that I wasn't the only one with a weapon.

His blade slashed at my arm and I screamed as it penetrated deep into my bicep. Falling against the opposite wall, I discovered the secret to his ability to see around walls. As I held my injured arm, I noticed someone had placed a mirror outside of their apartment. It looked old as if maybe they were throwing it out but hadn't carried it to the dumpster yet. My reflection looked back at me holding his shoulder as blood seeped into his shirt. Mr. Ventura had seen my moves before I could make them, and now that I could see into the elevator, I found that he wasn't alone.

A tenant that had been returning to the floor with a bag of groceries had been surprised when a man in a brightly-colored shirt with large flowers and jumped into the lift and put a knife to her throat. Using her as a shield, much of his face was hidden behind hers as a single eye peered out at me. His hunting knife moved up to rest against her cheek as she trembled in his grasp. I feel she would have screamed, but his free hand was clamped tightly over her mouth. As I stood in the hall holding my injured arm, I was unable to do anything except watch as the doors closed on the man smiling back at me. He may have escaped my home, but this wasn't over by a long shot.

Running down the hallway, I reached a door and slammed through it into the stairwell. Taking two steps at a time, I hoped to catch up with him in the lobby. After making it down two floors, I felt the blood pouring down my arm and knew this would be a problem. Pausing at the next landing, I ripped off my shirt and tore it apart to make a tourniquet. Synching it tightly around my arm, I ran bare-chested down the rest of the stairs. I was in pretty good shape, but after all the tussling in the apartment and now running down all the stairs, it felt like my heart was about to explode. It seemed that cardio just might be the death of me.

Finally, I made it to the bottom and exploded into the lobby entirely out of breath. I didn't see him anywhere as I stumbled around looking. At the front desk, the concierge stared at the shirtless, bloody man with the gun in his hand running like a maniac. I'm sure that the sight would be frightening if he didn't know who I was, but other guests in the building might not be as confident in their safety.

"Sammy," I shouted between gasps for air. "Did you see the man in the Hawaiian shirt come through here?"

"Yeah, he just left a few seconds ago," he said pointing towards the front of the building.

"Thanks," I said as I ran after him. Outside, I looked in every direction in the hope of catching a glimpse of him. When I looked south on Walnut, I located my target crossing over 10th street. Exhausting the reserves I had in tow, I pulled up every ounce of energy I had as I ran after him.

A man screamed curses at me as I bounced off him. Worse is that the commotion alerted my prey that I was still on his tail when he looked back and spotted me. He picked up the pace and began running himself as he turned west on 12th street. I chased after him and reached the corner just as he was turning south again onto Main.

Every part of me wanted to catch this guy. He'd broken into my home, tried to kill me, and also ruined a damn good shirt in the process. Continuing with all I had, I turned on Main and kept my eyes out for him. I paid no attention to the pedestrians staring at the shirtless madman running down the sidewalk with a gun. I didn't care about the calls to 911 that were surely lighting up the switchboards. All I was concerned with was catching a lunatic.

Spotting my mark only half a block away as he entered the parking garage across from the Midland Theatre, I followed after him. Inside were numerous exits on each floor of the parking structure that he might use to lose me. But I wasn't prepared to give up, so dug deep for another burst of speed to catch up. After entering the garage, I stopped and listened. After a brief second, I had him. Going left towards the sound of shoes slapping pavement, I tried to reduce his lead on me.

After running up the ramp to the second tier of the garage, I came around the corner and finally had him in my sights. I knew I was just about out of gas, so I raised my gun and in a final ditch effort I yelled, "FREEZE!"

I should've known it was a pointless venture. He refused to stop and this time I was clear of collateral damage, so I fired off a round that clipped him in the bicep. It caused him to stagger, but he still didn't stop. At the back corner of the garage, he sprinted towards an exit and I followed. As I reached it, I noticed a couple cowering behind an SUV.

"Call 911," I told them. "Tell them to get to Detective Alexander Saint's apartment immediately. He's in pursuit of subject." The man pulled out his cell phone and started to dial. "Got it!?! Alexander Saint!"

"Yes sir, it's ringing now."

Flying through the door, I ran out onto the street and looked for any sign of him. In the middle of the Power and Light District, I was surrounded by late-night bar patrons, but I didn't see Ventura. I thought I spotted him for a moment, but the colorful designs were from a woman's dress. Spinning in circles, I felt a heavy pit in my gut as I came to a realization that I didn't want to accept. I was bombarded by a crowd of those seeking Kansas City's nightlife, but the man that tried to kill me was nowhere to be seen. The heaviness in my stomach got worse as I had to face the fact that I'd lost him. "FUCK!!"

I walked back up towards the car garage spouting more profanities to myself. I couldn't believe that I'd let him escape. This now made two in a handful of days that got away. As leaned against a wall to catch my breath, I was shown how my pity party could quickly get worse.

I saw the gun pointing at me just as the voice told me to "Drop your weapon!"

Chapter 21

The night had started off in spectacular fashion. Not only had I enjoyed a night of poker with the guys, but I'd even won the pot as well. The only thing that would have made it better would be a woman in my bed to be the icing on the cake. As I thought about it, icing on a woman in my bed would be quite the delectable treat as well. But the explorations of another's body was not the hot and sweaty I was granted on this night.

Instead I'd been tied up in a very non-BDSM kind of way by a moron in a brightly colored shirt and a hockey mask. It was like *Jason Voorhees* was back from his tropical vacation just in time to murder another high school kid. After the struggle, I'd run all through the P&L trying to catch the bad guy just to lose him in the crowd. To make matters worse, my sweaty-and-shirtless condition had me feeling like John McClane at Nakatomi Plaza. The torn piece of cloth was still wrapped around my arm with visible blood seeping through it. And now I had a gun pointing at my back.

An off-duty street cop doing moonlight security for extra scratch had happened upon my Die-Hard cosplay in the middle of downtown and didn't react well to it. With the gun still in my possession, I kept both hands in plain sight as I responded, "Relax, officer. I'm Detective Alexander Saint. I was pursuing a murder suspect, but I lost him in the crowd."

"I said drop it."

The guy wasn't taking any chances as he stood vigilant. His weapon was steady as he studied me for any indication of fighting. "I'm telling you I'm a cop."

I pleaded for him to listen as I wasn't in the mood to deal with this. Getting shot on top of the laceration to my bicep wasn't exactly the nightcap I hoped for. The thought of a bullet made me force myself to focus on the situation from his point-of-view. I had to let go of my frustration at losing my would-be murderer and work with what was happening in the present.

"I'm lowering my weapon and placing it on the ground," I said as I slowly knelt and placed it on the sidewalk. "I'm now going to stand back up and take two large steps away from it so we can both feel safe." I rose very slowly and took two steps to my left. I kept the weapon in my vision so I didn't lose it, but also made no move to reacquire it as I didn't want anything rash to happen in the heightened stress of an unknown male running through the city with a gun.

"As I said," I began as I turned to face him, "I'm a cop. My name is Alexander Saint."

"Show me some identification."

Frustrated, I looked down at myself and then back at him. "Do I look like I'm in state that I'd have ID on me? My badge is at my apartment a few blocks away." I caught myself before I said anything I'd regret and regained my composure.

"Sorry, I know you're just doing your job. Give me a couple minutes to catch my breath and you can escort me to my apartment if you wish. There should be a couple inside by a blue SUV that can corroborate my story for now. I told them to call 911."

"That doesn't make you a cop," he said as he picked up my gun without taking his eyes or weapon off me. Placing my pistol in his holster, he repositioned to stay a few feet away from me.

"Maybe not, but by now that call should be on record. You can call it in to check. It's all I can do right now to prove who I am."

"Turn around and face the wall."

"Seriously?" I could feel the anger rising again.

"I'm willing to check on your story, but I'm not going to do it while holding a weapon on you. For everyone's safety, I'm going to cuff you and set you on the ground while I call everything in. I'm going to take a chance on your story instead of hauling you in, but only if you cooperate."

"Fine," I said as I turned to face the wall and placed my hands on my head and spread my feet apart. I knew the drill after performing it on others enough that I did what I could to speed it along. He holstered his weapon and stepped closer to pull each of my wrists behind my back. I heard more than felt the clicking of my new bracelets before he helped lower me to the pavement so I could sit with my back to the wall. Only then did he get on his walkie to ask about my story.

I listened for five or ten minutes as he spoke with dispatch. Finally, my lungs had cooled the fire in my chest and my breathing returned to normal. The short, bald man kept me in his sights as he was on the horn. I overheard confirmation of the 911 call from the couple in the garage, but that didn't prove who I was. But the voice that suddenly patched in must have heard my name come over the grapevine.

"Let me speak to him now," she said to the officer.

"Yes, ma'am." He pulled the microphone from his shoulder and held it front of my face as he held down the receiver.

"Hey, cap," I said.

"What the hell is going on, Alex?"

"Should I start at the beginning with my attempted murder, or jump to the present where I'm sitting in handcuffs on 13th Street?"

"I have people on route to your apartment. Get over there and fill them in immediately. There better be a good reason you were running through downtown with a gun. Give me back to the officer."

I looked up at the man as he pulled the microphone back. "Yes, Captain Hawthorne?"

"Let him go," she said. "He is who he says he is. Get him where he needs to be on the double."

"Yes, ma'am," he said just before releasing me from the second time I'd been constrained that evening. After helping me up, he me escorted back to my apartment.

It was squad-car city in front of my apartment building as my armed escort and I approached the front door. It looked like Stacey pulled out all the stops when she got the call from the couple in the parking garage. I counted ten different black and whites, plus a few others that could be unmarked vehicles. All the surrounding structures were lit up red and blue as faces appeared in the windows wondering what was going on. The block of pavement in front of the building was blocked off from traffic, but there weren't many cars out this late.

Stepping through the building's front doors, I entered a rave that I hadn't purchased tickets for. Bodies were packed in the lobby as the lights flashing outside reflecting off the wall tiles like a dance party. I wouldn't have been surprised if ecstasy tablets would start getting passed around to take advantage of the light show.

I spotted Bronson in the lobby who took custody of me from my escort. It nearly made me laugh since I wasn't under arrest anymore, but I appreciated it all the same. Re-acquiring my weapon from the officer before he left, I checked the safety and placed it in the waist of my pants before walking with Bronson to the elevators.

"So, what the hell happened tonight, Saint?"

"Long story; probably should save it and tell everyone at the same time."

Bronson pressed the arrow to call for the lift. "No problem," he said. "The captain's waiting in your apartment anyway."

"Did she call in an 'all cars' or something?" I asked, gesturing towards the outside. "Shit's nuts out there."

"Something like that. I was already upstairs with her and I know we didn't leave that mess, so I'm guessing this will be a riveting tale." He paused as his eyes looked me up and down. "You couldn't have cleaned up a bit before inviting us back over?"

The light-hearted jab was its own special language one learned after being on the force. The job was serious enough all by itself without the heavy emotions from brothers or sisters in blue. The rapport you developed with each other became one of belittlement. But in reality, we all knew that it was a way to avoid saying the real things like I'm glad you're okay. Each of us knew what the other was really saying beneath the words. This was just Bronson's way of acknowledging what happened and offering a hand of support.

Back upstairs, I found the door to my apartment guarded by two uniformed officers that nodded when I passed. Inside, the room was filled with forensics techs and the men I'd seen mere hours earlier. My partner was in the middle of a conversation with Pinick in the kitchen while Captain Hawthorne stood a few steps away on her phone. They were going over every inch of my home with care because an attack on one of their own was an attack on them.

As I walked up to them, I realized that Delgado hadn't changed since the poker game. Bronson and Pinick appeared to have made it home for a shower and fresh pair of clothes, but my partner hadn't been granted the same luxury. Bronson was in a fresh polo and jeans while Pinick got style points with his *Vans* tee and sweats. It was a safe bet that his attire was the least of his concerns when he got a call that I was in trouble.

"Evening everyone," I said stepping into the kitchen. "Anybody want a beer?"

Stacey turned to see me an immediately hung up the phone. She dropped the pad she'd been writing on onto the counter and walked up to me. "Are you ok?" she asked. I nodded. "What the hell happened?"

With my usual flair, "That seems to be the question of the night. I throw a party and next thing I know I'm being swarmed by cops. What's your deal with harassing law-abiding citizens anyway?"

A few chuckles came from the peanut gallery, but Hawthorne wasn't amused. She had her not-in-the-mood face fully activated. Awkwardly clearing my throat, I decided not to poke the beast.

"I went to the market after the guys all left," I began. My eyes wandered the room as I recanted the events. I didn't want to miss any details. "I was out of coffee so I went to pick up a fresh bag of beans. Afterwards, I was walking back home when I got a call from Eric. He told me about the file you had put on my desk," I said to Hawthorne. "When I got back here, I found the door was unlocked. I assumed I'd forgotten to lock it in my haste to get coffee beans. But when I walked into my room, I saw blood on the wall just before getting clocked in the head. Next thing I know, I'm waking up tied to one of my poker chairs."

I walked all of them through the events from my encounter with the Hawaiian wonder all the way to my short time in handcuffs a few blocks away. When I finished, it was Pinick that asked the first question.

"In the garage, you said you fired off a single round at him, correct? And it hit him?"

"Barely. It grazed him at best."

"I need you to take us to where this happened."

"Why?"

"Do as he says," commanded Hawthorne.

Instead of asking for an explanation, I did as she said and took a ride with them to the parking garage. At the scene, Edward Pinick was in full-detective mode as he had me once again recant the tale of what happened. He asked that I go over everything from when I came into the garage until I was back outside. I started with them at the entrance and the followed me as I went through all the details of how I'd run up the ramp after the man.

Along with the detectives, forensics followed along with flashlights moving across the concrete. They continued canvassing the first floor as we went up to the second. It had only been an hour since everything happened here, so I could see it all with fresh eyes. When we arrived at the part of the story where I'd fired my service weapon, I explained that I'd aimed at his shoulder before commanding him to freeze.

"I was out of juice and couldn't continue chasing him, so I hoped to slow him down or even stop him. That's when I took the shot."

"Can you stand in the same place you were when you shot him?" asked Pinick. I obliged and took a few steps away from my current position to where I'd been. "Okay, now aim the same direction you were facing when you fired your weapon."

I held up my hands in a mock display of holding a weapon out complete with thumb and forefinger. With my makeshift gun, Pinick stepped behind me and peered down the barrel of my finger. He squinted one eye as if looking through an imaginary sight. "Are you sure this is exactly where you were positioned, and exactly where you were aiming?"

"I can't exactly get it down to the exact millimeter, but it's the best you're going to get. I wasn't exactly doing a building survey to map the landscape." Taking one more glance down the barrel of my faux gun, he walked off in that direction. "Are you going to tell us what you're on about?"

He didn't respond, but instead just continued walking. I looked over to the others for answers, but they just shrugged before following him on his trek through the garage. Only Stacey seemed to be two steps ahead as she conferred with a forensics tech and pointed towards Pinick who had made it all the way to the opposite wall.

Running his fingers across the concrete, he remained silent until he paused on a single area. As the tech came up next to him, he pointed at the spot and said something that I couldn't hear. As he spoke, the tech opened the case he carried and pulled out a tool that looked like a long silver spike and a plastic bag.

"Pinick," I said. "Come on already."

"When you fired your Glock," he said, turning back to face us. "You said he staggered a bit but kept on going. That doesn't sound like it hit anything vital like a bone because that would have floored him. Since you felt it only grazed him, the bullet could still be here. And sure enough, I found it lodged in this wall." He pointed at the area the tech was now working on.

As if on cue, the forensics tech stepped away from the wall with the bullet held up by his forceps before dropping it into the evidence bag. He examined the jacket through the clear plastic before nodding at Pinick, "You were right, sir."

"And now we have a sample of his blood," Pinick smiled.

Bronson finished the thought for him. "Which means we have his DNA. If the database gives us a hit, we'll find your *Ace Ventura* with a *Voorhees* fetish."

For being the only one who thought to look for the bullet to get a DNA sample, Pinick felt big in his britches as he grinned from ear-to-ear and stated, "Yep."

Chapter 22

Captain Hawthorne ordered me to go get a hotel and let the other detectives handle the investigation. I say ordered because she had asked me more than once to get some rest once they had my story and began working the crime scene. Since there was still a forensics team in my condo, that meant I wouldn't be allowed to sleep in my own bed either. She had offered to have someone drive me wherever I wanted to get lodging for the night, and I had refused. Eventually she had to turn the request into a command just to get me to leave.

I respected Stacey's concern for my wellbeing, but my state of mind had only sharpened. Catching the man that decided it was perfectly acceptable to invade my home and damage a good dress shirt while he was at it, wasn't a subject I was going to drop. But she was right that I should get some rest. It was just past midnight and I hadn't had a good night's sleep in days. This time of year always had a habit of interrupting my REM cycle.

Tonight, wouldn't be any different because how does one just lay down and take a load off after the high-stakes evening I'd just went through? Surely my mind wouldn't be capable of just easing back into neutral simply by placing the back of my head on a pillow. I'd very nearly died tonight, and even with the life on the KCPD I'd never had a brush that close.

It was true that I'd used my service weapon on the job before, and even taken more than my fair share of bruises. But I couldn't think of any time before that I'd truly felt like it all might be coming to an end. As I walked along the sidewalk in a fresh set of clothes I'd changed into before leaving the apartment, I could still feel the bindings around my chest as the knife was readying to relieve my body of its life-giving fluids. It was an experience that made me look back at my life so far.

Tragic events always came with the added weight of questioning what a person has done with their life; the choices they've made. I was no different. Waiting at a crosswalk for the signal, I thought of the life I'd led so far and the dedication it gave to those lost. I watched as a couple walked past holding hands. The woman was dressed simply in jeans and light blue shirt under her jacket as she smiled into the loving gaze of the man she cuddled up to. There was a love there that I'd never allowed myself.

The man looked at me and nodded in acknowledgement of my presence before looking back down at her and returning her smile. He wrapped his arm around her and kissed her on her head as they disappeared around the corner. I didn't consider how I must have seemed as I continued looking at the last spot I'd seen them until people started shoving past me to cross the street. The commotion caused me to shake out of it and notice the flashing indicator to walk.

I quickly crossed over the street and pulled my phone out of my pocket, but it started ringing before I could press anything. On the screen was the name Kathryn Morrison. My thumb hovered over the green icon a moment as I considered if I should answer, but I knew she'd be worried if what happened that night had made it back to her, so I pressed it and held the phone up to my ear.

"Oh my god, Alex. Are you ok?"

"I'm fine, Kat."

"Are you sure? I just heard about what happened. Did they find him yet? Why did he target you?"

The questions came at me in rapid-fire succession as I tried to calm her. It was like a pummeling to my ears that wouldn't stop. I did everything I could to assure her I was living to fight another day as I hailed a passing cab. Taxis weren't as prevalent in Kansas City as they were in places like Manhattan, but you could find one occasionally while downtown.

As I opened the back door and slid into the leather seat, I covered the phone as I gave the driver my destination. After seeing the couple on the street and getting the call from Kathryn, I knew where I needed to go. I had to see her.

"I don't know for sure," I said, returning to my conversation with Kat. "Apparently he'd seen me on television working the Blood Week case and decided to come after me."

"So, it was him then? The vigilante?"

"I highly doubt it. It was more that he was trying to pin a body on Blood Week and then paint me to be the vigilante all so he could get away with his own murders. Something about his demeanor told me he wasn't sophisticated enough to behind the real Blood Week deaths. Not to mention some of the other items like the hunting knife that didn't fit with previous bodies."

"I should be there with you right now," she said. "I can't even imagine what you went through. You shouldn't be alone."

As Kathryn said this, my ride pulled into the driveway and I handed him a wad of cash before stepping out and walking towards the front door. "My place is a crime scene right now, so I can't even stay there myself let alone have guests. Your fellow lab techs are combing over everything as we speak."

I stepped up to the Tudor style home and knocked on the front door. As I waited, I heard footsteps inside coming closer. "But I promise you'll see me soon enough."

The door opened and she stood before me in all her splendor. Tears immediately filled her eyes as she sprang forward, wrapping her arms around my neck as she buried her face in my shoulder. As she held onto me so tenderly, the voice coming through the phone repeated her question.

"When will I see you?" Kathryn asked.

"Soon," I promised. "But right now, I should get some rest. I'll talk to you later." After I ended the call, I walked with Amy Doyle into her home to spend the night.

Chapter 23

I watched as the car pulled up to the intersection. The setting sun reflected off the blue paint causing flecks of silver to sparkle like stars in the night sky. The man driving leaned over to the woman with him and kissed her on the cheek. As he pulled away, an arm came in through the window and pressed a cold barrel to his temple. I wanted to scream for help, but before the words could come out, I felt the pistol on my skin.

Death's goodnight kiss was puckered and ready to bid me farewell. I felt the cold leather of the steering wheel between my fingers. Before I could save myself, the trigger pulled and released the firing pin into that ignited the metal tube in a flash of light. Instantly, I was back on the sidewalk watching the struggle as a loud bang was followed by the interior of the windshield splashing red.

Time inched by as it appeared to stop in that moment. Everything froze for that instant before death. The slug shrieked in the night as it bored into flesh and bone. The geyser that was his life sprayed out like a fire hose as the force of the bullet snapped his head to the side and caused the man's dying body to fall into the passenger's lap.

Again, I tried to stop what was happening. The man was lost, but I could still save her. I ran towards the vehicle, my chest heaving with the effort, but I didn't get any closer. From across the street, I could feel the life draining out as the blood spilled onto the floorboards. The woman was screaming as the gun turned on her. I ran harder as my vision began to blur from the strain. Reaching out as if my fingers could somehow stop all that was happening, the gun rang out for the second time as I shot up from the sheets screaming.

I woke up out of breath and covered in sweat. It was the same dream again that kept me from sleeping in peace. Lying beside me in the bed, Amy slept soundly. If nothing else, I was happy to see that my commotion hadn't stirred her as well. Leaning back onto the sheets that were soaked in perspiration, I looked over at the clock on her side table. There was still another hour before I needed to get out of bed, but deemed it better to wake now than falling asleep to relive the nightmare once more.

Letting my eyes rest on Amy as she slept, I felt like a part of me could be happy here with her. The whole idea of the family with the white-picket fence wasn't something I'd envisioned for my future since I was a teenager. But watching her chest rise and fall while her exhales caused the brown strands of hair laying across her cheek to dance made me wonder what could be. However, in the end I knew that I could never be what she deserved. I may put on a show of something better, but inside I would always be damaged goods.

Rolling up again, I swung my legs over the edge of the bed until my feet rested on the grey carpet. I grabbed my cell phone and checked for any missed calls or texts, and all I found were a few from Kathryn still wanting to see me. She again inquired about my condition, but it was too early to worry about responding to her.

I also found a voicemail from Hawthorne that gave me a small reason to rejoice. Forensics had finished up, so I would get my house back later that afternoon. Although I knew Amy was happy to host me while I was essentially homeless, I didn't want to be a burden on her or anyone. My preference was always to take care of myself, and that meant getting out of her hair as soon as possible. Luckily, she only had to provide a roof for me for a single night.

Standing up, I walked out of the bedroom and around the corner to her bathroom. As is standard with any man waking in the morning, I took my complimentary morning piss before turning on the shower. I waited until the temperature wasn't that of an icy blizzard before pulling back the curtain to step inside. Before I could start washing off the sweat from last night and my nightmare, I heard a whistle behind me admiring what she saw.

"Oh, I'll take me a piece of that," Amy winked. She leaned against the entrance to the bathroom with her arms crossed and still naked from a few hours earlier. "Mind if I join you?"

Yanking back the curtain, I waited for her to step in as the water splashed against my back. As we started to wash one another, I was shown the importance of getting stiches when you're supposed to. In all the action of the night, I hadn't taken care of getting the wound from the hunting knife in my shoulder sewn up. When the bandage was taken off my arm to clean off the dried blood, the scabbing was pulled back and reopened the cut. It wasn't spurting blood like a bad kung-fu flick, but it was enough to drain down my bicep and drip off my elbow. The droplets spread out like an amoeba on impact as it swirled in the water and headed for the drain.

"Fuck," I said as I saw it happening.

"You really need to get stiches."

"I know."

"Why didn't you get them last night before coming over? If not for that bandage, you'd have gotten blood everywhere."

"Because I'm stubborn."

"And pig-headed," she added.

"And pig-headed," I said.

"I'd take care of it," she said as she dried it off and wrapped a fresh bandage around it, "but I don't have any supplies here."

"Don't worry, I'll get it taken care of today. I'll just have to live with the gauze wrap for now."

Out of the shower and with my muscles aching, I had more difficulty drying off than I could handle, so Amy helped. I felt like a toddler needing Mom to take care of me. Once I was dry, Amy laid out a spare suit she had from the last time I'd spent the night. It took more time than usual, but I was able to get dressed and added my gun harness and a splash of cologne before putting on my sport coat.

The elevator chimed as the doors opened to the bullpen. Despite all the events of the last twelve hours, I remembered that Eric Masters had left a file on my desk and wanted to get to it. As I maneuvered around a group of people chatting while sipping their morning coffees, I avoided joining in and kept my eyes on the prize. As I neared my desk, I could see the yellow folder lying next to the keyboard, but I was ambushed before I could get to it.

"Are you ok? You never returned my calls. I've been worried all night about you."

Either Kathryn had either snuck up behind me after waiting for me to arrive, or I was so focused on seeing what Eric left for me that I'd walked right past her in the bullpen. Regardless, her surprise arrival kept me from the information on my desk a few minutes more. I was eager to learn what had come back on the hair found on Judge Matthews, but first I had to deal with a woman scorned.

"Morning Kat," I said turning to look at her. Her brows were pulled in tight as she stared at the cause of her frustration. She crossed her arms in what could only be a physical committal to not move until I spoke with her. She'd wanted to see me last night, but that hadn't been in the cards.

"I'm alright. I'm sorry I didn't get back with you, but I'd already told you I was ok and just needed to get some rest. I wasn't in the mood to go over everything again after having to do it for the crime report. I was all talked out and kind of lost in my own head, you know? I wasn't happy that I'd let the guy get away."

"I can understand that," she said as her muscles relaxed. She looked around to see if she'd caused a scene. The eyes that had been watching darted back to their work to hide their voyeurism. She stepped closer to me and dropped her voice to a caring, yet sensual, whisper. "Want me to come over tonight? I could get your mind off things for a while if you'll have me. I just want to take care of you."

She rested a hand briefly on my chest and looked up at me until she remembered that there were other people that could see us. Suddenly dropping her hands to her side and taking a step back, her eyes wandered everywhere around me but my face. "That is, if you want me to take care of you," she said.

She bit her bottom lip as she waited for my answer. If I was honest with myself, I wasn't keen on the yearning I saw in her wandering gaze. It felt like she was experiencing more from our pairing than I was willing to give. It was similar to what I saw in Amy's eyes, but this seemed more desperate.

"Ok, just let me know if there's anything I can do to help," she said trying to mask her disappointment when I didn't answer fast enough.

"Let me think about it," I said quickly to console her. "I have a lot of work to do today, and I don't know how I'll feel later. I'm still sore from the entire ordeal as well. Just let me think about it and I'll let you know, ok?"

She nodded with a concerned grin and her eyes lingered on mine in an attempt to sway my decision. Getting nothing concrete in return, her face went slack as she turned and walked away.

Kathryn could easily offer a wonderful distraction that would surely work wonders on any normal day. But my state of mind was out of tune lately, and the longing I saw in her eyes wasn't something I was prepared to deal with. I was serious about giving the idea of her company some thought, but for now I was more concerned with the information on the hair from the crime scene.

Plopping down in my desk chair, I picked up the folder and cracked it open. As the day continued to work against me, I was once again interrupted before I could finish reading the first line on the page.

"Edward and Richard spoke with the lady in the elevators," said Marcus as lowered himself into the extra chair beside my desk. Setting a coffee in front of me, he leaned back to sip at his own before continuing. "She said that after your skirmish, when the guy used her as a shield, she was forced to stand with her nose in the corner like a kid on timeout as the elevator descended to the lobby."

Closing the file again, I thanked him for the mocha as I took a drink. As he gave report, I laughed at myself for forgetting about the other hostage from last night. In all the commotion, I hadn't even thought about what might be learned from the woman he'd used as a shield in the elevator during his escape.

"He told her to stand there with her eyes closed because if she saw his face she would, quote, 'seriously regret it.' When the elevator opened again in the lobby, he just left without saying anything else."

"I'm guessing she didn't get a description of his face then."

"Nope."

"And all I got of his face was blocked by hers, so we've got nothing to go on."

"Yeah, but if the blood on the bullet brings anything back, then that won't matter. Also, they took the clothes she was wearing at the time into evidence as well. It's unlikely that we'll get anything from them, but with the brawl the two of you had beforehand, you never know what might come back."

"Good thinking," I said.

"I'll let you know if anything else develops," he said as he stood back up and walked to his desk. With no further distractions or reports, I was finally able to read through the report I was still holding. As I scanned through it, I discovered that Eric was absolutely right when he said I'd be shocked.

The hair came from a Tara Williams, which would normally link her as our prime suspect to the murder. But another detail in the report also proved that it was impossible that Tara could be our killer. This Arizona native had resided for the last eighteen years in Scottsdale Cemetery after her own murder.

"I checked it three times because I thought I'd made a mistake, but I didn't. The hair belongs to Tara Williams and she is, in fact, deceased."

Standing in Eric Master's office in the lab, I held the file open as I went over the facts with him. I wanted to be positive that the information was genuine, and he assured me it was. After having pestered him about the facts, I took him at his word and apologized for the third degree. Luckily, he understood as he too had had a hard time accepting the information at face value. How would a hair from a woman that died almost two decades ago appear on a murder victim?

Tara Williams was born and raised in Scottsdale when her life was cut short by another Arizonian; Brett Davidson. Brett was tried and convicted of shooting Tara twice in the chest with a 9mm handgun. Although he claimed everything had been an accident, the prosecutor ran the entire jury through what happened and baffled them when asking how he could've shot someone on accident...twice.

The final ruling that sent Brett to prison took little time to come to the unanimous decision. In addition to the evidence from the prosecution, Tara's brother Trent had given crucial testimony. He'd hammered the final nails into Brett's coffin when he teared up on the stand and gave testimony against him. On the last few lines of the file, it said that the presiding judge on that case was the one and only Judge Joseph Matthews.

Back in the bullpen, I found a pleasant sight seated in the chair beside my desk. The precincts lovely coroner, Amy Doyle awaited my return. She noticed my approach and smiled with a hint of concern as her eyes wandered to the shoulder where I'd been stabbed.

"I haven't got the stitches yet, but I promise I'll get it taken care of," I said to console her. I pulled out my chair and swiveled to face her.

"Besides wanting to check on you, I've also got some results on the rug man from your apartment." She held up another folder for me then laid it on my desk. "The DB's ID came back as Trent Smith, but I got a hit when I pulled him up in the system. Apparently, he'd been living in Kansas City under witpro."

"Why was he in witness protection?"

"I spoke with Edward before you got here, and he made a call to find an answer to that question. He found that Trent had received death threats over some case pertaining to a local gang and the cops in his hometown didn't have sufficient evidence to do anything about it. But after an attempt was made on his life, he agreed to testify against them and was put in protection. Oh, and Eddie also learned his last name was actually Williams."

"So, we're calling Pinick Eddie now, huh? Should I feel jealousy about—"

I stopped as the name suddenly registered with me. Grabbing the file I still had from Eric off my desk, I flipped through the pages. When I came to the section I was looking for, I looked back up at Amy. "Did you say the victim's name was Trent Williams?"

"Yeah, why?"

Springing from my seat, I scanned the room until I found my team coming from the breakroom with fresh mugs of coffee. "Guys," I hollered as I flagged them down. "Get over here quick."

Detectives Marcus Delgado, Richard Bronson, and Edward Pinick all hustled over to my desk at the urgency in my voice. I informed them of what Amy had said as she sat listening to me. Clearly intrigued at what had agitated me, she sat quietly as I consulted with my team. "As I'm sure you've heard, the hair found on the judge belongs to a deceased woman named Tara Williams, but Amy just informed me that the body from my condo was her brother Trent."

Shock splashed across the three of them in unison like a wave at a baseball stadium. "That's not all, this guy also helped to put away his sister's killer whom I found out was released from prison not long ago."

"Sounds like we need to get a location on Brett Davidson immediately," said Delgado.

"I can call witpro again and see if they know anything about Trent and his sister's case." Pinick was already on his way to a phone before he'd finished the sentence.

"Great," I said. "Richard, can you check with the parole board and find Brett's current location?"

"On it," he said as he turned to take care of his task.

While the other detectives made calls, Marcus and I took a trip to Kansas so we could speak with Mrs. Matthews. It was possible that she may have more information on the judge's connection to all of this now that more information had surfaced.

Back in the Matthews home, Marcus and I sat on a leather couch in the living room with the judge's wife in the loveseat across from us. Just before we arrived, Bronson had called to inform us that after Brett Davidson was released from prison a month ago, he had moved to Kansas City but they were trying to get hold of his parole officer to get a current address. The news made Brett our prime suspect, and the information aided us in our meeting with the judge's widow.

Placing a few photos on the table, "Ms. Matthews, do you recognize any of these men?" As she studied them, I added, "Please, take your time." But time wasn't something she needed when her eyes landed on the third photograph.

"This one here is Trent," she said. Her eyes darted up to me as a hand went to her mouth. "My God, Trent didn't have anything to do with this, did he?"

Marcus jumped in, "Not that we know of, ma'am, but he was found dead yesterday." He waited a moment as her mouth dropped and a small gasp of air escaped. She recovered her composure slightly as the news sank in. "Can you tell us how you knew him?"

She told us that Joseph and Trent were very good friends as she wiped a single tear from her face. They met at the golf course, and Joseph was hesitant to have anything to do with him at first. Ms. Matthews never understood why, and Joe never elaborated. Marcus and I already knew that the assumption could be that the judge remembered presiding over Trent's case while still in Arizona.

Ms. Matthews informed us that she and her husband moved to Kansas City after Joseph was offered the district judge position. At the time he had met Trent at the golf course, they didn't know many people in the area and when the judge's uneasiness had faded, the two men became good friends. Trent had started joining them for dinner on a weekly basis and was often accompanied by his girlfriend.

"Wait, girlfriend?" I asked. "Would you happen to have her name?" As she gave us the girlfriend's information, my phone sounded off with a text message from Simmons. Thanking her for her time, we excused ourselves and treaded back to my SUV.

Once we were back in the vehicle, Delgado was the first to ask the obvious question. "Do you think Brett found out that Trent was living here and friends with the judge and tortured Matthews to find Trent?"

"It's a definite possibility," I said as I tapped the message on my phone. Simmons found that there was another Davidson living in the city as well. Brett had a brother and we had his address.

"And I think I've got someone that could help answer that question." I keyed the address into GPS and pulled away from the curb to follow the route to visit the other Mr. Davidson.

It was about twenty minutes later when I steered up to our destination. After parking the car, Delgado and I walked up the driveway to a ranch-style home with a garage on the left. The house was a hunter green that made me think of army camouflage. After a few knocks at the maroon door, a dark-haired woman with pale skin answered. The sight of two strangers at her door had her visibly tense.

"Hello ma'am," I said. "I'm Detective Saint and this is my partner Detective Delgado. Is Peter Davidson home? We'd like to ask him some questions about his brother."

Appearing relieved, "You here to take him back to prison? I want that murderer out of my house. Peter's at work, but feel free to haul Brett back to jail."

"Is Brett here?"

"No. I don't want that criminal in my home."

"And you are?" asked Marcus.

"Martha. I'm Peter's wife."

Could you tell us where your husband works?" I asked.

"As long as you're getting that killer back to where he belongs, I'll give you anything you want." She wrote down where we could find Peter and gave us the slip of paper. Thanking her, we went back to the vehicle to continue following the breadcrumbs, but Marcus paused near the front corner of the SUV and stared at me with a puzzled look.

"What?" I asked.

"Are you bleeding?"

I looked down at the sleeve of my left arm and saw a line of red seeping into the fabric. "Fuck, my bandage needs changed again. That asshole stabbing me is really starting to screw with my day."

"Sorry your chi is out of whack, but did you ever get it looked at?"

"Yeah, I had it cleaned and everything," I said.

"Not by the EMT, did you ever go to the hospital like Hawthorne told you to?"

"No, I haven't got around to it yet. I'll get it taken care of, but there are more important matters to attend to. For now, the bandage will have to do."

"Alex, you need stitches." He insisted that I get it taken care of immediately and pressed the issue when he took my keys and drove me to the hospital to get stitched up. He said he would speak with the brother alone and pick me up afterwards. I tried fighting him on it, but I knew he was right. And I didn't need to keep hearing about it from so many people. Besides, it hurt like hell too. Maybe I could get some painkillers while I was there.

Marcus left me at an urgent care clinic to get patched up while he went to speak with Peter Davidson. When I got inside, I informed the nurse at the front desk that I was there to get stitches in my arm. Once she realized I was a cop, she said I'd be pushed to the front of the line.

"I can't jump in front of the people that have been waiting already. Just put my name on the list and I'll get in there when it gets to me. What is the wait time?"

Informed that it would be twenty minutes if I waited, I thanked her and took a seat in the lounge. Looking for something to pass the time, I picked up one of the magazines and flipped through the pages. Periodically looking at my watch, I found the wait ended up being a little longer than expected. I started to wonder if I should've jumped the line after all so I could get back to work. I tossed the magazine down to get a status update and, as I stood, a nurse stepped in and called my name.

She put me in a room and told me that the doctor would be in shortly, but the fifteen minutes that passed while I sat in the room didn't feel that short. The predicted waiting times didn't seem that accurate to me, but the doctor did eventually join me. In the time it took the doctor to look at my arm and stitch it up, I'd been at the urgent-care facility for over an hour. By the time I got outside, Marcus had already returned to pick me up. "Get it all stitched up?"

"Yeah, what'd you find out?"

"You're going to love this. I spoke with Peter at the factory he works at and noticed a pretty nasty bruise on his face. He said he was hit by some steel piping that came loose from a fork lift. The important part though is that he gave me a location on his brother. He's staying at a hotel downtown, and I figured I'd pick you up before we went to see him.

"Thanks. Let's go nail this bastard."

Chapter 24

The ride across town put us right in the middle of the lunch rush. It seemed like everyone in the city was trying to make it somewhere to eat and back to work during that hour. We carved out our path through idling vehicles and hurried pedestrians to a budget hotel where our suspect was staying. Marcus had called ahead and learned that Brett's room was currently unoccupied because he'd stepped out about an hour prior to our call. With this in mind, we decided to stakeout the hotel and wait for him to return.

It didn't take long until stomachs started growling, so I left Delgado to watch for our man while I picked up some sandwiches from a deli across the street. I scanned the menu above the counter before settling on the tuna salad sandwich my partner requested and a roasted turkey on wheat for myself. Adding a couple bags of potato chips and two soft drinks to the mix, I started to pay for the food when I noticed the basket of cookies near the register. Tossing a chocolate chip into the bag, I handed the man a twenty and rejoined the waiting game already taking place in the Tahoe.

Stakeouts were a boring, yet required, part of the job. They made you long for something fast-paced and exciting, but every cop knew that it was grunt work like this that brought everything home. You had to put in the time with all the monotonous aspects before you could get the sweet satisfaction of hearing the perp being fit for bracelets.

"I got you a little something extra," I said as I slid back into the passenger seat. I dug into the bag and pulled out the cookie to present to Marcus.

"Fuck, man. I love chocolate chip."

"I figured as much, I've seen your sweet tooth. I'll just be sure not to tell the wife." Delgado touched his nose to indicate it was our little secret before pulling back the wrapper and taking a large bite. "I guess dessert comes first?"

"I haven't had a decent cookie in days," he said while chewing. "Rita is on this health kick and throwing away all my sweets. It's hell, man. I've had to resort to keeping little stashes around so I don't have to drive to the gas station every time I want a cupcake."

"Just call me your new supplier, but only the first taste is free." I smiled as I unwrapped my sandwich. As I prepared it, I noticed a raised eyebrow from Marcus as I applied a layer of chips that I then smashed down with the top of the bun. It made a satisfying crunch as the salted chips prepared to complement the turkey sandwich.

"Don't knock it 'till you try it," I said just before taking my first bite. I sat back and enjoyed the crunchiness as we multi-tasked our meal while keeping watch for Mr. Davidson.

Swallowing the massive mound of sandwich in my mouth, I asked my partner, "So when are you going to bring in the family for us to meet? I figured Rita and Victoria would want to see where you work eventually."

Laughing slightly, "Yeah, sorry about that. Most of my free time has been spent unpacking. You never realize how much stuff you own until you have to deal with all the boxes. The stacks of them are like a mini cardboard city."

"I can imagine. Well, we should have a barbeque or something with your family, as well as Edward's and Richard's."

"And you could bring Amy."

"Or some other date," I responded with a side glance at Marcus' implication."

"Fine, Kathryn it is. Oh, come on," he said after I raised an eyebrow at him. "It isn't any secret that you're fooling around with both of them."

"Maybe not, but no need to let them know that," I joked.

"I'm pretty sure they already know."

Before I could ask what brought him to that conclusion, we saw our target cross the street and pass right in front of our vehicle. Packing away our food, we hopped out of the car and followed him into the hotel where we loitered a few minutes in the lobby as we waited for him to turn down a hallway.

We wanted to make the arrest as quietly as possible to avoid causing a scene, so the idea was to catch him somewhere in the hotel that wasn't as busy as the main lobby. Normally it wouldn't have been an issue, but a few months ago there had been a small uproar after an officer used what witnesses called 'obsessive force' to apprehend a suspect. Just in case Brett put up a fight, it was better to do it away from so many spectators.

Once he had gone up a short flight of stairs and disappeared down the hallway, we quickly followed. On the next floor, we entered the hallway and proceeded along the multi-colored carpet, in dire need of replacement, until we caught up to him standing in front of room 108. Brett fished around in his pocket for a room card as we approached. With him preoccupied, he didn't notice us coming up to him until he inserted his card key into the magnetic-strip reader.

"Brett Davidson?" asked Marcus.

"Yeah...?"

"I'm Detective Delgado and this is my partner Detective Saint. We'd like you to come with us; we have some questions to ask you."

"What? Why? I haven't done anything."

"Sir, unless you want to make this an arrest, I suggest you come with us."

"ARREST!?" Brett appeared shocked at the idea, but his hand on the door handle kept me ready for a chance that he would try to run. "What would I be under arrest for?"

"The murder of Joseph Matthews and Trent Williams. I'm sure you recognize those names since they were both related to your conviction for murder."

"Wait, they're dead? How? And why would I be a suspect. I've been here since I got out of prison. You can check with my parole officer."

"Both of these men were living in Kansas City too," I said. "And they were found dead two days ago along with a hair that led us to you."

"But that doesn't make sense. I haven't seen them since my conviction. How could my hair be on them?"

"We'll explain everything at the precinct," I said. Pulling out a pair of handcuffs, I held them up to him. "So, how do you want to play this?"

Looking at the silver bracelets dangling from my finger, Brett calmly agreed to come peacefully and avoid an official arrest. We walked him out through the lobby and to the waiting SUV like a trio of friends going out for lunch.

Standing in the viewing room, I watched Brett through the glass as he sat in interrogation, fidgeting with his fingers and looking around nervously. Delgado gathered the files containing all the case information thus far, while I measured our man. The vibe I was getting wasn't that of a hardened criminal. He acted like a first-timer that legitimately had no idea what was happening, but that didn't necessarily mean he was innocent. Many suspects have made an art out of this routine, and I was still trying to decide if Brett was an artist. Either way, I was certain of one thing. This wasn't the man that attacked me in my apartment.

Brett didn't have any facial hair, which could have easily been shaved, but he also didn't have a bullet wound on his arm.

This wasn't the man I shot, but that didn't rule him out of the deaths of Joseph Matthews or Trent Williams.

A knuckle rapped the door and I turned to see Marcus waving the file at me through the window. Following him out and around the corner, we entered the interrogation room to join our suspect who snapped to attention when the door opened. Closing the door behind us, my partner slapped the file onto the table, startling Brett.

"So, Mr. Davidson," Marcus began, "you've been in town for roughly three weeks now...visiting family, correct?" Brett nodded his head. "Can you give us your whereabouts last night? Let's say from eight to midnight?"

Although I knew Brett wasn't my guy, I didn't interrupt as there may be something useful that springs free from the questioning. Nervously looking back and forth at the two of us, he slowly answered Delgado's question.

"Umm, well I got some barbeque at the place around the corner from the hotel around 8:30. After that I stopped at a bar for a few beers and then went for a walk. You don't get to have alcohol in prison so I've been there a couple nights this week." I wrote down the names of the restaurant and bar while Delgado continued.

"Any reason you decided to take your walk last night?"

"Same reason as the beers; after all that time in lock up, you forget the simple joy of being able to do something as mundane as take a stroll."

"What time did you go for this walk?"

"I don't know, around 10:30? Can we get to why I'm connected to all this? I told you I haven't seen the judge or Tara's brother since I was in Arizona. It's been almost twenty years."

"You say that," I said, "but it seems rather suspicious that you come into town and the people who put you away show up dead."

"I agree, but it has to be some kind of coincidence because I didn't kill them. I had no reason to even hurt either of them because I'm not like that."

"Well that's your first lie," said Marcus. "You've already killed before, so how can you say you aren't the kind of guy that would hurt someone? You spent fifteen years in prison based on Trent's testimony? Are you really going to tell me that you don't have a motive here?"

"You think I'm angry about any of that?" he said. Both of us looked at him without responding, "Look, I bear no ill will towards them over anything. How could I after what I did? I deserved what happened. Yes, I killed Tara, but I'm not a murderer. I never meant to hurt her. Her death was an accident." Not breaking our stare, he took us back to the beginning of the night the Williams' family lost one of their own.

In the open desert of Arizona, loud music blared while local teens emptied kegs one cup at a time around the large bonfire. Attendees to the event showed up in cars, after nightfall, for what was meant to be the party of the year. It seemed like the entire town's teen population drove up to the destination that was over twenty miles from the nearest city. A young Brett Davidson showed up with his brother, Peter, after hearing about it through the grapevine.

As they walked up to get their first beer, they noticed that Tara Williams and her brother, Trent, were also in attendance. The brother and sister were acquainted with the Davidson boys since they attended the same school, but didn't normally run in the same crowds. Trent gave the traditional teen greeting of 'what's up' as the brothers grabbed cups to get their first drink of the night. The booze flowed freely and blood-alcohol levels rose as everyone enjoyed the party.

At some point in the night, everything escalated when Peter thought it would be fun to shoot off his father's gun. He'd snuck it out of the house without anyone's knowledge—including Brett's. A small group of around twelve ventured away from the main gathering area to fire off some rounds, and Brett, Peter and Tara were among them.

With the smaller group, Brett and Tara got better acquainted after an abundance of flirtatious glances throughout the night. Now he was free to talk to her while the others took turns with his Dad's pistol. They sat beside each other on a rock and Brett lost himself in her beauty. Her hair was red like the morning sun and he marveled at the cute freckles on either side of her nose. He wasn't sure if it was the beer talking, but he really wanted to kiss her.

As they talked, the time got away from them as dawn approached. Many of the cars had already left with only a handful of people still drinking and enjoying the waning fire. Brett, Peter and Tara were the only three still sitting near the shooting range after everyone left and Trent slept off the booze in his car. All the beer had gotten to Brett too because the last thing he remembered was sitting down with the gun to load a few rounds and suddenly feeling nauseous. He decided to lie down until his stomach stopped turning summersaults.

He kept his eyes closed to help, but he must have passed out. The next thing he knew, he was being pulled off the ground by police officers who placed him in handcuffs and read him his rights. As the bright light of the morning sun stabbed at his eyes, he found his extremely hung-over vision difficult to get to cooperate. Shapes were abstract and blurred in color as he asked what was happening. He figured he was being arrested for underage drinking, but something was off. Even through his inebriation, he could see that nobody else was being cuffed.

It was when one of the cops stepped between him and the sun and casted a shadow over him that he was able to focus on an image that was forever burned into his mind. Lying it what could only be described as a bloody jumble of limbs was Tara's body as paramedics near her packed away their supplies. Trent sat beside her and pulled her limp form to his chest as he cried. There were two spots on her chest that had soaked her clothes and the dirt dark red. That's when he was told that he was being arrested for her murder. He had no recollection of the two bullets he'd put into her during his drunken state. It was at the trial during Trent's testimony that the gaps in his memory were filled in.

Trent had come to check on his sister after his nap, and what he found was Tara on the ground struggling for breath with nobody around except Brett who still had the gun in his hand. When Trent screamed for help, Peter had come running and it was he who'd called 911.

I could see the regret in Brett's eyes as he told us how a party had ended up destroying all their lives. It was after hearing this tale that I'd made the decision that this man was no killer. As I thanked him for his time, I had the regrettable task of informing him that he would be staying with us overnight. "You are still our primary suspect due to the connections to Tara, but I'm sure that you'll be free to go once we can confirm your whereabouts during the judge's death."

With sunken shoulders, Brett said he understood as Marcus escorted him to holding. What was one night in holding after fifteen years of it? We knew that all we had was circumstantial, but we'd have to release him in 24 hours if nothing solid comes up anyway. No DA would ever try to prosecute a man with this little evidence because they would lose. Needing a jumpstart, I poured myself some coffee in the break room before going to my desk.

"Saint," said Pinick as he caught me leaving the break room. "The results came back on the bullet we found in the parking garage."

"Great, did we get any hits?" Before the answer passed Pinick's lips, I could see the disappointment painted all over his face.

"No. We didn't even get a chance to test it. The lab told me the sample was contaminated by a fungus or something on the wall. I can't even pronounce the stuff, but we won't be able to make any kind of ID with it at this point."

"God damn it."

"Tell me about it, but before you continue with that thought, I do have some good news. You remember the clothes we collected from the woman in the elevator? Well, we found blood on them too."

"Edward, tell me we're having better luck with the clothes than the slug."

He paused long enough to form a huge grin on his face, "The sample was good. Kathryn is running it through the database as we speak."

"What the fuck, man? Why didn't you lead with that?"

Pinick shrugged, "Just being thorough."

"Just let me know if, and when, we get anything."

"Will do," he said, walking back to his desk.

Back at my little slice of real estate, I took another sip from my cup as I sat in my chair. Looking at the stack of papers on my desk made me wish I could be anywhere else in the world. I was not the least bit in the mood for paperwork right now, but there was one place I could find what I did want to do. Carrying my coffee with me, I went to the elevator and pressed the round, plastic button that would take me to the morgue. Descending, the bell chimed as the doors opened and the person I was on my way to see bumped into me as I tried to step out.

"Afternoon gorgeous," I said as Amy stopped in her tracks, noticing it was me. She smiled in that way that could melt everything away until it was only her.

"Afternoon yourself. What are you doing down here?"

With a complete lack of trying to hide my intentions, I stepped forward and wrapped her up in my arms. Our eyes stared deep into one another as I leaned in to meet her lips. Before I could press my mouth to hers, my phone started ringing. Detective Edward Pinick couldn't have had worse timing.

"Done already?" she asked as I answered the phone. "Talk about quick draw over here."

We both laughed. "Duty calls," I said, "rain check?"

"I don't know. You might have to sweet talk me first," she said walking past me into the elevator. The doors closed as she gave me a wink, and then she was gone.

"We're going to have to work on your timing," I said to Pinick. "What do you got for me?"

There was always a measured amount of suspense when new information came out on a case. Each new piece could make or break an investigation, but what he had to tell me was a piece that could blow everything wide open.

"We got something back on that blood sample. It doesn't belong to anyone in the system, but it's not a total dead end." A momentary pause allowed him to build up the gravity of what had been discovered. "We got some unexpected results that you'll want to see for yourself. But first, I'd recommend you pull your suspect back out of holding."

"I'll be there in two minutes."

Chapter 25

I stepped through the elevator doors before they finished opening and found Pinick waiting for me. News that a blood sample didn't come up with any hits wasn't out of the ordinary, and it was something every cop learned to live with. There was no way to have the DNA of every person on the planet, so you started to assume that blood wouldn't get you anything in the beginning. But Edward's news from Kat was anything but normal.

Waving Delgado over to join us by interrogation 1, I skimmed the file from Pinick as he went to join his partner in the observation room. After filling in Marcus on the news, we entered interrogation together to question our guest again. I was anxious to see how he reacted as he eyeballed us coming in to join him.

Curiosity crept across Brett's brow as he wondered why he was back in this room again. He was completely lost on the reason, but I was there to enlighten him as I stepped up to the table and sat in front of him. "Mr. Davidson, we have some exceptional news for you."

"What?" Before I laid everything out for him, I inquired about his siblings. "I have my brother Peter that you've already met, why? What's this all about?"

"Please...humor me."

Brett told a story of the wonderful man that stood up for him at every turn. Peter visited Brett every Saturday in prison like clockwork before they moved to Kansas City together. He'd come in with news of the family, how the Cardinals were doing, and even brought in home-cooked meals on occasion. Peter was the only one that ever looked at him the same after what happened to Tara. He was the only one that kept in touch and always looked after him.

"The only reason I made it through prison was because of him. Having a piece of my family still with me is what got me from one day to the next. He even promised to get me a job at the factory he works at. I'm telling you, I'd have been found in a noose a long time ago if it wasn't for him."

"Peter sounds like a standup guy to have as your brother," I said.

"He is," Brett and I both heard a short chuckle from Marcus. "He *is*," he said eyeballing Delgado. Looking back to me, he continued, "Now, why did you want to know about him?"

"Well, Mr. Davidson, we got the results back from a DNA panel that we ran on a blood sample. It was retrieved from the man that we believe murdered Joseph Matthews and Trent Williams."

"He also attacked a detective in his home while transporting Trent's body," added Delgado. As Brett stared at him, his brow wrinkled as he attempted to connect the dots. "He tried to kill him; a police officer. But we weren't able to get a match on the DNA in our system."

"I don't see what this has to do with me."

"I'm getting to that. While we didn't find a complete match, there was a familial relationship found."

"What are you getting at?" Even as the words came out, I could see that Brett didn't want to hear the answer. The dots were forming a picture, and he didn't like where the crumbs were leading him.

"The sample had markers in common with your DNA, which means the blood belongs to a direct relative of yours. More specifically, a male sibling."

"It's your brother," I said, filling in the blanks for emphasis.

"What do you mean it's my brother? Why would he go to your house? You must have made a mistake."

"Perhaps he thought we were onto the two of you and—with Saint being the lead detective on the case—he made the absurd attempt to frame him for the recent murders."

"I already told you, I didn't kill any of them. You've got the wrong guy," pausing, he added, "wrong guys!"

A tap came from the mirror directly behind me. "We'll be back," said Delgado. "How about you think about what we've said and see if you have something better to tell us."

Stepping out to the bullpen, Simmons waited excitedly to give us his news. A call had come in from the forensics team at Trent's home. When they arrived, the rooms had been torn apart like it had been burglarized, but it was hard to say if anything had been stolen. All the major electronics and a savings jar were undisturbed. But Simmons now believed the burglar hadn't found what he was looking for because of what the techs discovered.

A single pillow on the couch gave the impression that Trent had slept there recently, and inside was a hidden USB drive. Our forensics team didn't cut corners, but we were lucky that the person who broke in didn't share this trait. When the pillow had been pulled from the case, they found that the pillow had been cut down the center, and inside was where they located the memory stick.

"Now why would someone hide a flash drive in a pillow?" asked Simmons, rhetorically. "They discovered it was password encrypted, but that didn't stop them. Twenty minutes after Eric got hold of it, we had full access to what was stored on it." Simmons grinned as he held up a sheet of paper with a transcript printed on it. "Alex, we have a full accounting in Trent's own words of what really happened the night his sister died, and this version has an alternate ending."

I took the transcript from Simmons and held it where Marcus and I could both read through it. He was right, this completely rewrites what happened that night.

"This was everything on the flash drive?" I asked. "How do we know it's authentic?"

"Because the drive was a video of Trent confessing the truth. This is just a printout of what he said. Eric did a query to see when the video was recorded, and I think this may be why he's dead because it was less than two weeks ago. His death was to cover up the truth."

"Do you have the video with you?"

"I thought you might ask," he said, holding up a department issue flash drive.

"Great, let Pinick and Bronson know too. Are they already on route to get Peter?"

"Will do, and yes. When they heard the confirmation that Peter was Brett's only sibling, the left immediately."

"Good." Grabbing a laptop, Marcus and I reentered the room to show Brett what had developed.

"Brett," I said as I started setting up the laptop on the table. "What if I told you there was a possibility you're not a murderer after all?"

"That's what I've been telling you. I had nothing to do with Trent or Judge Matthews."

"No, you don't understand. I mean that you've never killed anybody."

"Except for Tara, right?" he said glumly.

"No, I mean your hands are clean of everything. You've never killed anyone...ever."

Brett's head tilted and he leaned back in his chair like a bad smell had just wafted through the room. His eyes studied me as I finished with the computer and plugged the drive that Simmons had given me into the USB port. Slowly, he leaned forward with his elbows on the table and worked his lips as if rediscovering how to form words.

"What exactly are you getting at?" he finally asked.

Turning the computer around, I pressed the spacebar and allowed the video to play for him. On the screen was an image of an older Trent since the last time Brett had seen him. "My name is Trent Williams, and I've done something terrible..."

In the Arizona desert, time had gotten away from the young Brett and Tara as the party slowed down and dawn approached. Many of the cars had already left with only a handful of people still drinking and enjoying the waning fire. Brett, Peter and Tara were the only three still sitting near the shooting range after everyone left and Trent slept off the booze in his car. All the beer had gotten to Brett too as the last thing he remembered was sitting down with the gun to load a few rounds and suddenly feeling nauseous. He decided to lie down until his stomach stopped turning summersaults.

He kept his eyes closed to help, but he soon passed out. With Brett lying in the dirt, Peter decided that Tara was now fair game. He knew that she had been eyeing his brother all night, but now it was his chance to move in on her. Brett couldn't do anything if he was unconscious, and Tara was extremely attractive. Trent returned and picked up the gun to fire off a few rounds while Peter started hitting on his sister.

"Why don't we go back to your brother's car and have a little fun. Everyone else was hooking up tonight. There's no reason you and I shouldn't get a little action too."

The only problem was that Tara wasn't even slightly interested in sleeping with Peter. For starters, she informed him that she wasn't a 'damn slut', and—if that wasn't enough—she had really liked talking to Brett. She thought he was cute and had hoped he might ask her out. Brett was sweet and she could tell how shy he was. It would be funny to talk about their first night together when he passed out drunk, if they started dating.

And if he didn't ask her out, she was going to ask him to a movie when he woke up.

Peter wasn't happy to hear her rejection and pressed the issue again. Scooting in close to her, he rubbed his hand along her thigh and asked for sex again. Again, she didn't give the answer he wanted. In fact, she outright refused him and smacked his hand away in disgust. He didn't like that and forced himself on her as he tried to kiss her. Grappling with him, Tara pushed back and slapped him across the face.

Angered, Peter fought harder to get what he wanted whether she liked it or not. Shoving Tara onto the ground, he pinned her to the ground and tore her shirt apart, exposing her bra. He pulled the straps over her shoulders to free her breasts as she fought to escape. With her arms pinned under his weight, she was too weak to free herself and screamed for help. Alerted to what was happening, her brother shoved Peter who smashed his elbow into Tara's would-be rescuer's face. Trent stumbled backwards as he tried to get past the stars filling his vision.

Before she could get to her feet to run, Peter re-acquired his position on top of Tara to finish what he'd started. "Stop struggling, bitch. Just lay back and enjoy what daddy's going to give you. I've been watching you all night. I know you want it."

"I'm going to call the cops, asshole!" These words stopped Peter in his tracks as he stared down at her. Without response, Peter rose to his feet and walked over to where Trent and fallen. As he paced, Tara started to dial her phone as her face streaked with tears. She shook from sobs at what had happened.

Before she completed dialing 9-1-1, she heard something animalistic in Peter's voice. "It's in your best interest to hang up the fucking phone before you make things worse."

Appalled at what had transpired, Tara asked how he could do anything worse to her. He'd tried to rape her and she was not going to let him get away with it. Trent rolled over to help his sister, as a united front against her attacker, when he heard the loud click of Peter sliding a loaded magazine into his Dad's pistol.

He watched Peter's arm raise with the gun pointing at Tara just before two rapid flashes came out of the muzzle. His sister's chest exploded as she was knocked backwards. Screaming her name, Trent sprang to his feet to rush to her aid. He had to stop the bleeding, but he was stopped in his tracks when Peter stepped in his way with the gun now pointing at him. What happened next would forever fill Trent's life with guilt.

"You have two options," said Peter. "You can help me out of this, or you can die right here...right now."

"Fuck you!"

"Okay, if that's how you feel." Peter's finger started to squeeze the trigger, but Trent urged him to wait. He wanted to save his sister and have Peter pay for what he'd done, but the fear of death played tricks on people. It had a way of making people agree to things that made them sick because nobody wants to die.

"Fine," whispered Trent.

"Speak up. I didn't hear that."

"I said I'll do it. Please don't kill me."

Trent sat helpless with his sister as she drew her final breaths while her murderer started working up the story for the police. He placed the gun in Brett's hand as he concocted a tale that left Brett as the person behind Tara's death. In exchange for Trent's life, he was instructed to say that he'd watched Tara repeatedly rebuff Brett's sexual advances and then he found him standing over her body with the gun.

To ensure Trent stuck to the story, Peter looked him square in the face and said that he would still kill him if he didn't do what he was told. "You'll suffer her fate if the truth ever comes out," he said. After those words, Trent spent the rest of his life feeling like a silent stalker was constantly watching him.

Through every passing day after her death, Trent wanted to come clean and save an innocent man from persecution. But each time he thought about telling the truth, the haunting memory of Peter's eyes would leave him trembling. He hated the coward he'd become after that night, but he was too frightened to do anything about it for a very long time. The guilt weighed heavily on him as he watched Brett accept that he killed Tara although he had no memory of ever mistreating her. Peter's plan had worked so far as to convince his own brother that he'd killed a girl.

"I wanted to tell the court the truth as I testified," Trent said on the computer monitor. "But I could see Peter in the room as he stared back at me. His eyes were filled with a darkness that I can only describe as pure evil. I truly feared that he would kill me right there in front of all of them if I didn't stick to my script. So, I did as I was told."

"Years later—after witnessing a mugging that ended in death—I again found myself giving testimony on what I'd witnessed. Word got out to the suspects' partners, and I started getting threats. I couldn't let another murderer go free, so I testified in exchange for protective custody."

"That's when I was moved to Kansas City, and after befriending the judge from Tara's case all those years ago, I realized that Peter no longer knew where to find me. I found strength in my friendship with him and in meeting my girlfriend that I knew I could finally tell the truth about that night in the desert. And that is what I planned on doing, but when I went to Joseph's recently, I saw a man outside his home that reminded me of Peter. I'm recording this now as a way of safeguarding the story in case anything happens. When I know it's safe, I'll take it to the police. Brett deserves the truth."

"MOTHER FUCKER!!" Brett screamed at the computer screen. "How the hell could he do this to me...to her?" Instead of calming him, we let his emotions flow in whatever way they needed. I couldn't imagine finding out the last twenty years of your life were a lie. I felt bad for him, but we needed his tirade to push him to cooperate with us in bringing his brother into custody.

"I always thought he was just giving me support, but he was actually giving penance or dealing with his own guilt over what he did to me. I can't believe this. I thought he loved me. We never talked about that night again after it happened. Was it because it was all his fault? I hope you nail him to the fucking wall. What do you need from me?"

Before I responded, my phone vibrated with a text from Pinick. 'Peter Davidson not at work. Boss says he went home, but not here either. Get down here. Found another problem.'

Chapter 26

I entered Peter's home knowing that we could have apprehended him already if we'd had the facts earlier in the investigation. Marcus was particularly upset about the situation because he had been the one to speak to him about Brett's location. Knowing that we could have prevented this had him pacing with his arms crossed in frustration. The discovery of the USB with Trent's confession came too late for us to react fast enough.

As a cop, I dealt with the guilt and regret of not getting someone off the streets when we could've, but it was the victims who paid the permanent price. I'm reminded of this first hand, as forensics worked around the congealed pool of blood that surrounded Peter's wife like a moat. I didn't need the medical examiner's report to see that she'd been stabbed three times in the abdomen and her throat slit, but I listened to Amy anyway.

"Liver temp puts her TOD about an hour ago. We also found this under the body," she said, handing me a small, handheld tape-recorder with a slip of paper taped to it with the words *play me* written in pen.

Moving to a circle with my fellow detectives, I pressed the button and the tape began with shuffling and static before we could hear a door open and close.

"Honey you home?" we heard a voice call out.

"I think that's Peter," said Delgado, but it was quickly confirmed via the playback.

"Yeah, Pete. I'm in the kitchen." Said a distant voice that sounded like it was standing across the room. *"What're you doing home already?"* My eyes met my partner's and knew that he also recognized the voice of Peter's wife Laura.

"Got off early. Can you stop what you're for a minute? I need to talk to you about something."

"Ok?" Sounds of footsteps on the linoleum got closer to the microphone until we could hear her as clearly as if she were standing next to us. "What is it, sweetie? Did the cops pick up your brother?"

"I believe so, but that means bad news for us."

"What do you mean? I don't see how that murdering brother of yours getting arrested is a bad thing."

"They'll connect the dots. I couldn't find anything at Trent's house, and I know he made something telling the truth."

"What dots? And who is Trent?"

"It's all his fault. If he'd kept his mouth shut, none of this would be happening," said Peter.

"Baby you're starting to scare me. What is all this about?"

"Brett never killed that girl in Arizona."

"Yes, he did. You and her brother witnessed it...is that who Trent was? Was he that girl's brother that saw Brett kill her?"

"It wasn't him. I just blamed him for it. I killed Tara."

A long moment of silence passed before she responded, "Peter that isn't funny."

"Do you hear me laughing," he asked. "I'm not making jokes over here. I killed that girl because she disrespected me."

"Disrespected you? What are you talking about?"

"She refused me because she wanted Brett. She was just like every other girl."

"Peter, I don't understand."

"She threatened to call the cops on me," he shouted. "The bitch got what she deserved, and I wasn't going to prison over that snatch. There was only one person that knew the truth, and he was going to spill the beans. I couldn't let that happen, so

I tried to clean everything up. But he died before I could find where he put it."

Frightened, Laura's voice started to tremble. *"Why are you telling me all of this?"*

Clearing his throat, *"Well...now that I know the heat will inevitably be coming down on me, I have a few last-minute loose ends to tie up. I can't leave anything behind that could lead them to me."*

There was a burst of static as Peter shifted and the microphone rubbed against fabric. As the question arose, Laura's reaction told us where the story was going. This recording would end with her dead body on the kitchen floor.

"Oh God, Peter, what are you doing?!?"

"I told you...loose ends."

She screamed over crashes and shuffling of a struggle before a loud thud as the two wrestled as Peter attempted to kill her. From the body in the other room, we already knew who won that battle.

"NO; Please, God...NO!!" Her screams were muffled over by a loud gurgling like water running down the tub drain. Each of us visibly cringed as we listened to a man murder his wife. She choked and gagged until the sounds dissipated and all we could hear was loud gulps of air as Peter caught his breath. After a moment, his voice spoke.

"Did you like that, Mr. Saint? I didn't realize we'd be in touch so soon after my visit to your luxurious apartment. In fact, I just assumed go back to my life since you never saw my face. Thanks for sending your partner to question me so I could have this chance to get away. A part of me will miss Laura, but she wasn't good enough for me. She was overweight and kind of fugly. She was nothing like Tara, am I right? So, I guess this is goodbye. Happy hunting, detective." The tape clicked and went silent as the recording ended.

"We need to find this asshole and now," I told everyone. I knew they were all thinking the same thing. "Bronson, you and Pinick talk to the neighbors; see if they heard anything or know where Peter may have gone. Marcus and I will look for more here; report back in twenty."

With everyone understanding their assigned tasks, we broke to perform them and find leads. I began by calling in an APB on Peter Davidson and requested Eric to see if he can ping the GPS on his cell phone. If luck was on our side, we'd pick him up quickly. Making calls, I peered in the kitchen and saw Amy finalizing her report so she could get Laura's body transported downtown.

Twenty minutes passed with Delgado and I having nothing new to show for it. All we'd come up with was that Peter had packed up his clothes and personal items before he split. We already knew he was on the run, so that didn't help anything. Our counterparts returned while I was on the phone checking the cell trace. Eric couldn't find anything on the signal, but he'd keep monitoring in case it popped up. I hung up and hoped to get better news from Pinick and Bronson, but they were just as empty handed as we were.

Canvassing the area, they found a next-door neighbor that heard yelling earlier, but he just assumed they were arguing again. They were often fighting about things, so it was nothing out of the ordinary. While Bronson explained this, Pinick received a call and stepped aside to take it. Once the story was through, and we were up to speed, I heard him say "Great, thanks" before hanging up.

"Good news, we found the girlfriend." Wondering what he was talking about, he continued "Trent Williams' girlfriend saw the story on the news. She's down at the station now; thought you might want to talk to her," he said looking at me.

"Yes, we'll head back there now. Can you guys wrap up here?"

"Sure thing, see you back in the bullpen." Marcus followed me out so we could try connecting another piece of the puzzle; Trent's recently discovered significant other.

Stepping off the elevator, the familiar smell of sweat, cheap cologne, and coffee greeted my nose. We were spotted by an officer who turned to intercept when we walked in. When he caught up, he informed us that Samantha Winchester was waiting for us in the break room. She was taken there to get something to drink instead of placed in interrogation like a suspect. It allowed us to speak to her in a more comfortable environment.

She sat on the couch, holding a coffee that looked untouched as her lips trembled to maintain her composure. The smudges in her eyeliner told me she'd been crying, but she was trying to keep the walls up long enough to talk to us. It was very brave of her to come forward considering what had happened to her boyfriend.

"Samantha Winchester?"

Looking up as if she hadn't noticed us until that moment, "Yes?"

"My name is Alexander Saint, and this is my partner Marcus Delgado. We're the detectives working Trent's case. Ms. Winchester, we were hoping to ask you a few questions about him."

"Absolutely," she said scooting up on the couch and setting her coffee on the table. "But please call me Sam."

"Very well," I said as we both sat opposite her. "To start, could you tell us about your relationship with Trent?"

"He was my boyfriend."

"My understanding is that you just found out about his death today, correct?" She nodded. "When was the last time you spoke to him? He died a few days ago, so I'm curious why you didn't realize he was missing before you heard it on the news."

"Yes, of course. He'd been acting strange lately, standoffish, you know? I figured he was second guessing our relationship, but he wouldn't talk to me about it. I wanted to know what was going on, so we had a huge fight and I told him we needed to take a break. I said he could call me if he decided he actually wanted to be with me."

Samantha grit her teeth together and put her balled fists up to her eyes as she fought to keep everything from collapsing. Her emotions were doing everything they could to burst past the dam she'd built up, but they were kept contained for the moment. Swallowing hard, she returned to the shaky composure she was retaining and continued.

"When he never called, I figured that was his way of breaking up with me. I never knew it was because he was..." She paused again, but the container she'd shoved everything down into was beyond capacity and the walls burst. The dam overflowed and the flood sprang free as her eyes glassed over with tears. "...that he was dead," she choked out. Her body convulsed with each cry and I grabbed tissues for her.

"Ms. Winchester...Sam, there is no way you could have known what was going on." Her makeup smeared as she wiped her face with a balled fist before taking the tissues I handed her. "You can't blame yourself for what happened. It's Peter Davidson that's at fault, and I promise he'll pay for what he's done."

Giving her a moment, she calmed slightly and blew her nose. Taking more tissues, she wiped at her face before looking back at me. "Thank you, detective. I just wish I could bring him back."

"I understand. I lost my parents when I was young, and I can say that it does get easier with time." She smiled before looking back down at her hands as she fidgeted with the tissue. "Is there anything else we can do for you?"

"No, thank you. I just want to go home if I can."

"Of course," I told her. "I'll have the officer outside escort you to your car." She thanked me as she stood up and slowly walked out.

"Poor girl," said Marcus. "It's horrible that she has to go through this." I agreed. "So, what now? We still need to find Peter. For all we know, he might go after his brother next."

I suddenly had an idea. I flipped through the notepad I'd been using for notes when talking to each person of interest and found the phone number I wanted. Punching the numbers into my cell, I waited as the phone rang. Delgado's curiosity got the better of him as he tilted his head at me. Holding up a finger to him, a voice came over the line. "Hello?"

"Yes, Mr. Davidson? This is Detective Saint, I was hoping you were still willing to help us locate your brother." Brett was eager to assist and supplied a few places that he knew his brother frequented. The leads were thin, but it was the best we had. Before I let him go, Brett asked if I could let him know when we caught the 'bastard.' I assured him that I'd keep him on speed dial.

"Got a list of possible locations for Peter." Ripping the list in half, I handed a piece to him. "How about we split up to cover ground faster?"

"Agreed." He took the slip and we both headed for the elevator.

Chapter 27

It was after dinner by the time I'd finished my list of hotspots and none of them had any bites on Peter. Unlocking the door to my apartment, I had a surreal feeling of coming home and the deadbolt still being locked. It would take time to feel normal coming to a place that had been violated by uninvited guests. Inside, I dialed Delgado's cell to see if he had anything, and if he wanted to grab a bite to discuss our next moves, but he sounded out of sorts when he answered.

Marcus answered completely winded and trying to catch his breath. "You ok?" I asked.

"Yeah," he said through depleted lungs. "I decided to go for a jog to clear my head."

"Seriously? I didn't take you for the jogging type."

"I've got to make up for the extra donuts I had this morning. Rita will start asking questions if I'm still keeping up the weight when all the sweets were removed from the house."

"Fair enough. Well, I was going to meet the guys at *Flying Saucer* in half an hour. Want to join?"

"Absolutely, I can meet you there."

"You might want to take a shower first," I joked before hanging up.

After thinking about it, I decided that I could use a shower as well after the day I'd had. A quick pass through the water and then I'd be off to the pub. Forty minutes later I was in a fresh suit as I exited my building to walk to the saucer. A great thing about the downtown KC was that practically everything I needed was within walking distance. The proximity of so many businesses and skyscrapers reminded me of Manhattan. It only lasted a few blocks, but the feeling was the same. With the similarities, New York was like Kansas City on steroids.

After only fifteen minutes, I was walking up the steps of the *Flying Saucer* Irish pub. The green doors opened to the hustle of one of the busiest bars in the Power & Light. Not catering to the club crowd, you would often see a variety of ages from all backgrounds in attendance. The walls were covered with plates that commemorated the frequent customers who'd reached milestones in beer consumption. Numbers were displayed proudly of the variety of beers consumed by each plate's namesake.

I spied Bronson and Pinick at a booth in the corner and I crossed through the decently sized crowd to join them. "Where's Marcus?" asked Bronson as I slid into the booth.

"He'll be here soon, but let's get a few drinks while we wait."

"We've actually already ordered a round," stated Pinick. "Wait until you see the waitress we've been blessed with. Richard and I are taking wagers that she's up your alley," he said with a smirk. Still smiling, his eyes darted over my head and his voice dropped to a whisper, "Here she comes."

A gorgeous drink of water approached our table carrying a tray with four beers. Her blonde hair was streaked with dark strands that dipped down to her shoulders. My eyes followed up her body to her face as she arrived at the table, and that's when I saw how striking she truly was.

"Wow," I said as she arranged the bottles on the table for us. "It's amazing how you light up the room."

She passed a large smile impressing upon me the shape of her jaw line. Her round cheeks dimpled slightly as she thanked me for the compliment before asking if we needed anything else. "No, thanks," said Pinick.

"Ally, huh?" I asked as I read the nametag on her black polo. Her matching shorts revealed runner's legs that flexed as she shifted her weight.

"That's what my boyfriend calls me." Subtle.

"Well, your boyfriend is an extremely lucky man from where I sit."

"Thanks, but if anybody's lucky, it's me. He's a wonderful man."

"I believe you. I apologize for how forward I may have been. It's difficult to not seem like a Neanderthal when beauty like yours walks my way, but should that be your fault? I'll stop bothering you, but make sure your boyfriend knows how well off he is."

"I will," she said blushing. "Are you sure there isn't anything else I can get for you?"

"Not just now, but thanks for the drinks." She nodded and went back to work. As I turned back to my cohorts, I found them grinning at me.

"Shot down," Pinick laughed as Bronson simulated a falling rocket followed by an explosion on the table.

I couldn't help chuckle, "Well, you can't win them all. At least she seems happy. I can't really feel shot down in a situation like that." Looking back one more time at the ravishing girl as she filled another drink order, I saw Marcus come through the front door.

Once Delgado had joined us, we began discussing the case and the dead end we were sitting at. I told them my leads didn't amount to anything and theirs were just as pointless. Feeling a bit warm, I stood up and removed my jacket to hang from the booth hooks.

"Alex, is your arm bleeding again?" asked Bronson.

Looking down at my sleeve, I cursed as I realized that I must have popped my stitches. "Damn it; this was a good shirt too." Grabbing one of the cloth napkins from the table, I unbuttoned my shirt and pulled down the sleeve. I did my best to tie a temporary tourniquet to the wound before re-buttoning the shirt and replacing the jacket to cover the stain. I decided to not worry about it for now since the shirt was clearly ruined. My wardrobe wasn't having the best of weeks.

As I lifted a hand to call the waitress back for another round—I was in serious need of alcohol now—all our phones chirped simultaneously. We all received the same text from Captain Hawthorne with an address where Peter Davidson had been located.

Flagging our waitress on the way out, I apologized to her again for my behavior before handing her a folded bill to cover what we'd had thus far. "Take that boyfriend out on the town at my expense."

"Oh my god," she said looking at the extra $100, "I couldn't possibly."

"Don't worry about it. I'm a bit of a romantic." Before she could argue further, I walked away to join the other detectives on the sidewalk. Marcus had already pulled his car around and the three of us hopped in.

Arriving at the address, we found the rave party of flashing lights lining the streets once again. Where was a pair of glow sticks when you needed them? Passing the yellow tape, I saw Stacey waiting for us on the porch. "Hey, Cap. What do we have here?"

Gesturing for us to follow her inside, we entered to investigators going over the room with a fine-tooth comb. On the floor, my favorite coroner examined a body, but I couldn't see the face past her. "Who's the DB?" I asked the captain.

Amy was the one that piped up after hearing my voice. "It's your guy, Alex. Peter Davidson. But he was the one to get the necktie treatment this time. Based on what I've seen so far, it appears to be self-inflicted."

"Look at what he's wearing," Pinick added. "It's the clothes from the traffic cam; the one we found near Big King's place."

"He was our *Guns N' Roses* fan?" asked Delgado.

"Looks like it," I said. "Did anyone find the backpack he had in the cam footage?"

"I can answer that, sir." The voice came from behind us as a Latino officer filled us in. "When I arrived to check on a B&E call from the neighborhood watch, I found the door was open. I heard a commotion inside, so I announced myself and entered the home just as someone ran through the kitchen and out the back door. I caught him trying to hop the back fence and when I tried to pull him back down, he caught me with a surprise hook that knocked me over. He was gone before I was able to shake it off."

"Can you get us a description?" asked Bronson.

"No, I never actually saw his face and he had a hood over his head.

"What about the missing backpack from the photo," asked Delgado. "You said you could explain that?"

"Yes, the runner had it with him."

"Backpack or not, that hunting knife is the same blade he had at my apartment," I said pointing to the knife in Davidson's hand.

"Yeah, we're bagging it to test the blood residue," said Kat who I hadn't noticed up to that point. She looked up at me and then back to Amy again. I didn't want to make a different kind of scene at the crime scene, and was saved by the captain's interruption.

"Congratulations, gentlemen. You got a killer off the street, or at least found him off the street. Now, if only there weren't a dozen more out there. Kathryn, I want a rush put on that sample to see if we can ID our runner."

"Yes, ma'am."

An hour later, the rushed blood samples came back with residue from Joseph Matthews, Trent Williams, Laura Davidson, myself, and Peter Davidson who was killed with his own knife. It was great to close the cases on so many deaths, but we weren't finished yet. Now we were left with whomever killed Davidson, and Pinick let us know that that wasn't all.

"So, the different MO and what Davidson said to Alex before trying to kill him tells us that he wasn't the Blood Week killer." We all agreed with this point. "But has anyone paid attention to the fact that we only got four bodies? There was Sullivan, Big King, Jackson, and the castrated man, but that leaves three more. Every year there are seven bodies, but this time the vigilante didn't finish. Are we sure that Davidson isn't somehow connected to that?"

"Holy shit," said Bronson. "Do you think the guy that ran off was the vigilante? Did he get wind of the frame job and put all his efforts into finding Peter?" None of us had an answer, but we were all curious to find out.

Chapter 28

After a long day, I was happy to have some time back home to relax. Turning to the tried-and-true sounds of the Chairman of the Board, I pressed play on the stereo and waited as the display came to life. After a scratch of static, the band played him in as I sang along. *"Would you like to Swing on a Star? Carry moonbeams home in a jar...and be better off then you are. Or would you rather be a mule?"*

My fingers snapped as I danced my way across the room towards the kitchen to pour myself a couple fingers of bourbon. I adjourned to the bedroom with my drink and changed out of my clothes. The sultan of swoon continued in the other room as I crawled into bed and grabbed the book from my nightstand. Not realizing how tired I was, my eyes started drooping before I finished the first page and I was out before I knew it.

I watched as the car pulled up to the intersection. The setting sun reflected off the blue paint causing flecks of silver to sparkle like stars in the night sky. The man driving leaned over to the woman with him and kissed her on the cheek. As he pulled away, an arm came in through the window and pressed a cold barrel to his temple. I wanted to scream for help, but before the words could come out, I felt the pistol on my skin.

Death's goodnight kiss was puckered and ready to bid me farewell. I felt the cold leather of the steering wheel between my fingers. Before I could save myself, the trigger pulled and released the firing pin into that ignited the metal tube in a flash of light. Instantly, I was back on the sidewalk watching the struggle as a loud bang was followed by the interior of the windshield splashing red.

Time inched by as it appeared to stop in that moment. Everything froze for that instant before death. The slug shrieked in the night as it bored into flesh and bone. The geyser that was his life sprayed out like a fire hose as the force of the bullet snapped his head to the side and caused the man's dying body to fall into the passenger's lap.

Again, I tried to stop what was happening. The man was lost, but I could still save her. I ran towards the vehicle, my chest heaving with the effort, but I didn't get any closer. From across the street, I could feel the life draining out as the blood spilled onto the floorboards. The woman was screaming as the gun turned on her. I ran harder as my vision began to blur from the strain. Reaching out as if my fingers could somehow stop all that was happening, the gun rang out for the second time and my body jerked as the alarm on my bedside woke me.

Slapping the alarm, I rolled up to sit with my legs hanging off the side of the bed. I peered up at the window that glistened with morning dew. It was always the same damn dream each year. I'd had it so many times that it was like a movie reel that kept repeating. It was something that I didn't dwell on anymore because there wasn't a point. Life happens, and then it goes on. I could smell the freshly-brewed coffee in the kitchen and decided I could use some.

With my cup of java, I stepped out the balcony and enjoyed it as I waited for the morning beams of light to breach the horizon and dance across the glass of the buildings around me. I admired the beauty of the morning sun until I'd finished my coffee, and then I went back inside to get ready. I was already imagining all the talk and conspiracy theories that would be coming out about the vigilante and why he hadn't finished Blood Week. Maybe he was having a change of heart? Only time would tell.

I arrived at the precinct an hour later, refreshed and dressed to impress. A good suit had a way of making a man feel like a million bucks. It also didn't hurt with creating admirers out of the ladies, but that was another story altogether. Dealing with Amy and Kathryn, for me right now, was like visiting the dentist. It wasn't that it was painful, but it could wait for another day.

My morning started in the bullpen just as I predicted, surrounded by my fellow detectives discussing the possibilities of the vigilante. "I'm telling you that he got exactly what he deserved," said Bronson. "Killing some poor girl because she didn't want to have sex with him and framing his brother? That is fucked up. I'm glad our vigilante took him out."

"Are you sure that's what happened?" asked Marcus. "You're still assuming the runner killed Peter. Forensics didn't find any prints on the hunting knife, and it could just as easily have been suicide. Don't get me wrong, the fuckhole deserved to die, but I still think he took the coward's way out. He should have gone to prison and got the kind of justice that's dished out to rapists and child molesters; justice from the inside."

"In other words," I started, "you're both saying he deserved to be tortured, beaten and killed?"

The two of them froze like I was a Tyrannosaurus and my vision was based on movement. I could see the questioning look in their eye as they pondered if their conversation had gone too far, but I decided to ease their tension rather than letting them squirm. "Can't say I blame you. People like that deserve what's coming for them."

As relief passed amongst them, I asked what they thought about the idea of taking Brett out to lunch on the department. "I want to thank him for his assistance and try to paint the police in a more positive light than what he's become accustomed to. He spent much of his life feeling like the bad guy whenever he saw a badge. I think it's about time he gets something better."

"You don't think it's eighteen years too late?" asked Bronson.

"Only one way to find out," I said. "Besides, it may start the healing process." With no arguments, I counted them both in and made the call to make arrangements. When I got him on the line, the first thing I wanted to do was pass on the information of my condolences. He'd been told of his brother's death when we found him.

"It's ok," he said. "I'm oddly alright with it. Honestly, I'll probably have a break down that I'll have to discuss with a therapist at some point, but right now I feel like he was dead to me when the truth came out."

"I can understand that. Well, there is another reason for my call. Because of your cooperation with us and all the bullshit you've had to deal with in your life, we were wondering if you'd be interested in letting us buy you lunch today."

"Seriously?"

"Yeah. Maybe we can get a better track record between you and the cops starting with the KCPD."

"What happened to me isn't the police's fault. They just did their job."

"But still…" Brett thought it over a moment and figured a free lunch is still a free lunch. I was surprised with how amiable he was with the situation, but it had to be one of the first times a man with a badge wasn't trying to arrest him or tell him to go back to his cell.

"We can pick you up at your hotel at eleven. I figured we could get some good ol' Kansas City BBQ." If I'm going to treat someone to lunch that's recently moved here, it's going to be a signature KC classic.

When the time came, I flagged down the dream team and we all wrapped up whatever was being worked on and hit the elevators. I chose Papa Jack's BBQ on 22nd off Main, which meant we had to drive further than usual for lunch, but it was worth it. There were many places to find BBQ in the area, but some of them like Papa Jack's shined above the rest. Situated on the opposite side of the train tracks from Union Station, the restaurant was an old station with red-brick walls. For those that didn't know better, the area of town didn't seem like it'd have such a booming place to eat, but Papa Jack's was always hopping.

The sweet scent of their signature sauce floated into the cab before we'd even parked. So well hidden among the buildings that you'd drive right by if you didn't know it was here, it didn't stop Papa Jack's from becoming a household name. I had plans to order a slab of slow-smoked ribs and the baked beans served with small pieces of rib meat. Just the thought of it already had my mouth watering.

Once we'd been seated and placed our orders, Brett took the kindness of our gesture to heart. "I wish I could do something for the families of the people my brother hurt. The best I can do is apologize and offer my condolences, but I don't see how that could do anything to make up for the pain and suffering he's caused."

"You never know," said Marcus. "It might do more than you'd think."

"Maybe, but he was still my brother. I can't help but wonder if it just might make things worse to come from me. It's funny...in a twisted way that's too fucked up to be considered funny, but Laura hated me so much and always called me a murderer. It must have been strange to find out that she was fucking the guy that really did it." Brett's face went slack as he absorbed the words and immediately regretted it. "Oh god, that wasn't very nice of me. We can't blame her when she didn't know any better; none of us did."

"It just goes to show that people are more complicated than we realize," I said. "Most people mean well in their hearts, but there will always be a few bad apples out there to weed out."

"And that's why we exist," added Delgado.

After our meal, we returned Mr. Davidson to his hotel where he thanked us for the gesture. Assuring him it was our pleasure, I heard a buzzing from my phone in the center console. Waving him farewell, I answered and was greeted by the sweet sound of our resident coroner. "Alex, I've found something on Peter Davidson's body. Could you guys swing by here when you're done? You should see this in person."

"Sure, we just dropped his brother off and can be there in twenty minutes."

"Okay, I'll see you in twenty."

"That was Amy," I said to Marcus after ending the call. "She was vague with the details, but she wants us to meet her at the morgue. She said she found something important."

My estimate was damn close as we stepped off the elevator to the basement and turned to walk through the doors into Madame Amy's Palace of Death. The pungent aroma of decay and formaldehyde crept up my nose and decided it would stay there for the next few hours. We entered through the large double doors just as Amy was putting on a fresh pair of medical gloves.

"Afternoon, gentlemen, you're going to love what I've got for you." She stepped behind the table where Peter Davidson's body lay so she could face us. "So, I just started the autopsy today because we've been a little backed up down here as you can understand." She wasn't going to get any argument from us. With all the bodies turning up lately, it wasn't a surprise that there'd be a traffic jam. "If you look here," she said, pulling a magnifying lens with a built-in light attached to the table towards Peter's neck. "You'll see what surprised me."

"Is that from a needle?" asked Marcus.

"That's precisely what it is. I ran a tox screen on him after finding it and discovered sodium thiopental in his system. Then, I looked at everything closer and found something else." Opening his jaw, she tilted the head back and shined the light inside. "Look at the roof of his mouth." As clear as day, REUS was cut into his palate.

"I think we've found the answer to that second gunman theory," I said.

Amy pursed her lips and leaned forward. "I heard you guys were debating about if this was a suicide or not. So, who was right?"

"Richard," said Delgado with disdain. "I bet on suicide."

"Well," she said rising back up for professionalism, "if I hadn't noticed the puncture mark, I may not have found the marks inside his mouth. Since the death had clearly come from the knife wound, I'd nearly missed them."

"Do you know what this means?" asked Marcus.

"Yeah," I answered. "It means that Peter here was just a carbon copy and the original is still running loose, but we already assumed that."

"The evidence tying him to the first two murders was just circumstantial, but why was he in the clothes from the tape? All that was missing was the backpack."

"Turnabout is fair play," said Amy.

"Agreed," I said. "Peter tried pinning extra murders on Blood Week and the real vigilante decided to turn everything back on him. Looks like we have our missing fifth victim. Blood Week isn't over."

Chapter 29

In the bullpen, everyone worked to find anything that could possibly lead us to the murderer. Any overlooked piece of evidence or previously disregarded fact could break the case wide open. So, the rest of the day was spent pulling the original files on all the murder cases to compare previous notes with newly discovered information. When it had all been compiled, we found that even with the revelation that Peter was the fifth body, we were still going nowhere.

Davidson's idea to flip the bird to police by leaving Tara's hair on the judge's body was the first domino that ended with his death. The clues were there from the beginning that he wasn't the real vigilante. Now that it was confirmed, the bullpen was filled with cops doing the grunt work. The mission was to find that loose thread that would lead us to another arrest.

As I scanned through and responded to emails, one popped up with an urgent label. I clicked on the icon because it could be a new development about the case, but I noticed that the return address wasn't from a KCPD domain once it expanded on my screen. I didn't think much of it first other than it probably wouldn't be new leads on Blood Week. This was confirmed when I started reading it, but it could be something even stranger. I had put out feelers when I felt that Marcus wasn't being entirely honest about what he was doing in Kansas City.

My new partner was an amazing detective, but I didn't understand why he was hiding his true intentions behind his transfer to my precinct. Everyone was entitled to their privacy to a point. Something about his brush off rubbed me the wrong way, and I wanted to know why. It seemed now that that itch in the back of my mind was right, and I had just struck pay dirt. The real reason that Delgado had come to Kansas City had nothing to do with issues with his prior captain. Marcus had been lying to all of us, and I now knew why.

Delgado had been the first one out the door when the day shift had ended. Seeing his partner putting in overtime as he entered the elevator, he chose to take the evening instead of sticking behind for more paperwork. It would still be waiting for him in the morning anyway. As he descended to the garage, his phone chirped with a message from his wife asking him to call her. Hitting the recall icon on the screen, he waited for the call to connect.

"Hey honey," he said when Rita answered. "How was your day?"

"Great, actually. I wanted to let you know that the plumber came and fixed that leak this afternoon. Also, your daughter brought home an A on her math test."

"That's wonderful. She's really adjusting to her new school. What do you think of doing something special for her to celebrate?"

"Sounds good to me. You want to pick up some noodles and garlic bread? She's been wanting another spaghetti night, and I already have what I need to make the sauce."

"Sure thing, babe. I'll swing by the market and be home in about an hour. Are you sure there isn't anything else you need?"

"No, that should be everything."

"Ok, I'll see you soon."

The doors opened at the garage level just as he was shoving the phone back into his pocket. Marcus wondered if he might make the night even more special as he walked to his car. While it was true that Victoria loved spaghetti night, he'd seen an advertisement that the circus was coming soon to the *Sprint Center* in a few months. It wouldn't cost too much to pick up a few tickets and surprise her with them at dinner. It could be the perfect way to congratulate her on her good grade. It wasn't that she needed something special every time she did well on an assignment, but with everything going on during the move across the country, he wanted to do something nice for her, so he decided to swing by the ticket kiosk before it closed.

Pulling in the driveway, he saw a gorgeous seven-year-old burst through the front door and run out to his car with a huge smile. Before Marcus was completely out of the car, she slammed into him and wrapped her arms around his waist with a squeeze. Victoria had barreled into him and nearly knocked him over with the biggest hug she could muster up, and he was happy to see her too.

"Welcome home, daddy. I'm so glad to see you."

Lifting his daughter up to fully embrace her, "Thank you. I'm happy to see you too, baby girl." Pulling back from their hug, he looked into the girl's twinkling eyes and congratulated her. "I heard you got an A on your math test."

"Yep, sure did cause I'm smart," she said, grinning from ear to ear.

"You are super smart, and if you get much smarter, you'll have to start tutoring me instead of the other way around."

"I could never have a brain as big as yours, daddy." Marcus laughed at how matter-of-factly she'd made her statement. He face was so serious as if the idea of being smarter than her father was preposterous. It was the cutest thing he'd seen in days.

"Oh, I don't believe that for a second. I bet you're going to be so much smarter than me that they'll have to make up a whole new word to say how smart you are." Victoria giggled. "But until then, would you like to help me carry in the grocery bags?"

She nodded eagerly, and Marcus set her back on the ground and pulled the two bags from the back seat to hand to her. "Here you are, one for you and one for me."

"I can carry both."

"I know you can, honey, but I have a couple surprises in here for you and Mommy."

"What is it, daddy? What is it?"

"I'll show you as soon as we're inside, ok?" Lifting the bag up, she carried it squeezed to her chest like a long-lost friend as she scurried up the drive. Anxious to hear about her surprise, she moved as fast as her legs could carry her while Delgado followed close behind.

"Honey, I'm home," he called out after closing the front door.

"Yes, Vicki made that quite clear when she bolted for the front door when you pulled up," she smiled as they entered the kitchen. Giving her husband a welcome-back kiss after a tiring day, she took the grocery bag from their daughter and tossed the noodles into the pot with the water she'd already started boiling. She then placed the garlic bread on a cooking sheet and placed it in the oven before turning back to her family.

"Sparkle Cider!! Is this for me?!?"

Marcus looked down to see Victoria peeking into the bag he was still holding. "Aw, you caught me," he said in playful disappointment at the spoiled surprise. "I got it at the market for you when I heard about your grade."

"Thanks, daddy."

"You're welcome. How about you put it on the table and we'll pour some while we eat dinner?" Not waiting a second longer than needed, she took the bottle and moved across the kitchen with great care to not drop it while Marcus grabbed three glasses from the cabinet. "That's not the only surprise I picked up for my ladies." He placed the glasses on the table and pulled an envelope from his back pocket. Pulling out its contents, he held the three tickets in the air. "I bought tickets for the circus in a few weeks."

Victoria bubbled with excitement as she gave daddy another big hug and endlessly repeated "thank you." When she finally felt her gratitude had been displayed, she climbed into a chair and waited as Marcus poured her a glass of sparkling apple cider. After handing her the glass, she took a long sip with her eyes closed. She loved her 'sparkle cider.'

"That was a wonderful thing you did for her," Rita said, kissing him on the cheek.

Delgado's phone chirped with another text as his wife returned to finish cooking dinner. His face was grim as he read through the message and he felt lucky that Rita hadn't noticed. "I need to make a call in my study," he said.

"Be quick because dinner will be ready soon."

"I will," he said as he walked away. The message he'd received was important, and it meant he had some planning to do with little time to do it.

The spaghetti dinner was enjoyed by all, especially Victoria who ate a shocking three plates. "You must be going through a growth spurt to eat that much, young lady", said her mother.

"Was it good?" asked Marcus while checking his watch. Victoria did her best to nod and smile without showing any of the food stuffed in her cheeks, which made her mother laugh.

"Did you see that, Marcus?" Her husband swiped at the screen on his phone and didn't respond. "Marcus?"

"Huh?" he said, shaken from his bubble. "What did you say, honey?"

"Nothing, you missed it." She shook her head at him and started to clear the table. "Why don't you guys go play for a bit while I do the dishes? Vicki hasn't had much time with you the past week with your late nights."

"It's the case," said Marcus. "I've been really busy."

"I know, but all the staying out late and not getting back until early in the morning has our daughter missing her daddy. I can already tell that you're going to be out late again, so before you do, how about a little family time?" Marcus looked at his phone a moment and then checked his watch before nodding in agreement.

A half hour later, Rita called out to the prince and princess in their backyard castle that it was getting late and the princess needed to get ready for bed. Rita's notice of approaching bedtime for the princess caused Marcus to curse as he looked at his watch.

"Sorry, sweetie," he said to Victoria. "It's time to go back in and get ready for bed."

"Can we read again?"

Delgado rubbed his head as he looked between the house and the little girl wanting to spend time with him. She stared up at him with pouty lips as she waited for him to respond. His heart melted as he looked at her expectant eyes looking back at him. With a heavy sigh, "If you're quick about it, we can get through a few more pages. But I'm serious, you need to be in your pajamas and have your teeth brushed on the double." The little girl sprinted towards the house like an Olympic Champion in preparation for him to continue Wizard of Oz.

"So, did the prince save the princess from the tower?" asked Rita as Marcus came back inside.

"Almost, I was in the middle of slaying the dragon that trapped her there when the gods on high recalled me back from the royal kingdom."

"Well darn, I'm sure you'll get him next time," she laughed.

Kissing his wife on the cheek, Delgado asked, "Do you think you can read to her? She's wants to continue Wizard of Oz, but I really need to get going. I've got an appointment to keep."

"She wants you."

"I know," he said, looking down at his watch.

"Look," she said, drawing his eyes up to her as she wrapped her arms around his neck. "I don't know what's been going on this past week, but you've been out every night. Just take this one to read to her a little bit, and then I'll explain why you had to leave. Ok? Please?"

Marcus bit his lower lip as he felt himself lose the battle. It was hard enough to not give one of his girls what they wanted, but right now they were a united front and all they wanted was a little time with him. He glanced at the clock on the stove behind her before looking back into those pleading eyes.

"Fine," he said. "But I can only get through a couple pages and then I really have to go. I have business again tonight, but I promise you that everything will be back to normal soon." Kissing her on the mouth, he smiled before leaving her to walk down the hall to the stairs that led up to Victoria's room.

As he passed the second-floor bathroom, he heard the water running and glanced in to see Victoria brushing her teeth. Continuing into her bedroom, he grabbed the hardback from the shelf and sat in the rocking chair by her bed to wait. From the bathroom, the water stopped and a toothbrush tapped against the counter before being placed in the brush caddy. Feet slapped against the hardwood floor as the little girl came running around the corner on the way to her wardrobe. Tearing open the drawers, she pulled out her pajamas and changed into them in a flurry of flying clothes before diving into her bed and pulling the covers up to her chin.

Once situated, she looked up at him and stated, "I'm ready."

"I can see that," he said, pulling open the pages to where the book mark held their place. "Let's see…ah, here we are. Even with eyes protected by the green spectacles," he read aloud, "Dorothy and her friends were at first dazzled by the brilliancy of the wonderful City." After a few pages, Marcus saved their place for another night and placed the book back on the shelf. Calling to his wife, he informed her that they'd finished reading and she came into the room to say goodnight to their princess.

"Sweet dreams, honey," Rita said after many hugs and kisses.

As she left, she turned out the light and closed the door behind them. When finished, she realized that Marcus was already down the stairs and heading for the garage. Following him, Rita opened the garage door to find her husband moving things around in the back corner of the garage and he stopped in his tracks when she asked, "What are you doing out here?"

"Nothing sweetie, I noticed the car was little low on oil so I'm just checking to see if we have a quart to top it off before I leave."

"Okay, but please don't stay out too late."

"I shouldn't be long, maybe an hour or so. Maybe more…" He trailed off momentarily as his eyes flicked around him and back to Rita. "Do you need me to pick anything up while I'm out?"

"Not that I can think of. Just be sure to hurry back, momma needs some alone time with daddy." She smiled briefly and went back inside.

Marcus listened as her footsteps carried her away and glanced at his watch again. "Fuck," he whispered as he turned back to the wall of shelving behind him. On the bottom shelf behind the lawn mower, he pulled back an old tarp to get to the large trunk hidden underneath. Inside was an assortment of old blankets and quilts that were hand-stitched by Rita's great grandmother.

Pushing aside the family heirlooms, Marcus pulled out a black backpack before returning everything to where it had been. Slowly opening the door back to the hallway, he peered around to make sure Rita wasn't around before quickly walked down the hall and out the front door. At the car, he tossed the backpack into the passenger seat and started the engine. He had another long night ahead of him, but the week was almost over.

Chapter 30

A large paddlewheel that spanned two stories splashed against the water pool beneath it as it rotated. It was a tourist attraction that once propelled the side-wheeler steamboat Arabia before being set up in the museum in the River Market. On September 5th, 1856, the Arabia struck a submerged walnut tree that caused the craft to sink so quickly that only the smokestacks and pilot house were still visible after a day. There weren't any fatalities that day on the Missouri River, but the craft was swallowed up by the river mud and eventually lost to time until it was rediscovered and exhumed over a century later in the late 1980's.

Watching the paddlewheel turn, a woman marveled at its twenty-eight-foot diameter as she leaned against the railing on the second floor that overlooked the pool below. The atrium was just outside the gift shop where she could listen to each paddle as it slapped against the water. She found it quite peaceful, but was still elated when she was interrupted by her boyfriend handing her an ice cream cone.

She spun around to a tall man with a square jaw beneath a mop of dark hair that held a cone of vanilla goodness that she graciously accepted. Walking with him to the closest table, she smiled as he pulled out her chair before sitting himself. "Why, Keith, you're quite the gentleman today," she teased.

"Are you saying I'm not always a gentleman?" he challenged humorously.

"I guess you are; that's one of the reasons I love you so much."

"Well I love when guys leave you a hundred-dollar tip that you use to buy me dinner."

"I guess you're just a lucky guy then," she said, sticking out an ice-cream covered tongue at him. Ally was often hit on and flirted with at work, which was something she knew bugged him about her waitressing. However, he took it in stride since he knew they were working to make something better out of their lives. Keith never felt threatened, but that didn't mean it didn't scratch at him each time it happened.

Finishing the last of their cones, Keith tossed the napkins into a nearby trashcan while she walked back to the spinning paddlewheel. When he joined her, he wrapped his arms around her and kissed her delicately on the neck below her earlobe. Ally leaned back with her eyes closed and rested her head on his shoulder. She could be content in his arms forever. "I love you so much," she whispered.

"I love you too, which is why I have something for you."

When she opened her eyes, she saw his hand in front of her holding a small white box with a round lid. With his thumb, he pushed back the silver flower that latched the lid and revealed a princess-cut diamond resting on white gold. Ally gasped as she covered her mouth and turned to look at him.

"Ally," he said as he stepped back from her and knelt to one knee. "You're my best friend and the most wonderful person I've ever had the privilege to have in my life. With that in mind, I can't imagine living a day without you in it. From here until forever, I want you by my side. Will you marry me?"

Ally didn't answer as she struggled to catch her breath as her eyes filled with tears. The lump in her throat from the surprise made it hard to speak. She wanted to tell him that this was the happiest moment of her life, but she struggled to find the words, so all she said was yes.

Filled with pure joy, she leapt into his arms and squeezed him without ever wanting to let him go. The happiness in both their hearts warmed their embrace with a long and passionate kiss before they parted long enough for him to place the ring on her finger. They laughed as he hugged his fiancée.

Marcus walked past the atrium and noticed a man proposing to his girlfriend. He heard her say yes before he was out of earshot as he turned a corner to head out the backdoor. The parking outside was emptying as it was late and the shops were all closing. He tightened his grip on the backpack he wore as if it could steal away from him if he didn't hold onto it tight enough. Looking at his watch, he cursed himself and picked up the pace as he turned down the alley that ran behind the museum.

With the shopping center preparing to lock up, Keith took Ally's hand and escorted her outside. After descending the front steps, he wrapped an arm around her as they walked along the sidewalk with her marveling at her new engagement ring. Seeing how happy it made her brought relief to the stress he'd felt about popping the question. He had strong feelings that she was going to say yes, but that didn't make it any less scary to ask. It had been tormenting him since they day he'd picked the ring up from the jewelry store.

As they approached the cross street, Keith was excited when he noticed a dark blue Suzuki Hayabusa pull up to the intersection. Being a motorcycle enthusiast, he had dreams of one day owning a similar bike. Listening to the engine of the fastest production bike in the world as it idled less that fifty feet from him was marvelous. His infatuation with motorcycles rivaled that of his bride-to-be, and she smiled at the boy-like wonder that filled his eyes as he watched.

"I think you've fallen in love with two ladies tonight," said Ally. She laughed at his mumbled response. "It's a gorgeous motorcycle, honey."

"It sure is." The motorcycle revved as the rider tilted it to the side as he turned up Grand Avenue. "I can't imagine how much it must have cost, but it's not nearly as gorgeous as you," he said as he looked into her eyes and gave her a squeeze.

"Good answer," she smirked. "I can't wait to tell the girls about this." Ally held up her hand and admired the diamond as it sparkled in the moonlight. "They already think you're the greatest, but they will be speechless when they hear about the proposal. They're going to be so jealous." Keith was beaming with pride. "And with what you did tonight, you are getting SO much sex when we get home."

"Well, then there is not time to waste," he said as he picked up the pace. Ally laughed as he pulled the keys from his pocket, hurrying towards his car with her jogging along behind. They passed by a chain-link fence surrounding electrical transformers before crossing the street to get to the car. As they reached the passenger door, Keith started to open the door for her when a figure stepped from the shadows of a nearby building.

The black man appeared under the street lamp wearing dark jeans with large letters down the side, an over-sized white t-shirt, and a large medallion hanging from the gold chain around his neck. He stood near the driver's front fender as he flicked the roller on his lighter and lit the blunt in his mouth. The cherry started glowing as he took a large drag while Keith and Ally paused at the door. The two found the man's sudden appearance alarming.

When he exhaled, the smoke drifted slowly from his lips in wisps that danced on the evening air. His gaze was fixed on them in a way that sent chills up Ally's spine as she crowded closer to Keith, clutching his arm. He whispered that everything was alright as he unlocked the car, but his nerves told him that he'd just told his first lie to his fiancée.

"You guys got any cash on you?" asked the smoking man. "I need bus fare."

"No, sorry," Keith responded reaching for the door handle.

The man lifted his shirt to show the handgun stashed in his waistband. Pulling it free, he gripped the hilt and let it rest at his side. "Now that didn't sound very polite to me. How are we to move forward with our transaction without a little respect? What do you think we should do here, bro?"

Before Keith answered, another voice spoke from behind them. "I think they should make a large monetary donation to our charity fund." Ally and Keith both turned to see another man coming towards them also carrying a pistol. He was dressed similarly to his counterpart except that his shirt was red with splashes of black and white behind the outline of a bird. "It's called the give-me-all-your-fucking-money foundation." He lifted the weapon and aimed it at the two of them.

"I'm sorry," said Keith. "I don't have much money, but you can take everything that I have." His fingers shook as he pulled out the few bills he had from his wallet.

"Give me the whole thing," said the smoker. Keith handed the entire wallet to him and watched as he flipped open the leather and looked back at Keith with disgust. "Twenty-seven bucks? You're going to have to do better than that, asshole."

"How about we take the donation out of your bitch?" said the bird-shirted man. "I saw the way that ass was shaking as she walked across the street. I bet honey can give daddy a sweet ride."

Ally tried to cover herself as the man's eyes wandered over the surface of her body. Her lips trembled and her eyes watered as Keith tried to control the situation. "You're right, there isn't much money there. But how about you just take my car along with the wallet? That should make up for the lack of cash, right?" He held up his keys to him for acceptance.

"Tell you what," said the smoker. "We've got your wallet and we'll take your car; but that pretty little rock on your girl's finger is coming with us too."

"No, please just take what you the money and the car and go."

"Keith, it's alright," said Ally. "Just let them have the ring." She pulled it from her finger and offered it to the man behind them in hopes that it would leave them unharmed.

"Wait," said the smoker with a sudden exuberance. "Tyrell, maybe we should just let them go." His partner looked at him puzzled. "Seriously, man, give them their stuff back and we'll all go our separate ways."

"What the fuck are you talking about, Dwayne? I'm here to get paid or a piece of this bitch's sweet pussy. Why the hell would we let them go?"

"Just give them back their shit!" Tyrell stared at his partner as this sudden adlib seemed to come out of left field.

"Man, fuck you! I'm here to make some paper and that's exactly what I'm going to do."

"Damn it! Give them back their shit before this mother fucker kills me."

Ally gripped onto Keith as both were as clueless as Tyrell. "What the hell are you talking about?"

Dwayne was unable to respond as a loud flash of light exploded behind him and sent a bullet through the back of his skull and out his forehead with a splash of blood that painted the windshield of Keith's car red. Ally screamed and Keith pulled her away as Tyrell focused on his friend's body as it collapsed to the ground.

"HOLY SHIT!" Realizing there was another piece on the game board, Tyrell grabbed Keith's arm before he could get away and ripped him from Ally's grasp as she screamed.

Standing behind his human shield, he held the gun to Keith's head and shouted, "Who the fuck is there?!?"

Dwayne's killer stepped into the light wearing leathers and a motorcycle helmet. In his right hand was the gun that put the first dog down, and it was now aimed directly at the last one. "Let them go and I'll make it quick," said the muffled voice from inside the full-face helmet. "If you don't, I'll be sure that you suffer violently."

"Man, kiss my ass, bitch!"

"That's a quick way to make it through door number two. How about I sweeten the pot? If you let them go, you can take me as a hostage. I'll even take my weapon out of the equation." He pressed the side of the pistol with his thumb and the magazine slid out and fell to the dirt. Kicking it towards Tyrell's feet, he continued, "You only need one hostage anyway, right?"

"You know what, you're right. Trying to make two people cooperate would be a bitch." Tyrell fired a round into Keith's back and Ally cried out as what was to be the happiest night of her life unfolded into the worst. The man of her dreams fell to the ground and all she could do was watch as blood spilled out at her feet. Her tears poured out and all she wanted to do was run to him, but she stood rigid out of fear until Tyrell grabbed her hair and dragged her over to him.

"I think I'll take this here bitch with me," he said.

"You forgot the chamber, asshole." The biker fired his weapon and the projectile sailed above Keith's limp form and past Ally's thigh before shattering Tyrell's left kneecap. Screaming out in pain, he released his hold on Ally and grasped at his wound as he fell to the pavement.

The biker appeared by his side with a blade that he jammed into Tyrell's arm, forcing him to release the pistol amidst further agony. As he screamed, the biker unzipped a pouch on his right thigh and removed a needle that he swiftly pushed into the screaming man's neck. Within seconds, Tyrell passed out.

Ally's guardian tore the fabric of Tyrell's shirt into strips before moving alongside Keith and applied pressure to his wound. "Do you have a cell phone?" Ally nodded her head. "I need you to stay calm and call 911. Put it on speaker so your hands can be free to help."

She did as she was told, and set the phone on the concrete as she assisted the man aiding her fiancé. The emergency operator came on, and the biker reported what had happened and she relayed instructions to stay on the line as she routed police and emergency responders their way. Keith stirred, but he was barely able to concentrate on what was happening around him. The man placed Ally's hands over the wrappings and showed her where to apply pressure.

"I can't stick around with police coming," he said. "I meant what I said earlier. He's going to pay dearly for what he did; I promise you that."

"Thank you," she said between tears. As he lifted Tyrell onto his shoulder, she asked, "I have to know; who are you?"

"I'm a friend, Ally. That's all you need to know. Your fiancé is going to be fine; take care of him until help arrives."

With that, he carried the body past the fence surrounding the electrical transformers across the street, and disappeared. Ally watched him until she couldn't see him anymore. Looking down at the man she loved, she was thankful for the stranger that stuck his neck out for them. In a time where people didn't go out of their way to help anyone but themselves, this man did.

Chapter 31

Marcus leaned against the brick wall in the alley he'd disappeared into and reflected on what had brought him here. He began his career as a cop in California with the idea of eventually moving to detective. For most of his life, this had been his dream. Working hard to make a name for himself got him recognition and even a few medals when he was still in blues. This and his tenacity is what garnered him favor with the homicide captain that eventually took a chance on him to get out of the squad car and into the investigation side of police work.

Even with the accolades and seeing the realization of his dreams, he scoured at where the path had led him. Gripping the shoulder pads on his backpack, the fabric scratched against his nails. He hated all the lies to his family, but he was stuck in a bad position and needed to do things he didn't like to keep others safe. What was getting to him now was the waiting. While it was important that he was where he was supposed to be on time, the person he was meeting wasn't forced under the same constraints.

He looked at the time on his phone, and realized he'd only been standing there for fifteen minutes. Only. Just to give himself something to do, Delgado pulled the backpack off and unzipped the front pouch. He reached in and pulled out a chocolate cake roll. He had a few sugary snacks in the bag that he'd managed to hide from Rita. While he had the bag unzipped, he confirmed for the fifth time that the package he was delivering was also still wrapped up inside.

After putting the bag back on, he unwrapped his snack and was just about to take a bite when he heard a loud clap. He immediately paused and turned his head in the direction of the sound. Swearing just heard a gunshot, he strained to focus and listen for more. Just as he'd suspected, another gunshot echoed from a few blocks northwest of the alley he was in.

Delgado dropped the cake and sprinted in the direction of the gun blasts. Ripping his phone from his pocket as he sprinted, he called 911 to report the gunfire. Next, he made another call to inform the powers that be that he wasn't going to make the appointment. "I'll bring it directly to you in a few hours. And this will be the last time you demand I meet you all over the city. We're square after tonight." Hanging up, Marcus went to work.

Moments after the guardian angel disappeared, an ambulance arrived and paramedics loaded Keith into the back. They assured Ally that he should pull through just fine, but they were taking him to the nearest hospital for treatment. Before they left, three squad cars pulled up with lights flashing. They detained Ally for her statement while the ambulance pulled away from the curb and rushed Keith to the emergency room.

She listed to the siren growing more distant as she spoke with the police. As they began, Delgado came rushing up and flashed his badge to the officers. "I called in the shots fired," he said, trying to catch his breath. "What have we got?"

An Officer Gray caught him up on the details they'd received from dispatch and what Ally had told them so far. He walked with the officer back towards the blonde woman talking with the other uniforms when he overheard one of them questioning her.

"Did you say he injected him with something?" asked the officer.

"Yeah. Then he called the ambulance for us and carried the guy off that way," she said, pointing.

"Then what happened?" Delgado interrupted. She looked at him with a raised eyebrow. To her, he appeared like a random guy that just walked up off the street. "Sorry, my name is Detective Marcus Delgado. Can you tell me what happened afterwards?"

"He said the guy was going to pay for what he did to us. After he got past that fence, I couldn't see him anymore. That's really all I know. Do you think I can go to the hospital now? I want to be with Keith to make sure he's ok."

"Of course, one of the officers will escort you there." Marcus looked at Officer Gray who instructed one of the other officers to take care of it. After Ally was out of earshot, he continued with Gray.

"This sounds like the vigilante to me. We may be getting another body on our hands if I don't get to him first. Do me a favor and contact Captain Hawthorne and Detective Saint. Fill them in on what happened and get them down here. I'm going after him." Pulling a flashlight from one of the squad cars, Marcus ran across the street in pursuit of a killer.

Stepping around a large white metal silo, the biker carrying Tyrell heard an ambulance siren approach. They had arrived faster than he'd anticipated, which meant two things. First, the man that was shot would be getting medical attention, but it also meant that cops wouldn't be far behind. What he did tonight had been unplanned. It was a right-place-right-time moment, and that meant he was flying by the seat of his pants.

A chill on the night air attempting to subdue the humidity left from the day cooled the beads of sweat on his brow as he carried his unconscious baggage past a pair of metal silos. A conveyor for grains ran over Grand Ave and into a large brick building on the other side of the street. Looking for a place that would be private, he continued to lug the dead weight as he surveyed the surroundings.

Beyond the storage containers, the ground sloped down while Grand Ave went up an incline until it was a bridge over railroad tracks. At the bottom of the hill was an area that was out of public view, and under the cloak of night. It was the best place he was going to find on short notice, so he treaded onward.

He was drenched in sweat when he finally got to the bottom of the hill. The rocky slope caused him to slip more than once and nearly twist his ankle. That would have been a great way to end the night; unable to walk away. Dropping Tyrell to the ground, he landed with a thud as the biker stretched his muscles. The impact caused Tyrell to stir as consciousness pulled at him. As he woke, his captor removed his helmet and cracked his neck. When Tyrell's eyes fluttered open, he saw the face of his captor.

A white male with dark hair wore a breathing mask that covered his mouth and nose. The wrap was common with bikers to help them breath in high winds as they drove down the highway, but it was also useful in concealing one's identity. The biker pulled the hood from his leather jacket over his head to further conceal himself. Fully sheathed in the darkness, the undertaker could begin.

Gravel crunched under Delgado's feet as he walked along a chain-link fence enclosing electrical transformers. He shined the light on the ground a few feet in front of him in between swinging it to each side as he looked for clues. Near the center of the lot, he found a single drop of blood on the ground that was still wet. Marcus immediately shined the light around to find more. He struck gold when he found the second breadcrumb roughly ten feet away. He had a trail to follow.

"Do you understand where we go from here?"

"Yeah, I fucking kill you," threatened Tyrell from his knees.

"Close," laughed the man pacing in front of him. "You are correct that someone is going to die tonight, but you're mistaken on whom that will be. I'd venture a guess that the one that isn't tied up will be the victor here. Your abhorrent actions towards others won't go unpunished."

"A brotha's gotta get paid, asshole. Besides, it's fun too," he grinned.

Tyrell's head slammed to the side as a fist connected with his jaw. "I'll ask you to show a little more respect," said the vigilante. "After all, not caring how you've affected those around you is the whole reason you're in this predicament."

Tyrell spit blood onto the blacktop as he shifted his weight to get back onto his knees. His captor removed the backpack he wore and placed it on a large boulder nearby. He removed a pair of blue gloves and discarded the riding gloves he'd been wearing. Allowing the nitrile to snap against his skin, he pulled them taunt and continued.

"You've had your entire life to choose the man you wanted to become. The decisions you made has brought me here as a sort of...natural-selection process." Retrieving a yellow bottle from the bag, he aimed it at his riding gloves sitting on the ground and squirted a liquid onto them. He then lit a match and tossed it onto the ground, which caught the gasoline and the gloves aflame. "No need to leave behind evidence for the authorities."

"Instead of waiting for God or Mother nature to take care of things..," he paused, pulling the scalpel out that had already stabbed Tyrell in the arm. "I like to have a more immediate effect on the world."

Marcus continued his hike through the grounds as he followed the blood. Normally, pursuit of a dangerous criminal without backup was not something he would be doing. But the past week had taken a toll on him. He didn't like people putting pressure on others. The more he thought about the idea of a vigilante over the past few nights, the more he felt that law should be left to those that enforce it. Those that carried a badge were the law.

Criminals may fear the vigilante more than jail, but that just meant that the police needed to work harder at cleaning the streets. Where do you draw the line on injustice when you allow people to break the law just to make your job easier? No matter how you looked at it, murder was a crime against God and the civilized world. This wasn't allowed by a nation of laws. Marcus now knew where he stood.

Delgado stopped as he heard distorted voices nearby. He listened for a moment until he had a bearing. They were coming from the direction the blood had been leading him. He found them.

"I think we've reached the end of this riveting conversation," said the vigilante. "It's time Blood Week comes to a close."

"Man, fuck you!"

Stepping alongside Tyrell, he rested the blade on his cheek so he could feel the chill of the surgical steel. "I believe I recall saying something about being respectful." With a flick of the wrist, the blade left a gash that ran diagonally along the side of his face. Tyrell tried to scream in agony, but the hand covering his mouth muffled the sounds.

Tightening his grip on Tyrell's chin, he pulled his head up and prepared to finish the job. "I guess you'll never live to understand being a better person. You've made the bed of your life, and now it's time to go to sleep."

Chapter 32

"FREEZE," Delgado shouted as he stepped around the corner of the building. With weapon drawn, he kept it pointed at the vigilante as he advanced. He came down the hill slowly so he wouldn't slip and lose the bead he had on the man. "Put the blade down and step away from him, or I will be forced to fire."

"Ah, detective; how are you on this wonderful evening? I must say it's colder out than it has been; a welcome change from the blistering heat. Wouldn't you agree?"

"I'm not looking for a weather forecast." Marcus feet continued to search for steady ground as he proceeded down the hill. He was already half way down and didn't want to lose his momentum now. He was also surprised the suspect didn't run when Delgado had appeared. Perhaps the surprise had him guessing on a next move? Regardless, it gave time for him to stop another murder.

"Oh, come on, detective, it's like 75 degrees out here. Even you have to admit how wonderful it feels." The pleasantries continued while the blade still rested on Tyrell's throat. The momentary pause gave hope to the captive who had put up a brave front in the face of danger, but was on the verge of wetting himself.

"I have to admit that I'd hoped to finish with my friend here without interruption," said the man with the scalpel. "Might I ask how you got here so quickly?" Delgado didn't answer, so he continued. "No matter. I'm a man of information, and I could make a few guesses why you aren't at home with the family, but I'd rather finish other business I'm in the middle of. Do you think you could come back later? It would be a huge favor and I'd owe you one."

"You don't really think I'm going to leave, do you? Tonight's business is cancelled," said Delgado as he finished closing the gap between them.

"That's quite close enough, detective." Tyrell winced as the pressure of the scalpel on his neck increased, causing Marcus to stop in his tracks. He was close enough to see the pain on his face and blood dripping from the cut on his cheek. Delgado knew from Ally's testimony that Tyrell was a criminal, but this wasn't what the man deserved.

"I appreciate what you're trying to do," Delgado began, "but it's not the kind of help we need."

"That's not how you felt a few days ago." There was a slight tilt of the detective's head as he narrowed his gaze in confusion. "I told you I'm a man of information. And a little bird tells me that I actually have support in the KCPD. You agree that the justice system has too many holes that allow scum like this to squeeze through." He looked down at Tyrell and back up at Marcus. "This country has become known for murder and mayhem, and people like myself aren't taking it anymore."

"I do understand," said Marcus. "And I may have been sympathetic to your cause when I first got to Kansas City, but things change. At first, the idea of someone helping to put a stop to crime in the city sounded great. But you're killing people. You may be stopping their crimes, but you are doing so by committing your own. None of us are above the law, and I'm not going to allow you to continue."

"*Allow* me? You're not going to *allow* me? Are you trying to say that you have anything to do with whether this man dies?"

"From where I stand, you've brought a knife to a gun fight." Marcus nodded to his 9mm. "Who do you think would win in that matchup?"

"I believe that would depend on the conditions you're presented with." Tyrell was suddenly forced up to his feet, which minimized Delgado's target as the captive was used as a shield. Marcus mentally scolded himself for allowing it to happen. "Sometimes a knife can be a much more precise tool than a handgun. How well do you trust your aim, detective?" Marcus knew that taking a shot now would risk Tyrell's life. "Not well enough I see."

"We can still find a way out of this," said Marcus. "We can let the justice system deal with what this man as done."

"The justice system? Have you ever looked at how many people that deserve punishment get off without it due to our *justice system*? How can you act like the city isn't a better place because of what I do?"

"I can't contradict that some may see a benefit to what you do. I've heard the reports that crime has dropped while you're around, but that's only one week a year. People are onto your game and know when to stay off the streets. And that doesn't excuse the fact that you're a killer. That means I will do whatever I can to stop you."

"Even if you could stop me, it would all come back to bite you in the ass. Stopping me means that the real criminals in this city will be left without fear. People are safer with those like me around. Just ask Ally and her fiancé that is being treated for a bullet wound. I stopped that from escalating. We are the counterweights that balance the scales against the bad guys."

"We?" Delgado asked.

"Yes, myself and others like me." He cleared his throat, "The royal we." Marcus stared into the eyes that were barely visible in the shadow cast by the vigilante's hood. He couldn't put his finger on it, but something seemed forced about his response. The man was trying to cover something up that he nearly let slip. "People like me are needed to maintain balance," he insisted.

"That's what the police are for. We take a pledge to uphold the law."

"Really now...then I guess we find ourselves at an impasse. You want to stop me and you're welcome to try, but there is more to this standoff than you may yet realize. I have no intention of being taken into custody, nor do I plan on letting this man live."

As he spoke, Marcus began noticing a vague familiarity to the voice. It was muffled and slightly distorted, but there was still something he recognized. He'd heard this voice before, and the only way to get to the truth was to find a way out of the standoff. He ran all the scenarios through his head as he continued to reason with the vigilante.

"...better I be branded a murderer for what I've done than allow my victims to continue harming the innocent."

"Criminals or not, you're still a murderer," said Marcus. "Nemo est supra legis"

"Nobody is above the law? I'm impressed, detective. I see I'm not the only one who knows a little Latin. I believe you're shaping up to be quite the yin to my yang. Honestly, I'd love to continue our little back and forth, but I really must be going. So how about we test how much Latin you really know? Qui tacet consentire videtur."

He who is silent is taken to agree was the vigilante's mantra to drive forward with his cause. It was how he reasoned with himself that he wasn't the bad guy. And as he said it, he dug the blade into Tyrell's throat and ripped it ferociously across it. The move was lightning fast as it showered crimson that splashed on the dirt and brought another life to an end.

The vigilante shoved Tyrell's body forward, which crashed into Marcus and knocked him off balance. As he fell backwards with Tyrell's blood spraying out at him, he felt a hand grasping for his gun. His hand was twisted sideways and up with such force that it nearly snapped his wrist as the weapon came free of his grasp. As he looked up from the ground with the bleeding body on top of him, he saw his attacker remove the magazine and clear the chamber before tossing the empty weapon to the ground and turning to flee.

Delgado kicked at him and caught some luck as he managed to trip the vigilante who crashed to the ground with a puff of dust. Shoving the blood-soaked body to the side, Marcus pulled himself to his feet as his foe did the same.

Before he could attempt another escape, Delgado dove at the vigilante and slammed into the center of his back. Both men crashed down again and Marcus heard the familiar clang of metal as his opponent's blade bounced away. Without the scalpel or the gun, the altercation came down to brute strength. Punches flew in this game of fisticuffs as they rolled across the ground; each trying to gain the upper hand.

Or a roll that put Delgado on the bottom, he gripped both his foe's arms and used his legs as leverage to flip over as hard as he could. He rolled both of them to the side until he was above the opposition and shoved both the vigilante's arms into the hard ground. The man screamed in pain before punching Marcus in the chin with enough force to shove him backwards. He landed on the dirt and started to scramble back to his feet when he felt warm liquid on his palm.

Bringing it into the moonlight; he saw a line of blood across the width of his palm that hadn't been there before. When Tyrell fell, his blood hand gotten on Delgado's chest, but not his hands. He inspected it closer as the vigilante still lay on the ground a few feet from him. There weren't in cuts on his hands, so the blood had come from the man before him. Could that really be the answer? He stared at the vigilante with curiosity as the man grasped at his shoulder. Still in shock, he looked back at his hand and breathed deeply. "It can't be."

Chapter 33

In the bedroom of a fifteen-year-old boy, the walls were covered by posters of superheroes and famous musicians. In one corner was Miles Davis playing his trumpet while in the other was the Dark Knight perched on a roof top as he watched over Gotham. Beneath the watchful eye of the bat, a short bookshelf was filled with board games and YA books.

The room portrayed the delicate balance of school and play in the teenage boy's life. At this age he was dating, learning to drive, and researching colleges to attend. He was getting hints of what it would be like as an adult having to fend for himself. But for now, he was still able to fall back on the help of his loving parents.

On the bed, the boy was still sleeping as his mother watched over him from the doorway. Each morning when she was about to wake him, she paused for a moment to view how peaceful he was as he slept. Working the late shift at the hospital meant she was waking him up for school before turning in herself. Her son had an alarm set to wake him, but she always liked to do it herself. It wouldn't be long until he was off on his own and she wouldn't be afforded the luxury.

Just before the clock read 7:00, she deactivated the alarm on the side table and shook his shoulder to wake him. He rubbed his eyes to adjust to the light before looking up at her.

"Mom, do you always have to stand there watching me? It's a little creepy."

"I can't help it, sweetie. You're just so cute. Did you sleep alright?"

"Yeah, but another hour would be awesome."

"I'm sure it would be, but it's a school day so get up, mister. Your father told me about the movie marathon you guys had last night. Did you have fun?"

"Yeah, we watched the *Star Wars* trilogy again."

Chuckling, she added, "You boys and your *Star Wars*. How about you get yourself cleaned up? After you're dressed I'll have some breakfast for you in the kitchen."

"Oh, could you make that sausage-and-pepper omelet you made a few days ago?"

"Sure, but first you need to get your butt out of bed," she said, swatting him on the behind.

"Love you too, Mom." Smiling, she left him to clean up.

Thirty minutes later, he came into the kitchen showered and dressed with the scent of apple-smoked sausage permeating the air. His mother was a pretty decent cook, but her omelets were like a little slice of heaven. He slid up to the kitchen table and poured a glass of orange juice as his mother set the plate holding his omelet on the table.

Adding a layer of hot sauce and a side of hash browns with ketchup, he shoveled forkfuls into his mouth. He savored the flavors that mixed together from the crispy potatoes and spiced eggs. Just about the time he was finishing up the last bite, his mother looked at the clock on the wall and told him it was time to go.

"You should get moving if you expect to make it to school on time." Swallowing the last bite, he washed it down with the rest of the orange juice. After placing his dish in the sink, he grabbed a blueberry muffin from the counter for the road, and kissed his mother on the cheek before rushing out the front door.

Outside on the sidewalk, he walked towards the school listening to his Walkman. Jamming to the latest from *Guns N' Roses*, he bobbed his head and lip-synced along until his vision went dark from someone's hand and the headphones were pulled back. He felt her lips on his cheek before he saw her. "Guess who," she whispered in his ear.

"Hmm, I'm thinking Lauren? No, it's Rose...or maybe Heather? You know, it's hard to narrow it down with all the girls that like to kiss me."

This was met with a swift smack to the back of the head as Shana stepped into view. Although she stared annoyingly back at him, all he could do was laugh. "Oh, baby, it's you," he said sarcastically. "I mistook you for someone else."

Looking at him as if she might hit him harder, "Don't make me smack you again." She knew he liked to joke, so she enjoyed ribbing him right back. Taking her hand, he pulled her in close and kissed it as an apology. The sparks of young love burned between them as they walked the rest of the way to school with their fingers intertwined.

After lunch, the young man took the east stairwell to the second floor for his philosophy class. He'd been taking it three times a week at third period for about a semester and thoroughly enjoyed it. The class discussions this week had focused on ethics.

Applied ethics was an area of particular fascination to him; specifically, that of Bioethics. It governed matters of controversy such as abortion or euthanasia, and the weight of decisions over such conflicted situations intrigued him. How does one make a choice when there isn't a clear answer?

On the way to class, he passed Shana at the top of the stairs as she headed to biology. "Are you doing anything tonight?" he asked. "It's my parents weekly date night, so I was wondering if you'd want to go out too. Maybe we could get some burgers or something?"

"I don't know, I've got like five guys lined up for tonight so I'll have to check my schedule." He smirked at her jab from that morning and stuck his tongue out at her, which made her laugh. "Tell you what, I'll just cancel on all of them and have you meet at my house at 5:30. Will that work? We can walk to the diner down the street."

"That sounds great," he said as he continued up the stairs towards philosophy. "I'll see you tonight." Giving her a smile and a wink, he parted her company to get to class before the bell rang.

The rest of the day went by quickly and the final bell rang before he knew it. Most of the students were packed up and ready to leave well before then, but he had been so deep in thought as he considered the lesson that day that the bell and startled him. His classmates had already cleared out to the hall by the time he finished packing his books into his backpack. He told Mr. Rafferty to have a good evening and headed for home.

After walking in the front door, the young man heard voices down the hall while grabbing a soda from the fridge. Following the sounds, he found his parents sitting on their bed looking at papers in a red folder as they discussed where to have dinner.

"Come on, Erica, which restaurant would you prefer?"

"I could go for the Greek or Chinese. Do either of those sound good to you?" As she glanced back up to her husband's face, she saw her son standing in the doorway. "Douglas, I think we have a visitor."

His Dad looked up at him, "Hey, bud. How was school?"

"It was good. Lined up a date with Shana tonight."

"Oh, that sounds fun," said his mother. "What are you two going to do?"

"After I meet her at her house, we're going to walk to the diner."

"Well make sure you guys be careful."

"We will, Mom," he said as he turned to head to his own room. "Oh, and you guys should do Chinese; you had Greek the week before last."

She looked up at the ceiling as she thought back. "You're right." Turning back to Douglas, "Chinese then?"

"Anything for you, babe," he said giving her a kiss.

"Come on, guys," the boy exclaimed with a slightly disgusted look. "Let the minors leave the room before you start that. Keep it PG for the sake of the children."

He walked towards his room sipping his soda as he heard his parents chuckling behind him. As he passed, he tossed his bag onto his bed and continued to the living room where he dropped onto the couch in front of the TV. After a long day of knowledge-building, it was time for some after-school programming.

As he perused the boob tube, he lost track of time until he happened to glance at the wall clock to realize he should have left for Shana's ten minutes ago. Springing from the couch, he ran to his bedroom and turned his closet into a whirlwind of clothes flying through the air as he pulled out an outfit befitting a date. Throwing it on, he included a splash of cologne before rushing out the door.

Running the entire way to her house, he was thankful that Shana didn't hold his tardiness against him. It didn't hurt that he'd picked a few wildflowers for her on the way. The smile he received when presenting them to her gave off the affection he'd hoped for instead of the irritation he narrowly avoided. Regardless, he still apologized for his tardiness, which she waved off as not a big deal.

As she held his arm, he escorted her to the diner as a gentleman. After the main course, they shared a strawberry milkshake over smiles and playful banter. When they'd finished, he paid the bill and held the door for her as they left. He learned early from his father that you always treat women with respect, and Shana was a girl that he wanted to shower with everything he had.

Taking her hand, they walked together along the sidewalk with the setting sun painting the sky orange and pink. The romantic nature of the colors was like the gods blessing their union. There could only be one thing that would end this night with perfection. He'd been thinking about it for a while, and tonight felt like the perfect time to take the plunge.

He opened the gate to her front yard and prepared to wish her goodnight, but he paused as he searched for courage. Usually he'd get a small peck on the cheek before she went inside, but tonight felt like it was time for more. It was an experience he'd yet to experience with anyone, and his nerves started to get the better of him.

As if she could read his mind, Shana didn't immediately lean in to kiss his cheek like usual. Instead, she played with her house key and told him how much funs she'd had tonight. She stared at the keys as she fidgeted with them and bit her lip as she waited.

In that moment, Shana was the most beautiful thing he'd ever seen. Courage swept over him like a wave as he admired her and he threw caution to the wind. Placing his hand on the small of her back, he stepped in closer to her. As her gaze rose up to meet his, she could feel the warmth of his breath on her skin. As her eyes penetrated into his soul, he seized the moment and pressed his lips to hers. With the explosion of flavor from her cherry lip gloss, they each experienced their first real kiss.

Two blocks from home, the boy was still smiling ear-to-ear after leaving Shana. A first kiss was a landmark occasion every youth experienced, and tonight had been his turn. It was softer than he thought it would be. He'd been given plenty of kisses on the cheek and given in return, but it was a different feeling when it happened with another pair of lips. He was on cloud nine with the greatest night of his life.

Rounding the corner, he saw an empty police car parked in front of his apartment building. He wondered what could be going on, but shrugged it off as he entered the lobby. As he was on his way towards one of the elevators, he heard the lady at the front desk say his name. Next to her was the police officer that probably belonged to the car outside.

"Son," said the officer as he walked over to join him, "I'm going to need you to come with me."

"Why? Did I do something wrong?"

"No, something has…happened to your parents."

Taken aback by the insinuation, the boy volleyed a barrage of questions at the officer as he was escorted to the squad car. "I don't have all the information, son. Once we get to the station, someone will be there that can tell you more."

"But are the ok? What happened?"

The officer insisted he wait until the 'someone' he mentioned was there to speak to him. The ride felt like an eternity as he circled over all the possibilities that sprang into his head. They ranged from a traffic ticket that got out of hand to an abduction by aliens. The lack of details was excruciating, but there was a light in the tunnel when Rae greeted him at the station.

Rae was a family friend that used to babysit him a lot when he was younger. She was a friend of his parents mainly, but she had spent so much time in his life that she was like an adopted aunt. He was happy to see her, but the tears in her eyes filled him with dread. Along with a detective and an assigned social worker, Rae struggled to get the words past her lips as she told him the news about his parents.

While he was having his first kiss, they were being ripped from this world. What he thought to be the best night of his life had become the worst. The feeling in his legs escaped him and he wobbled before collapsing into Rae's arms.

"That place was delicious," said Erica. "We should go there all the time." She looked at her husband tapping on the steering wheel with his thumb as the light allowed cross traffic to pass.

"You say that every time we eat there," Douglas laughed. "They should just have a table for us on standby at all times as often as we're there."

"Hey, do you think they'd do that?" She looked at her husband with an incredibly wide smile. She was putting on a show for him, and he knew it. Their marriage was a collection of inside jokes, innuendos, and just plain goofiness. The way she always made him laugh was one of the things that made him fall in love with her. And if he didn't love her already, he would be falling now with how radiant the orange of the setting sun made her look that evening.

Douglas leaned over to kiss her as they waited for the light to turn. She smiled as his moustache tickled her cheek. Pulling back, he started to say how much he loved her when Erica's face filled with panic. As she screamed, he turned to see the person leaning in his window and the gun he held.

"Get out of the car," the man said as he aimed the pistol at Douglas.

"I'm not giving you my car. I'm a city prosecutor and the best thing for you to do right now is to turn around and walk away."

"Wrong answer."

The bullet exploded through his temple, snapping his head to the side with such force that his body fell into Erica's lap as she screamed. His blood covered the windshield, the dash, and her dress as more spilled out onto the floor around her feet. His death had been instantaneous and the terror she felt was brought to burn as the gun turned towards her.

The bullet sliced through her chest like a burning coal that melted the flesh in its path. As the man was about to pull their bodies from the vehicle, he heard shouts and noticed someone at a payphone calling the police.

Spooked, the gunman ran off and left the couple to deal with the aftermath.

Erica choked on her own blood as she stared into the lifeless void that had been her husband seconds ago. Her eyes filled with tears as visions of the boy she left at home flashed through her mind. As unconsciousness swallowed her, a lone droplet slid off her eyelash and down her cheek.

"Mom, please don't leave me," the boy said as he held her hand. Paramedics had arrived in time to get her to a hospital. Doctors worked relentlessly to save her life, but after hours on the table, there was nothing else they could do. She was dying.

"I need you," he said through sobs of despair. "Who's going to watch over me when I'm sleeping?" He stroked her hand and buried his face in the side of her leg as he wept.

Erica held on for three days before succumbing to her injury. In all that time, the young boy never left her bedside. Despite what the surgeons had told him, he had waited expectantly for her to open her eyes. He needed her to wake up; to hear her voice tell him that everything was going to be ok. But she never woke, and her words never came.

The next few days were a blur as Rae took care of everything for him. In a foldout chair under a green canopy, he felt the freshly mown grass crunch through the soles of his wingtips. His suit which was bought only yesterday was tight on his shoulders as his hands rested in his lap. On either side of him was Rae and his

Aunt Cheryl who'd come in from Arkansas after hearing about her brother and his wife. Coming from a small family, she was now his only living relative.

Standing near the pair of oak caskets, the priest spoke to the gathering of friends mourning Douglas and Erica's passing, but the boy wasn't listening. His eyes rested on their names that had been etched into the large gravestone along with the inscription 'Beloved Mother & Father'.

As the ceremony ended, he placed a single tulip on each casket as he struggled to contain himself. Saying his goodbyes, he turned and left behind the two people that could no longer guide him through the labyrinth of life. He walked through the crowd of onlookers and noticed Shana waiting for him. She reached out her arm to draw him in, but he passed by without saying a word.

In the passing weeks, Cheryl made the preparations to move him to Arkansas with her, but he wouldn't have it. During that time, his sixteenth birthday had come, and so she made a deal with him. As long as he stayed with Rae, she allowed him to emancipate himself so he could stay in the city where he'd grown up. But by the terms of his parents will, the estate would be governed by his aunt until he reached 21 years of age. The terms were agreeable, and so he moved in with Rae, but that wasn't his only problem to overcome.

The police hadn't found the man that murdered his parents. Their loss had drained him of his lust for life and left a gaping hole that he didn't know how to fill. It also drained into his personal relationships as he gave up his ties of friendship to be left alone. Shana tried to be there for him, but he was too deep in sorrow to take notice or deal with anything else.

Reluctantly, she eventually moved on when she could no longer bear the cold shoulder. After waiting for him to open up for months, it tore her apart to leave him but that is what she had to do. Shana wished she could have done more for him, but she had reached a point that she couldn't continue spending nights crying for the boy she loved. She could see the anguish he felt each time he looked at her and was reminded that they were dying while he was having his first kiss. He would always be her first love, but it was time for her to move on.

Things got worse when he learned that the police knew who was behind his parent's deaths but weren't doing anything about it. He didn't care that the witness had recanted their stories about what they saw, nor did he want to hear about the rumor that it was because they'd been threatened. Without proof, there was nothing they could do about it, but all the boy heard was that Phillip Donner wasn't going to be punished for his crimes.

Even with his priors for assault, the case dissolved without witness cooperation. And without the weapon for ballistics match to the murders, the investigation died with his parents. The boy spiraled further into his seclusion and began to show violent tendencies towards others. As this was going on, Rae searched for a way to help him snap back. It wasn't until she found plans in the boy's room of how he was going to set the world right that the idea came to her.

Initially she was appalled at the idea, but she'd been hurt by the loss of Erica and Douglas too. As she tried to reason with the boy, he actually won her over to his side, and that's when the planning began. Rae taught the boy everything she had learned about laws, city regulations, and how to become invisible. He spent over a year learning tracking methods, biology, forensics and martial arts. He trained both his mind and his body to gain the knowledge and strength for what was to come.

As he learned all the concepts he would need, a philosophy of life began to form in his mind. There were many ways to punish the wicked, and his way was the swiftest of justice. He also came to realize that staying hidden meant not leaving traceable clues. Guns were loud and bullets could be traced through ballistics. A clumsy tool such as that was not right for what they were doing. They needed something more precise, and the boy chose a scalpel from his mother's tools as a surgeon.

With this newfound philosophy came a mantra to keep his vision forward. It would steady his hand and mind to know that his actions were to balance the scales. He would tell the man who murdered his parents that his despicable actions were being returned in kind, and he found this in his father's books of Latin. He recalled a phrase his father had used many times when telling his son why he'd become a lawyer. If you do nothing to make things better, you ally yourself with those causing the problem. He who is silent is taken to agree.

The day finally came on the two-year anniversary of his parent's death. He knelt in the bushes in front of a house across town and heard the television blaring inside. He looked up at the stars as he steeled his courage before peering through the window at Phillip Donner washing down a burrito with a bottle of whiskey.

They boy bode his time well as he waited in the dark for the man inside to pass out. When he watched Phillip's eyes close, he still waited. It was when the empty glass slipped from his fingers and bounced across the floor without waking him that the boy knew it was time. As Donner slept in the recliner, the boy picked the lock on the front door to gain entry.

Wearing latex gloves like his teacher taught him, he kept his fingerprints to himself as he entered the home. His heart began beating rapidly as the adrenaline seeped into his body while he stepped through the living room. It felt like his heart could jump out of his chest at any moment, but a few deep breaths kept him in control of his actions.

From the backpack he'd once used for school supplies, the boy pulled out a fresh roll of duct tape and secured sleeping beauty to his chair. The liquor had done a good job of keeping the man asleep as he did so, but it was time to wake the beast. The boy raised his hand and slapped him as hard as he could muster. The blow shook Phillip awake and he struggled against his binds when he tried to sit up.

"What the hell?" He looked down at the duct tape and shook with all his might before noticing the boy. "Who the fuck are you? What are you doing in my house?!?"

"I assure you we've never met, but you knew my parents for a brief time. You see, you shot both of them two years ago today."

"I didn't shoot anybody you crazy fuck."

"On the contrary, Mr. Donner…you know what, I don't think we need to be formal, do you?"

"How do you know who I am?"

"Well, Phillip, you murdered my parents when they wouldn't give you their car. Their names were Erica and Douglas." Donner watched the boy intently as he was putting the pieces together. "The witnesses were ready to put you away, but once they received threats on their lives…" the boy trailed off as he saw recognition in his prisoner's eyes. "Ah, so you do remember them, don't you?"

"Yes…I mean no…look he should have just got out of the damn car; just like you need to get out of my damn house. Bad things happen to those who don't do what they're told, boy."

"It's strange making threats from the position you're in. How could you possibly follow through with anything? I'll tell you what, I'll even give you an easy target." The boy turned his back to him and placed his hands on his head. He waited a moment before slowly turning back around in mock shock that nothing happened.

"Oh, wait, you're all tied up, aren't you? Since your threats are meaningless, how about we keep having our conversation?"

"What do you want?"

"I think I'd rather show you." The boy ripped open Phillip's shirt before covering his mouth with duct tape as a precaution. Then, he cut into his flesh with his mother's scalpel as the man squealed in pain through his gag. "R...E...U...S...," the boy spelled out as he cut the letters into Donner's chest.

He stood up and admired his work. "You know, it's not bad for my first time. What do you think?" The boy waited for a second and then bonked his hand against his head. "Duh," he said, "you can't talk through the tape. Let me help you with that." He pulled the tape from his mouth as it fought to hold onto Phillips skin, but it eventually released its grasp.

"Please, you don't have to do this," he begged.

"This mark shows that you're among the guilty, and you will be dealt with as such. It shows that you will never hurt anyone else like you did my parents."

As he stood there, he thought he should say something more. Making it all the way here to simply spill his blood and leave would make him no different than any other murderer. If he was to do this, he had to stand out from the rest. Remembering his father's philosophy on life, he thought of his mission statement.

Stepping behind Phillip and placing the scalpel to his throat, he ignored the man's begging as he whispered, "Qui tacet consentire videtur."

As Phillip gargled with his own blood as it spilled out onto his chest, the boy ran out of the house as fast as his feet could carry him. He ran from the porch and down the street taking wild turns until he reached an abandoned field where his chest heaved to catch his breath.

Stripping down to his underwear, he tossed the clothes in a pile and pulled out new ones from his pack. After he'd dressed again, he sprayed the pile on the ground with lighter fluid and burned them. The flames took instantly to the fuel as the fabrics began to crackle.

He watched the embers float up from the disappearing evidence and realized how much he'd enjoyed righting the wrongs done by Phillip Donner. It wouldn't bring back those that had died, but it was a step towards preventing it from happening again. It sparked an idea as the fire burned up the clothes and started to die. Why did he have to stop at just one?

With the skills he spent that last year honing, the boy decided to work both sides of justice. He joined the police force to carry on his father's memory of upholding the law, but when the law came up short, he had other means to protect people. The emptiness he'd felt since the loss of his parents refilled with the lust for life that he'd thought gone forever. He had discovered his purpose.

Twelve years later, that boy was now a man clutching at his bleeding shoulder as he looked up at Detective Delgado putting all the pieces together. He stared at the blood on his hand

and then back to the man lying on the ground. With confusion in his eyes, he asked, "Alex?"

Chapter 34

This revelation had Marcus dumbstruck as all the facts slid into place to form a path that led directly to me. The fact that the vigilante seemed to have access to so much information on his victims, it made sense that he would have access to the police database. Then the murders stopped on the night that Peter Davidson broke into my home and held me hostage. The clues had been in front of them the entire time, but the idea of a cop hadn't occurred to him.

"Alex?" he asked still trying to come to grips with reality. As he looked down at the man he'd trusted, he became wrought with anger. "Alexander Saint?!? What the hell? It's been you the whole fucking time?"

Pulling myself up to a seated position, I let my hood fall back and removed the face mask. When the ambient light reached my face, it revealed what the detective had already deduced. "Well," I started as I unzipped my jacket ripped fabric from my shirt to tie around my bleeding arm. "I'm not really sure what to say here. After my parents died, their killer went free without any jail time. The short version is that it put me on the path to becoming the city's vigilante."

Wrapping the torn fabric around my arm, I cinched the knot tight with my teeth. "Any man going through what I did could easily end up like me."

"No, they really wouldn't. People die all the time and their next of kin don't start killing people! And I've read your file, it says your parents died in an automobile accident."

"BECAUSE THE ASSH-", I paused to calm myself. "With the right connections and a bit of money, paper records can be doctored. It's not so easy today now that everything is on computers, but the past were simpler times. The truth is that

Douglas and Erica Saint—my parents—were killed when a man tried to steal their car."

"How were you able to alter all the police and medical records that would have been connected to something like that?"

"Tenacity, but that is not what we're here to talk about, are we? You know as well as I do that everyone that I've killed deserved it. The badge couldn't touch them, but I could."

"You mean by killing them."

I pulled myself to my feet to meet Delgado's determined gaze. "You have to admit that my solution does result in a city that doesn't have to live in fear. All you have to do is watch the news. Have you heard a public outcry to stop me? While I may not be publicly endorsed, few try to stop me." I could see my words registering with Marcus, but the grinding of his teeth didn't seem to have him swaying in my favor.

"Our badge is meant to show our devotion to the law," he said. "Good intentions don't negate murder."

"Ex malo bonum."

"No, there is no good out of this evil. You can't try to put a positive spin on killing. It doesn't matter that you only prey on the wicked. Alex, you must understand this."

"I can see how you might think that, but I can't sit in silence while criminals skirt the law."

"Don't you see the hypocrisy in that statement? You can't let criminals skirt that law? That's exactly what you're doing!"

The point stabbed me like another knife through my arm. I bit my lip and thought of Amy. This past week had me thinking about her more and more. It was easy to tell myself that I was doing the right thing when I didn't have a family to worry about, but lately she'd become important to me. On the night I thought I could have died, she was the only person that

I'd wanted to see. After all I'd been through, being with her made me feel safe and loved like I used to when I was a kid.

"What's wrong?" asked Marcus. "You don't seem to be believing in what you're saying."

"You're wrong there; I fully endorse my actions. I believe that this needs to be done, but I know that everything ends at some point. I'm just not sure it's me that should be doing it anymore."

"Then let me take you in. Let's put a stop to all of this tonight. No more death."

"Qui tacet consentire videtur," I whispered.

"He who is silent is taken to agree? You said that earlier." Marcus glanced at Tyrell's body that was bleeding on the dirt a few yards away before looking back at me. "What is that supposed to mean?"

"It's something my dad used to say. He was a lawyer and he felt that if you had the ability to make a change and didn't, then you were culpable to what happened. That's why I do this. If I don't and these people hurt someone else, then my hands are just as dirty as theirs."

"It's not a perfect system, Alex, but it's the only one we've got."

"Don't give me that not-a-perfect-system bullshit. My father dealt with that constantly. I can't remember how many times he'd come home feeling regret over some prick that got off because of our imperfect system."

"Is that why you tag everyone as guilty?"

"Reus? Yeah. The courts failed in delivering the verdict, so I make it a part of them. They die knowing that justice is being served."

Marcus pressed for more information as he used me to connect the dots. "Who is helping you with this? I don't see how you could alter government records and keep the precinct off your scent alone."

I checked my field dressing to make sure the bandage was holding and ignored his question. "I thought I'd throw you guys off and maybe retire when I took care of Peter. I even dressed him in the clothes I'd worn the night I took out Big King so the implications might stick. I knew it was a long shot since I'd used a scalpel and he had a hunting knife, but it was worth a shot. It might have even been believed if I hadn't been caught fleeing the scene."

"So that was you then?" I nodded. "But why the sudden change of heart and urge to retire?"

"I thought you wanted me to stop? Now you question why I'd stop?"

"Alex, I'm just trying to get the whole story. You talk of retirement, and yet you killed two more people tonight."

"Tonight wasn't planned," I said, scratching my head. "I was just out for a cruise and saw everything unraveling for Ally and her guy. You remember Ally, right?"

"Yeah, she was the waitress the other night."

"Exactly, and I couldn't let something happen to them. So, I decided to do something about it."

"You're a police officer; you could have simply arrested them! Your testimony would have locked them behind bars."

"True," I said, looking at the body on the ground as I thought back on my decisions. "I guess I've been at this long enough that the badge isn't the first thing to cross my mind when I see a crime."

"Well, you're going to regret that because this area is flooded with cops by now. You've got no way out. I hate that our partnership is ending like this, but you made the decisions that led us here. Alex, you're under arrest."

"I can respect that, Marcus, but do you know what I learned before I killed the man that took my parents from me?" I took a step towards Marcus and turned my shoulder towards him as he shook his head. "Always have an exit strategy."

In one swift motion, I pulled a retractable baton from a strap on my thigh and swung it around to strike Marcus in the forehead. His hands held the side of his face as he hit the ground and tried to look up at me through eyes that would be seeing stars. I leaned down next to him so he could hear my words clearly, "I'm sorry I had to do that, but I'm not going to jail for what is right. And before you chase after me, you should know that I found out your secret. I know about the cash payments and the real reason you moved to Kansas City. Just know that the secret is safe with me as long as you don't pursue me."

His eyes flickered as sheer terror flashed through his eyes before being replaced with rage. "I'll stop you," he whispered as he tried to steady the world that was spinning all around him. "I'm done being threatened by assholes trying to force me to do what they want. I will stop you."

I guess that backfired, but I wasn't going to stick around while he reasserted his dominance. "Take care of your family and just forget about me." I sprinted up the hill that led back to Grand Avenue as Marcus screamed at me. I heard him tripping across the rocks as his sense began to clear and he attempted to pursue. I knew I didn't have much time until he was back at full capacity, so I put as much space between him and myself as I could. Just before I rounded the warehouse building, I realized he'd reacquired his gun and ammo as a loud bang followed with small chips ricocheting off the brick building as I passed. I guess my attempt to dissuade him from coming after me had the opposite effect.

I ran past the silos in the gravel-covered courtyard as Marcus reached the top of the hill and continued after me. To avoid all the cops that would be just past the transformers at the end of the clearing, I ran away from the flashing lights of the cruisers and cut through an alley nearby. After winding my way through it, I exploded into the City Market and glanced behind me to see Marcus still on my tail.

I didn't want to risk another physical altercation as I ran through the market square. When I heard him crash into and trip over a trashcan I'd passed at the end of the alley, I assumed the blow to the head was still affecting his vision. My bike was parked where I'd left it at the end of the lot and I leapt onto it without slowing. With Marcus still running and me sitting still on the motorcycle, the space between us was getting smaller by the second. Slipping on my earpiece, I inserted my key and revved the engine as I popped the clutch. The tires screeched as they spun rapidly before spitting me out onto the street in a trail of white smoke.

I thought I would lose him, but he spotted a stroke of luck pull into view as I was leaving. He flagged down the passing squad car and commandeered the vehicle after flashing his badge. Marcus threw the transmission into gear and floored the accelerator to follow me as I sped south on Grand.

With his black-and-white inching up on me in my side mirror, I sent a boost of power to the engine to pick up speed. Delgado followed suit as he attempted to match my acceleration as I weaved the Hayabusa through traffic. Not wanting to lose me, Marcus called in the chase on the radio for assistance. "Officer in pursuit of suspect south on Grand. Request immediate assistance. Suspect on motorcycle is Detective Alexander Saint. Repeat...Alex Saint is the Blood Week Murderer."

Hearing the call through the earpiece I put on back in the parking lot, I through a curveball in Delgado's plan as I slammed hard on the brakes at E 5th Street. My rear tire lifted off the pavement with the inertia of my speed for a second before I mashed the throttle again to swing the bike 180 degrees. I pulled a wheelie with my sudden burst of speed as I flew past Marcus in the opposite direction. I saw the anger on his face as our eyes met in the second that he narrowly avoided colliding with me going the wrong way. Tires screeched as he stomped his own brakes and cranked the wheel to correct his course and come after me.

"Suspect now heading north on Grand," said Marcus' voice over the radio. "I need the vehicles on 1st to set up a roadblock immediately."

Picking up speed, we passed E 3rd where Grand veered off to the right and I nearly laid the bike down when I hit an oil slick. Recovering after a slide, there was a slight wiggle before I was able to steady the rocket between my legs and throttle up again. The powerful engine echoed off the buildings as I thundered by in a blur.

Quickly approaching the roadblock starting to form ahead of me, I saw the fork in the road ahead. Going left would leave you on Grand while off to the right was E 1st Street. The tines of this fork were bent with one option going up an incline and the other down towards the train tracks.

As I sped towards the cars blocking Grand, I could see they were still attempting to get E 1st covered. A familiar voice came over my radio, which told me that the other detectives were on the scene. "Marcus, I'm pulling out in front of 1st to force him up Grand," said Bronson who was already pulling into the street when I spotted him.

The people trying to stop me had assumed there were only two options. Door number one would slam me into the side of Bronson's vehicle and that would lead to massive injury or death at the speed I was going. Door number two would have me stopped by a roadblock roughly thirty yards past the fork. I decided to go with a third option.

Chapter 35

Everything that came into the light over the past few weeks had built to this moment. I guess I always knew that my side business wouldn't last forever, but it had never occurred to me how it might come to an end. Something caused me to slip up on the details. An argument could be made that the monkey wrench was the unforeseen and impromptu introduction to Peter Davidson. No amount of planning could have prepared me for the dumb luck he experienced when trying to frame me for things I'd already done.

While that may have played a part, I don't think that was the first domino in fate's design. Despair from the loss of my parents left me feeling empty, and I filled that void with vengeance. It made me feel complete for a time, but it was slowly replaced when the despair began to be replaced with happiness and contentment. I began to love someone for the first time since I was a boy, and those emotions created a world where I no longer needed the vigilante.

I was still going through the motions, but it hadn't occurred to me that I was pretending until Peter broke into my home. He was the catalyst for the realization that I wasn't empty anymore. My feelings for Amy were deeper than I could have imagined. I think I may have been fighting it subconsciously by continuing my affairs with other women like Kathryn as a means to avoid accepting it. Thanks to whatever drove Peter to come after me, I couldn't pretend anymore.

Sadly, this doesn't mean that I completely threw in the towel. I couldn't stand back and watch a pair of young lovebirds be harmed, and for that reason I had a decision to make. With the engine screaming between my legs as I raced towards the fork in the road that had both escape routes blocked, Marcus thought he had me as he pursued in the squad car behind me. He was wrong.

Taking a left at the fork, Bronson watched me fly past him up Grand towards the black and whites waiting further up the road. I pictured Marcus smiling as I was forced to stop, but I was going to have to disappoint him. Thirty feet up the fork, I angled the bike towards the barrier between 1st and Grand. Racing straight for the point where the roads split with one going down the hill towards the railroad tracks and the other up over the bridge, I pulled hard on the throttle. My front tire rose off the ground just as the tires hit the barrier that ran up the edge of the dividing wall.

As soon as I hit, the bike sailed over Bronson's vehicle blocking the lower street and fell fifteen feet to land safely behind it. The Hayabusa wobbled slightly with the sudden stop when it hit the pavement. I stuck my legs out over the street to steady it like a tightrope walker with his long stick. After it had stabilized, I looked up the road just in time to see Marcus' car screeching to a stop to avoid wrecking into the wall. It was the last thing I saw before speeding off uninhibited.

Throwing it in reverse, Marcus backed up while shouting through the window at Bronson to move his car. Mashing the pedal and speeding past Bronson with barely an inch on either side of his vehicle, Delgado cursed at what happened. Fucking *Evel Knievel* wasn't going to get away from him without a fight. But after twenty minutes of driving in circles, he had to admit that the stuntman was gone.

Back at Grand, Marcus parked the borrowed patrol car and walked towards the huddle of detectives discussing the crazy stunt Alex used to get away. He was agonizing over what Alex knew, and what he could do to keep the truth from coming out. Could he really know why he came to Kansas City? The questions only fueled the fire of Delgado's desire to catch him.

"You should have seen him fly over the fucking car," Bronson said to Pinick.

"Must have been nuts, but are we sure it's Alex?"

"I'm sure," said Marcus. "I watched him kill someone in the gully over there before getting into a scuffle where I saw his face. It's him."

"How do you think we should proceed?"

"For starters, put a call into the bank to freeze his accounts and put a trace on his credit cards. We need to track him down. Edward, I'll need you to take care of alerting the airports. I've already called in the BOLO on all highways leading out of the city."

While Bronson stepped away to call the banks, Pinick asked, "Do you really think he'll try to fly out? Don't you think he's smarter than that? He has an exact copy of our playbook. He knows everything we're going to do."

"I know, but we're still doing this one by the book. These tactics are used for a reason. They get results...but it doesn't hurt to hope we'll get lucky." The sun started to peak over the horizon as Pinick pulled out his phone to work the airport angle, but Marcus knew that KCI would be a dead end. He squinted at the new light painting the sky orange and tried to think were Alex would go.

The city I loved was no longer a safe place for me, so I initiated escape protocols I had in place. Walking through the gym, one of the trainers asked if he could help me with a program. I shook my head as I went directly into the locker room and found the door marked 117. I pulled a brass key from my pocket and popped the lock to get to the large duffel inside. Carrying it to an empty corner, I unzipped it and checked the contents before quickly sealing it back up and tossing it over my shoulder as I left.

Cinching the bag tightly to my back, I threw my leg over the motorcycle and started the engine. Looking up, I watched the sun rise steadily into the morning sky and decided to marvel at it for a moment. I realized that this could be the last time I saw a sunrise over Kansas City, so I wanted to remember it. But eventually I had to leave and sent a mental goodbye to the city that had been my home for so long. After putting on my spare helmet, I rolled the bike out of the spot and sped off with the sun on my back.

"Marcus, we have a problem," said Bronson. "It's all gone; his bank accounts were emptied two days ago."

"How the hell could he have known to do that? There was no way for him to know all this was about to happen." He ran his fingers through his hair and screamed in frustration.

Leaving him with his thoughts, Bronson walked over to his partner who stood on the other side of the lot. "What do you think of all this?" he asked.

"All what?" asked Pinick. "You mean how the man we've worked with for years was a secret vigilante? How he was smart enough to evade the entire police force? Or how a part of me is happy we didn't catch him?"

"Well, all of that I guess. It's kind of nice to know he's out there."

With the detectives carrying on, they hadn't noticed the woman walk up to them. "Are you sure you want people hearing that?"

Both turned to see their superior standing beside them. "Captain Hawthorne," stuttered Bronson. "I only meant that he...well..."

"At ease, Richard. We'll skip the reprimands. You're free to think whatever you like. Just fill me in on where we stand with finding Saint."

The detectives informed her of the search, but they felt it was a lost cause with his training background. It wouldn't be easy to find him, but there was a BOLO out on him in the hope that they'd get lucky. He'd already been gone almost two hours with no news of any sightings. As they were finishing up the report, her phone rang and she stepped away to take the call.

About fifty miles outside of Columbia, Missouri, I pulled into a gas station along a dusty road to fill up. Removing my helmet, I looked around at the sheer emptiness of it all. Being miles from a decently sized city, the gas station was the only building in sight. I wondered how much business the tiny shack saw being in the middle of nowhere as I filled my tank. A loud *thunk* told me it was done, and I replaced the nozzle before stepping inside to pay for the gas and a sandwich.

I chose roast beef on rye and was about to pay when I saw a rack of prepaid cellphones. Grabbing one to add to my purchase, I went outside to eat and make a quick call. It rang a few times before the other end answered. "I'm safe," I said. "I'm already out of town and heading cross country."

"Aren't you glad I told you to prepare evacuation supplies in case something like this happened? You weren't sticking to your training."

"I know. I came across a distraction, but it won't happen again once the news hits."

"Yeah, I feel sorry for the lovely coroner. I liked the two of you together."

"I know you did. You'd never shut up about it, Rae Rae."

"You know I hate it when you call me that. I haven't used my middle name in years."

"I know, but you're a chore when you know you're right all the time," Alex chuckled.

"Meaning you like to torment me instead of just allowing the compliment?" The warmth in her voice was both chiding and playful.

"Can't pet your ego too much. You'll get too big for your britches. Either way, your recommendations came in handy."

"That's what I'm here for. Let me know where you end up." Saying farewell to Alex, she placed the phone in her pocket as she heard her name called.

"Captain Hawthorne," said Pinick, "would you like a ride back to the station? We're going to call the search now rather than wait; he's gone."

"Yes, Edward. Thank you". Following him to the squad car, she reflected on the man that Alexander Saint had become and the work still to be done.

Acknowledgements

The relaunching of this book with a new edition was both a fun and difficult journey. As my freshman outing into writing, I'll be the first one to admit that I made a LOT of mistakes. They ranged from grammar to spelling as well as issues with storytelling. I learned quite a bit from it though, and made the changes to how I write with the books I've released since. It was a torturous journey as I read through this novel and found all those mistakes. It stabbed at me that I made them, but also allowed me to see firsthand how far I've come.

As with all writers, there are going to be mistakes in our stories that are found after print. But learning from them lets us make fewer as we grow in our craft. The growth I've gained in this journey are owed to a small yet greatly appreciated group of people. It was them that kept me typing at the keys to put my tales to print. I wouldn't be where I am in my career without them.

The first person I want to thank is Bob Sixta. You were my first raving fan that made sure I knew how much you enjoyed my work. Each time I saw you, you drilled me about when I would have another novel out. Your thirst for books is something that drove me forward to bring more. What could have been a one-time outing turned into a career through your persistence, and I can't thank you enough for that.

Finally, where would any of us be without our mothers? Repeatedly reading my books as she painstakingly pours over each word to edit them is a gesture I'm eternally grateful for. I literally wouldn't be here doing what I love without you.

Proof

Made in the USA
Columbia, SC
10 February 2018